Cracker Jacked

A JULI BUTLER MYSTERY
BOOK ONE

BARBARA WITEK

To the friendships & shenanigans you can never forget.
May there always be a little mystery in your life, and a little love in
your heart.

One

Some days it doesn't pay to get out of bed. Believe it or not, I've had that feeling for the last month, and I haven't gotten paid, period. My phone is disconnected, and my landlord has been anxiously waiting for his rent. Too bad it won't be coming any time soon. After putting in overtime for the Galleries' special events, my greedy boss and ex-boyfriend, David von Hoffster, has yet to pay me for the two private showings and three after-hours cocktail parties I played hostess to. Typical, but I wasn't about to let it get me down.

Leaning out the window of my trusty Chevrolet, I breathed in deep the warm air. Summer in Boston; I loved it. Concerts in the park, seafood at the pier and fresh gelato from Spera's on the corner. Life didn't get any better. Well, it would if I ever got a paycheck, which was why I had my little bargaining chip tucked safely in the back seat. If David didn't pay up, I'd pawn my little piece of canvas and be sitting pretty until I figured out my next move. Since I'd basically told David to kiss off, any move I made was totally in the hands of fate at this point. After I reported him for tax fraud, one could only hope he'd cut me a check before the IRS froze his assets.

My short fuse has always been my downfall, and unfortunately David knew how to push my buttons. What he didn't know was the lengths I'd go to in order to see justice served. When I was growing up, my mother used to say I landed on my feet like a cat with nine lives to boot. Thank goodness dear old Mom had no clue about half of the crazy, awkward, and just plain stupid things I'd done over the last ten years in trying to "find" myself.

I parked outside my adorable brick flat on Maple Street, then grabbed my purse and the two canvas grocery totes from the back seat. Juggling my keys to find the right one, I stepped over a crater-sized crack in the concrete walkway and looked up to see a bright pink paper tacked to my door.

If it was another invitation to a Pampered Chef party, I would die. I wanted to support my friends' efforts, but one person could only have so many mixing bowls and spoons.

A smile crossed my face at the thought of my enormous kitchen gadget collection. I loved my apple-peeler-corer-slicer and couldn't live without my garlic press. They were the staples to my never-ending ideas for organic recipes. I dreamed of one day owning my own place and selling not only organically grown herbs and spices but treats for both people and animals. Everyone deserved healthy alternatives.

I focused on the neon paper, which was no invitation at all. In fact, it was quite the opposite. "Evicted?" my voice carried on the summer breeze as it shot up three octaves.

I ripped the notice from under the silver tack and held it between my teeth while I opened the door and stepped over the day's mail which had been shoved through the metal slot. "You have got to be kidding me," I said with the paper still in my mouth. The tub of organic yogurt teetered at the top of the bag as I set my groceries on the counter.

Yes, I was two months behind with my rent. I had a reason— thank you, David—and Lou usually understood. I steadied the yogurt, and out of habit, reached for the phone to plead my case.

The dead phone.

"Arrrgh!" I slammed the slim black handset into its cradle, then took a calming breath. I would stop and see Lou on my way to work tomorrow. "Good thinking, Juli, except odds are you don't have a job anymore," I reminded myself and knelt to scoop the pile of mail from the floor. Bills, bills, and more delinquent bills. How much worse could one day get?

"Excuse me, Miss Butler?" a voice crackled, and I looked up to see a well-dressed older man standing in my doorway. Mom would have a fit if she knew how many times I didn't lock the door or left it half open, like now. "Julianna Butler?" he repeated a bit louder. His gentle grey eyes didn't strike me as those of a serial killer. Then again, it was always the non-obvious ones you had to worry about.

"Yes, that's me," I replied and stood with my mountain of mail. "What can I do for you?"

"I have some very disturbing news," he began, and I froze. Goose bumps crept up my arms in a march of doom.

"Oh, no." I gulped. "Oh, no-no-no-NO!" Rushing to the window, I swept aside my teal, shaggy-chic curtains while trying to hold down the bubbling panic. "You can't repo my truck." The reality came out on a whoosh of words. I had one more year of payments on my cherry red pickup. "I called and made arrangements." Or was that the month before? "Please don't take my truck. I need it for my job." Maybe.

"You misunderstood, Miss Butler. I'm not here about the truck." I visibly relaxed against the window, feeling my pulse return to normal. "I'm afraid it concerns your mother."

"Mom?" I turned around slowly, stranger-danger clanging a red alert inside my head. I grew up in a small town where everyone knew everyone's business whether you wanted them to or not, part of the reason I couldn't wait to leave. I shot him a curious stare and nailed him with my safe question, "How do you know my mother?"

"Well, I don't personally." He swayed back and forth, his

patent leather shoes squeaking as much as my warped wooden floor. It took him a moment to meet my gaze, making me wonder if my safe question tripped him up or if serial killers became nervous before doing their deed. "I'm from the court," his voice broke through our awkward silence. "I've been sent to give you this." The man handed me a large envelope. "You're a very hard woman to track down, Miss Butler."

"Wait a minute." I waved my hands as I shook my head, relieved when he didn't murder me, yet confused by the thick missive only inches away from my fingertips. I hadn't talked to my mother in ages, reminding myself once again that I was the world's worst daughter. I'd call her tomorrow, I decided, but then again, that's what I always said. I silently vowed to do better since apparently, I wasn't going to become a statistic, when his words suddenly registered. "Is Mom okay?" I took the envelope from his hands. "Is this something I need to sign for her?"

"I'm sorry, Miss Butler, your mother passed away three weeks ago." His words hit me like a punch in the gut, and I couldn't breathe.

"What?" I wheezed, staring in disbelief. The mail cascaded—in a waterfall of bills that didn't matter anymore—to my feet. The only thing left in my hand was the crisp white envelope bearing a raised attorney's office insignia.

"I'm terribly sorry for your loss." And like that, he was gone.

Just like Mom.

———

WITH MY HEART IN MY THROAT AND EVERYTHING I owned stacked in the bed of my truck, I turned onto the highway and headed out of Boston straight toward New Hope, Connecticut. The morning sun broke through the clouds, casting beams of light to the quiet earth below. An old friend once told me this was the stairway to heaven.

I swallowed hard and tightened my grip on the steering wheel. I hadn't shed a single tear last night, and I wasn't about to now. There were many things to take care of back home and plenty of time for a meltdown after. Mom would want me to be strong, and for once in my life, I wasn't going to fail her. She was in a better place, I had to believe that. It was the only thing getting me through this.

Mom had always lived modestly. I couldn't imagine her having many assets to have to deal with an attorney. When Dad died five years ago, he'd at least made sure the house was taken care of. Funny how they split when I was in high school, never finalized their divorce, and never found anyone else to spend their lives with. Yet they didn't find their way back to each other, either.

I popped in a piece of sugar-free bubblegum as I pondered this and many thoughts of my own commitment issues. Before I knew it, I had long crossed the Connecticut state line. In another forty-five minutes, I'd be pulling into town.

Guilt plagued me with every mile. I'd always been a loving daughter, but I hadn't been a very dutiful one. I wracked my brain to remember the last time I'd spoken to my mother. Now, thanks to my own selfishness, I'd never have another chance. Tomorrow would never come for real this time.

A flood of memories I hadn't expected, yet cherished as they played like an old-time movie, occupied my concentration when I approached the roundabout at Confusion Corners. And, yes, I did the all-too-familiar rolling stop right before I punched the gas to merge and make my way home. The whir of a siren and flashing lights brought my attention to the rearview mirror.

"Perfect," I grumbled and pulled my truck onto the shoulder. While leaning over to retrieve my license, I practiced my pitiful look and plastered a sugary-sweet smile on my face. My best friend, Amelia, used to meet me for lattes and informed me several times this worked like a charm. Only, I wasn't Amelia and had never been good at being coy and flirty. I had no other options. There was no way I could pay for a ticket right now.

"Driver's license and registration, please," a deep voice echoed between my ears. Why did it sound so familiar? Well, no bother. I couldn't afford to get distracted.

Feeling ridiculous, but desperate enough to try anything, I was determined to put forth an Oscar winning performance and make Amelia proud. Batting my baby blues, I whipped my chestnut brown locks toward the open window with a smile so wide my cheeks ached.

"I'm terribly sorry, officer…" I paused to look at his rock-solid chest and the name badge above the pocket of his uniform, "Hargrave?" I choked out. My smile obliterated. No wonder his voice sounded so familiar. My shocked stare rose to his face. Standing before me, in all his grown-up glory, was my childhood friend and certified pain in my butt, Chase Hargrave.

"Juli?" he questioned, just as shocked, while looking over the rims of his department issued sunglasses.

Good Lord, he'd ventured into law enforcement? I'd always pictured Mr. Goody-Good going into some technical field or even becoming a doctor. No way did I ever picture our resident geek as the local sheriff.

"That would be me." I sighed, all pretenses of being a sweet young thing gone. Chase knew me too well to ever buy that act. My wooden bracelets clanked together as I draped my wrists over the steering wheel, trying to look as dejected as I felt. "So, how've you been?" I tried changing the subject, hoping he'd forget about my minor violation.

Of course, he didn't.

"Better than you, apparently," he said with a quirk to his lips as he scribbled something on a piece of paper. "You do realize you failed to stop back there." He motioned with his head toward Confusion Corners.

"Did I?" I said sarcastically at the realization he wasn't willing to cut me a break after everything I'd been through. He hadn't changed one bit. So much for knowing someone in law enforcement. He'd proved those rumors false.

"You did," he said without missing a beat and perused the inside of my truck as if he were looking for smuggled contraband or something. "You can cut the act. It's not going to work."

Act?

Ohhh, that did it! I started to protest, then clamped my lips tight, forming a stubborn scowl like I used to do when we were kids. When he didn't seem to react this time, I ground my teeth and shook my head. I had too much on my plate right now to play along.

"So, you're giving me a ticket? Really?" Chase ignored me, and I swear I saw the corner of his mouth twitch. I could feel my blood boil. After all these years, he was going to make me suffer.

"I'm debating," he finally said as he smoothed his brown mustache, attempting to hide his amusement. I bit my tongue. He was baiting me, and I knew it. Well, I wasn't going to bite.

"If you don't mind, just write me up and let me be on my way. It's been great seeing you, but I have things to do. I'm going home."

And that was all I had to say.

Chase slowly removed his glasses, and I saw sadness in those deep green eyes I remembered so well from my childhood. Living right next door, we'd always acted more like siblings rather than best friends, which was why we got on each other's nerves so much.

"I'm sorry about your mother. She was a great lady," he said in a soft, quiet voice full of sincerity.

"Thanks." I inhaled a deep breath through my nose to stifle the sob about to burst out. Friend or not, no way would I cry in front of him.

"Mind if I ask where the hell you've been?" His tone changed, catching me off guard, and I switched into defense mode.

"Living my life, if it's any business of yours."

"C'mon, Juli, I checked everywhere. All the numbers your mom had were old or disconnected with no forwarding address. No one knew how to reach you. Hell, it took my P.I. two weeks to find you."

"You hired a private investigator?" I wanted to jump out of my truck, except he was standing in front of the door. "I can't believe you!" I slammed my palms against the steering wheel and squeezed until my knuckles were white. "No, I take that back. That is so typical of you."

"What is that supposed to mean?" He stepped back, and that was my cue to swing open the door. A couple of cars passed by, and I'm sure they thought I was about to be cuffed and hauled away. Not exactly the first impression I wanted to make to the locals, but I was too mad to care at the moment.

"You know what it means. Mr. Switzerland has to stay neutral and do the right thing. Why can't you leave things alone? Or better yet, let the path unfold itself."

"Switzerland? Oh, that's original." His mustache twitched and were it not for fear of a life sentence, I would have killed him right there. "It's not always about you. This was your mother, Juli. I thought you'd want to know, since you haven't bothered to come home once in the last ten years." He stared me down, and I wasn't about to look away.

"Keeping tabs on the locals, Detective?" I jabbed my hands at my waist. So much for dripping sugar, this tasted more like venom, and I couldn't control the flow. "Stay out of my life, Chase."

"It's Sheriff, and don't worry. As long as you behave yourself, we won't have a problem." Chase started to walk away but stopped and turned briefly. "And just for the record, my parents always thought you were special. It was their idea for me to call in a professional."

I stood, dumbfounded, and watched him walk with his shoulders pulled back and a purpose to his step. He'd become quite the man, no sign of geekdom at all. Not that I cared, or anything. I shrugged off the uncomfortable observation when his words sank in.

"Wait!" I called and took a couple of steps forward, wanting to set things straight. The frustrated look he shot me just before he slid the dark shades over his eyes held me in my tracks. "Aren't you giving me a ticket?"

Even behind his sunglasses I could feel his glare. He stared at me for a long moment, and then simply said, "Let's just say you owe me one." Chase climbed into his car and pulled away, leaving me standing there like an idiot, wondering what the heck that meant.

I drove straight to the attorney's office, allowing the severity of this meeting to squash the strange feeling in my gut over seeing Chase again. Forty-five minutes later I emerged with my mother's information and the keys to the antique shop. Tomorrow I would check out my new place of employment.

Right now, I was going home.

Two

By the time I'd unloaded my belongings into the house, my next-door neighbor, Mrs. Bailey, had brought over a pitcher of iced tea and a plate of her famous radish sandwiches, complete with crusts cut off. We sat on the front porch, serenaded by the sounds of squawking and barking. Mrs. Bailey owned a feisty parrot, named Scallywag, after her late husband's tour in the navy. The Hargraves, on the other side of my house, apparently still had their sheepdog, Duchess. I remembered many sleepless nights during my senior year of high school because of those two crazy animals.

Mrs. Bailey didn't seem to mind the noise as she refilled our glasses. Then again, the sweet lady had to be in her mid-seventies now. She probably couldn't hear it.

"Now don't you worry about a thing, Juli." Mrs. Bailey reached over and patted my knee. "Your mother didn't suffer one bit. Just fell asleep all peaceful-like and never woke up."

"Maybe if I'd been here—"

"It wouldn't have made one bit of difference. There's nothing you could have done to predict a bee being in her bed sheets. She's the one who hung them on the line."

"At least she wouldn't have been alone. Her death just seems so unfair, dying from a bee sting reaction of all things."

"Life is unfair, Sweetie, we just have to make the best of the time we're given. Your mother thought the world of you, you know. She was constantly telling everyone in town all the wonderful things you were doing."

"Thank you, Mrs. Bailey." I rested my hand on the top of hers, her skin loose and warm. "I wasn't doing anything overly wonderful really, just being on my own."

"Justine loved your independence, envied it, actually." Mrs. Bailey started rocking in the chair, and I couldn't take my eyes from hers. "Oh yes, there were many a night we sat out here and talked about our flourishing rose beds, recipes for pie crust, and how she wished she'd been outgoing like you when she was your age."

"Really?" I asked, while my heart soared. I had never questioned my mother's love. Over the years I'd found myself wondering if she really understood me, or if I'd ever made her proud. Based on Mrs. Bailey's praises, I'd have to say yes, which helped ease my pain.

"Glad to see the Hargraves still have Duchess," I said, acknowledging the persistent barking, and looked toward the yellow house on the other side of mine.

"Oh, that's not Duchess. She died two years ago. They kept one of her pups, though. The nasty dog thinks he owns the neighborhood worse than she ever did."

"If I remember correctly, so does Scallywag." I winked, and we both laughed at the memories of Duchess and Scallywag. Seriously, between the two animals, I think the bird won pretty much every time.

"Scallywag gives him a run for the money that's for sure. That darn bird is worse than Houdini these days, sneaking out of his cage so much. The rascal has found his way out of the house, too, on occasion."

"Really?" I sipped my tea to cover a giggle. He most definitely was a Scallywag. I didn't dare tell her how many times I'd found him perched in the tree outside my bedroom window, and how many times Chase and I had returned him to his cage before heading off to school.

"So how long are you staying?" Mrs. Bailey asked and offered me a plate of oatmeal cookies I hadn't noticed earlier. Dusk was starting to fall, and a warm breeze wiggled the blossoms on hanging baskets of purple begonias. I reached for a cookie, feeling a tightening around my heart. Even Ida Bailey knew I was a free spirit and couldn't settle down for long.

"I don't know. I suppose I need to see the condition of Mom's store and probably contact the real estate agent."

"Oh, I understand." Her mouth drooped slightly, and she looked toward the plate of sandwiches. She was my mother's close friend and this loss had to hurt her as well. I didn't mean to be insensitive, but as I chewed the moist cookie, I knew for a fact I'd rather stay in my crazy disorganized world than have to deal with this heartbreaking reality.

"Don't get me wrong," I corrected, feeling a twinge of guilt, "once I deal with Mom's affairs, I'll figure out what I'm going to do. I never did like the antique store much. I'm sure this will take a while."

"Don't rush, dear. Things change. People change. This isn't the same town you left when you were eighteen."

"Good evening, ladies." A tall man stopped on the sidewalk and waved.

"Well, hello, Mr. Banks." Mrs. B returned the gesture. "Beautiful night for a walk."

"It sure is." He held up the camera strapped around his neck. "The sunsets are beautiful here, and I get to walk off some of Misty's dinner. I couldn't have picked a better place to stay. She's an amazing cook."

"Those are all family recipes, you know."

"She's making my job very easy, that's for sure." He flashed a smile and said, "Enjoy the rest of your night." With a final wave, he continued down the street.

"Oh, that Mr. Banks, such a nice young man."

"Is he new in town?" I asked, continuing to watch him walk away.

"Only temporarily. He's staying at the Sunflower Inn while his house is being built over in Port Byron."

"Port Byron? That's almost an hour away."

"His wife and kids are vacationing in Cape Cod until the house is done right before school starts. He's been here a couple of weeks and goes every now and then to visit them."

"Is he some kind of photographer? April is going to have a fit if she doesn't know already."

"I think he said he's a food writer or something like that. He stopped into the Sunflower for lunch and Misty's beef stew made an impression, so he stayed."

"Why is Misty cooking at the inn? I thought she had big plans after college."

"Her parents bought a place in Las Vegas, so Misty took over. She's really in her element, entertaining guests and cooking up fantastic meals. So much like her mother and grandmother."

"Good for her." I tried to sound positive even though I wasn't feeling it, which had more to do with me and this town than it did with Misty Shepard. "I'm just not sure what's here for me. I've never felt like I fit the New Hope mold."

"That's nonsense. You always fit in here. You were the lifeblood of this place, you and Chase."

"Chase?" I choked on what I hoped was a cookie crumb. "What does he have to do with any of this?" I looked suspiciously toward the house next door, noticing the barking had stopped. Why would I not be surprised if he or his parents put Mrs. Bailey up to this?

"Oh nothing." The silver-haired lady flicked her wrist. "I only remember you two running around on all sorts of adventures. The two of you were inseparable. The first year you were gone, I didn't know what that boy was going to do with himself."

"He went off to college," I scoffed. "He had to do the right thing, you know. And now he's back here making everybody else do the right thing, too."

"Is that so bad?" Mrs. Bailey poured us both another glass of tea. "He cared enough to come back and watch over of his town."

"There's more to life than New Hope." I hoped to plead my case, but I could tell by her soft brown eyes she knew exactly what I meant.

"And you've seen some of that, Juli. Your mother didn't do so badly here, you know. Her store did really well, and once she got on that there Internet, she had buyers from all over the world buying and selling with her."

"She did?" Wow. I hadn't known my mother knew anything about the Internet, let alone had a computer. To think she'd been so successful all on her own. "She never mentioned big buyers or sellers or that she was online." Of course, had I checked in with her more, I might have known.

"That's because it was always about you, dear. She wanted to know what you were up to, and that you were all right. The last thing you needed was to hear about her problems."

"Problems?" I set my glass down on the wicker table between us. "You just said Mom had been doing well. What kind of problems did she have?"

"Oh, nothing she couldn't handle." Again, Mrs. Bailey waved me off as if I were over- exaggerating. "Mark Walker came to your mother begging for a job because he needed to pay off some gambling debt. Justine flat out told him no. He came back three or four times trying to convince her. Your mother never budged."

"Mom must have had her reasons. The Walker family always seemed so respectable."

"They still are, but Mark has ventured down the wrong path. Ever since he lost his job, he's been pretty desperate, poor soul."

"I remember Mark, too. He was a few years ahead of me in school. Too bad things haven't worked out for him."

"And then there's that Sandy Perkins." Mrs. Bailey wagged a finger at a platinum- blond woman in a silver Mercedes as it cruised by. "Wonder where she's off to in such a hurry." The fire in the old woman's eyes was inescapable. "Now, she's one who's not as sweet as she appears."

"What do you mean?" I couldn't help but get caught up in her gossip.

"Everyone thinks she's this upstanding person, when she really has the mean streak of a viper." Mrs. Bailey harrumphed. "Your poor mother had a run in with her a couple of years ago over her pineapple cheesecake recipe at the county fair."

"Oh, I love that recipe," I reminisced and licked my lips, practically tasting the sweet, creamy dessert.

"Well, Sandy accused your mother of using non-whipped topping. Can you imagine? She was just being a poor sport because your mother won hands down, and Sandy came in third that year."

"I kind of remember Mom telling me about the pie-incident." I chuckled. "You know Mom, she was ready to make another pie just so Sandy could taste they were the same. Now me, I would have shoved her face in it."

Mrs. Bailey laughed and stacked the plate of cookies on top of the now empty sandwich plate. She looked at her watch and then west toward the setting sun. We'd spent a long time on the porch. It was like she'd known I'd need to have a piece of my mom on my first night back. I was grateful for that, and her.

"I'll leave you with the cookies and tea. You can bring the pitcher over tomorrow, or whenever you're done. There looks to be enough to share." That sly old lady winked toward the Hargrave house. What on earth was she up to? Smoothing the front of her lavender polyester pants, she leaned over to give me a hug. "I'm so glad you're home."

"Thanks, Mrs. B." I pinched my eyes tight and squeezed her frail shoulders. I was sure she was tired, yet I wasn't quite ready to face the empty house. She smelled like home-baked cookies and freshly starched laundry. The scent lingered and comforted me as I watched her walk across the lawn and into her house.

I stayed for a moment longer on my porch and listened to the night bugs chirp. The last time I'd been alone in my house, my parents had gone to Cape Cod to visit friends, and there was a huge thunderstorm. I'd gotten so scared when the lights flickered and thunder crashed, I'd called Chase and we'd both slept on the couch. I smiled softly at the memory, then my lips tipped down into a frown. I wasn't a child anymore. It was time to grow up. Taking a deep breath, I opened the door and went inside. No rain, no thunder, just me alone in my house.

My house.

No more landlords or rent to pay. This was mine if I chose to stick around. I could almost feel Mom wrap her arms around me as I turned off the lights and headed upstairs.

So why was my gut telling me something was wrong?

"Nothing," I mumbled with blurry eyes as I checked each cupboard. Mom had always been a tea drinker, but I thought for sure there would be a stray can of coffee somewhere.

Padding through the house in my Boston Celtics sleep tee and bottoms, I didn't think twice about venturing down the front walk to retrieve the morning paper. My Mom had been old school with still having the newspaper delivered. In fact, I was sure the entire town remained old-school. Part of its charm. The cool concrete against my bare feet helped wake me up, since I wasn't going to savor my cup o' caffeine. Far across town I heard a rooster from the Murphys' dairy farm.

"Morning, Scarlett," the deep rumble of Chase's voice cut through the air, startling me out of my brain-fog. I hadn't heard that name since high school. Chase had nicknamed me after the infamous movie heroine during our Civil War unit since my last name was Butler, and I stood in awe over him using it now.

"What are you doing here?" I flattened the newspaper against my chest, suddenly feeling exposed. My pace slowed and I eyed him curiously across the hedges looking spit-polished in his navy-blue uniform. He picked a newspaper off the ground and held it up for me to see. Seems we had the same idea, so I acknowledged him with a nod. "Well, tell your parents I said hello. I didn't get a chance to stop and see them yesterday."

"Sure thing as soon as I see them again. They're spending time with Angie's family since coming up from Florida for the funeral." He watched me closely as if he expected me to break down or something. I didn't, and I wouldn't.

"I'm sorry they had to cut their vacation short." My toes were cold from the walkway, and I suddenly wished for the escape of the morning news.

He looked confused and shifted his weight to the opposite leg. "They weren't on vacation. They live there now."

"They do?" My eyes grew wide as I looked from Chase to his front door, holding tighter to the New Hope Chronicle. "Then who lives here?"

"I do."

"You're kidding. After all these years I still can't get rid of you?" I blurted before thinking.

"I hired the P.I., remember? You'll never get rid of me, Scarlett," he added again just to annoy me.

"First, no coffee, and now I've got Marshall Do-Good living next door."

"It's Sheriff," he corrected.

"Whatever." I rolled my eyes. "Where's Deputy Goober?" I looked up and down the street for a possible sidekick.

He cleared his throat. "It's Gary, and he's back at the station. I relieve him in a while."

"Of course, you do." I smacked my forehead with the palm of my free hand. I'd been away from small-town America for too long.

"Coffee just finished brewing if you're interested. If I remember right, your mother was a tea drinker." He rolled the paper and gestured toward the house. "C'mon, you know you want to."

"Oh, why not," I said, totally caving. Hey, it was a free cup of much needed coffee. I hopped through the dew-covered grass and squeezed between his house and the hedge. Just like old times. With a quick peek toward the sky, I thought I saw my mother's face in the clouds smiling down at me.

Must be my goodness meter was coming out of hiding. A bit rusty, as Mom would say, but in working condition with just the right nudge. It must have been sweet Mrs. Bailey rubbing off on me, because the only thing Chase Hargrave ever did was annoy me on so many levels. I never quite understood why. I returned to New Hope to take care of Mom's business, never imagining Chase would still be here. I always envisioned he'd meet someone at college and have a life I'd never know about, a life he deserved after everything that happened.

Chase had put his stamp on the old homestead all right. My bachelor friend could definitely use a female eye in the decorating department. The numerous shades of beige, brown and white strewn in a variety of textures all around screamed testosterone. By the looks of all the family pictures placed about the living room, Chase enjoyed the outdoors and dirt bike racing. Never would have seen that coming. He'd always been too by-the-book. I guess even the local sheriff needed to let loose now and then.

A bass guitar sat propped in the corner. Something else I

didn't know about my old buddy. Without thinking, I walked over and strummed my fingers across the strings.

"My secret passion. Don't tell anyone," he whispered, and handed me a steaming mug. "Cream only, right?"

"How'd you remember?" I didn't hide my surprise. It had been so long since we'd shared a cup of coffee. I honestly didn't expect him to remember such a vague detail.

"You used to say no sugar because you were sweet enough."

"You're such a jerk." Losing all inhibitions, I slugged him in the shoulder and walked away from the guitar. "Sorry to hear about Duchess. Where's her naughty little offspring? Lucky for you he didn't keep me up all night." I peeked through familiar doorways, cradling my mug, wondering if the dog would run out at any minute.

"Outside. Most likely digging a hole."

"Ah, see? Evil is in the genes with that one." I sipped my coffee and scanned the many family photos on the wall.

"His name is Major. Want to meet him?"

"Duchess and I weren't exactly BFF's you know. I'm not sure about one of her puppies. Distemper could run in the family." I raised my hand in surrender. I'm sure it will take me most of the day to go through things between the house and shop and figure out what to do with it all."

"Hey, if there's anything I can do...."

"I know." I handed him the half drank mug. "Thanks for the coffee." That tone in his voice hinted to a conversation I wasn't ready to have. I couldn't get out the door fast enough.

Three

New Hope was the epitome of quintessential small-town America with its well-kept sidewalks, manicured hedges, and white picket fences. Bright colored flowers hung off black lacquered streetlights in decorative moss baskets. My hometown was quaint, peaceful and I had to admit...perfect. Maybe this was just the place for me to regroup, kind of like an extended vacation.

As long as it didn't last too long. I guess I'd inherited this trait from my father. Just thinking about letting the grass grow beneath my feet made me itchy for excitement. From the prior list of my phone numbers Mom had kept on the wall, I should have scars from scratching all those itches.

I continued my lazy stroll, taking everything in. It wasn't long before I found myself humming some happy tune from my childhood and my heart warmed at the memory of hot fudge sundaes on my grandmother's porch. I smiled, feeling more content than I had in a long time. I looked up at the clear blue sky and took a deep breath. This was going to be a beautiful day, exactly what I needed.

A tall, thin, old lady, wearing a green paisley dress and an apron, walked toward me. Her large, brimmed hat cast her eyes in shadow and in her gloved hands she carried a wicker basket filled with produce. She smiled sweetly as she approached, and I couldn't help but return the expression.

"Good morning, dear. You must be Justine Butler's daughter. You look just like her."

"Why, yes, I am." Wow, news traveled fast. "I'm Juli." I extended my arm, and the old woman adjusted her grip on the basket in order to shake my hand.

"I'm Tess. Tess McDermott. So sorry about your mother. The whole town has been at a loss." She pulled out a ripe red tomato and held it up. "You can't beat our local produce. Fred just loves my homemade salsa."

I bent down and sniffed the vegetable, not quite ready to talk about my mother with a stranger. Tess had given me a taste for a new salsa idea, and I couldn't wait to unpack my gadgets. If anything, it would further occupy my mind from missing Mom while waiting for all the legal formalities and figuring out my next move.

"Get yourself down to the market." She raised the juicy tomato as one last tease before setting it back into her basket. "They close at noon today. Go straight down Main Street and turn left on Park Ave. You'll pass the butcher shop and Harry's Hardware and then run right into it."

"Thank you, Tess. I think I'll check it out. I haven't been to the market in years." I licked my lips in anticipation of fresh garden vegetables. Nothing ever tasted better than homegrown.

"Well, just don't pay any mind to Mark Walker." Tess pointed from the direction she'd come, to a man in a crumpled business suit, throwing his fists in the air as he walked and then kicking a nearby trash can before sitting on a bench.

"Why?" Mrs. Bailey had mentioned Mark last night, and I wondered if things were worse than she'd thought. I hadn't seen the man in well over a decade. He appeared harmless enough sulking on the bench. Maybe he was waiting for a bus to go into the city or for someone to arrive.

"Looks like he had another late night and never made it home, not that he has a home to go to anymore."

I regarded the man for a moment, understanding how he must be feeling. Mom's death was the only reason I had a roof over my head right now. I still wasn't sure what to do about my own job situation.

"He looks a little sad." My attention focused back on Tess, and she harrumphed.

"He should be. Wife kicked him out since he lost his job and won't stop gambling. She won't take him back or let him see the kids. Who can blame her?"

"That's too bad." My gaze returned to Mark Walker. I tried not to stare, and instead sent some positive energy hoping things would look up for him soon.

"Well, I've got to get home to Fred. I've dallied long enough."

"Enjoy your day," I said as Tess walked away and I continued toward the farmers market. I passed the local library and post office, remembering to turn on Park Ave. Just past the butcher shop, a round man wearing a canvas apron turned away from his display of garden tools, looking just as friendly as I remembered.

"Welcome back, Juli!" He waved as I came closer. "Wish it were under better circumstances." Harry Henderson's gentle brown eyes touched my soul. I swallowed the lump blocking my airway and wondered when hearing condolences would get easier.

"Thank you, Mr. Henderson. It's a comfort to be back home. I somehow forgot what a pretty little town New Hope is."

"That it is. And please, call me Harry. You're all grown up and Mr. Henderson makes me feel old." He chuckled, and I smiled. "So, what brings you out so early this morning?" He returned to his work and straightened a couple pots of petunias.

"I ran into Mrs. McDermott who suggested I go to the farmers market, so that's where I'm headed."

"Nothing gets to the heart of our sheriff more than a good homemade meal." Harry seemed to blush and then added, "At least that's what my niece, April, says. They've gotten pretty close over the years."

"Really?" Chase must be the town's eligible bachelor. He'd make a good househusband to some workaholic, I mused.

"Oh, you won't have to worry," Harry's voice cut through my thoughts. "Now that you're back, I'm sure you've got Chase wrapped around your finger." He twirled his chubby pinky for effect.

Why would he even assume Chase and I were together? I let out a nervous laugh. Harry and Mrs. Bailey must be drinking out of the same tea pot.

"Wrapped around something, all right," I said under my breath, thinking Chase had enough on me to wrap me around his little finger if he wanted to. Then again, that's what best friends were for.

"What was that?" Harry leaned forward, tilting an ear in my direction.

"Love the garden gnomes." I rested my hand on the red ceramic hat of the statue, eager to steer the subject away from the town sheriff.

"Thanks, they're new this year. Got a shipment of wishing wells in the back, too. Friend of mine in New Hartford makes each one by hand." Harry knocked on the roof of a wishing well, and I blinked back to reality.

"Beautifully crafted." I couldn't resist turning the crank which lowered the small plank and metal bucket. I'd always had an eye for detail. Working at Gallery 02116 and my various stints as a personal shopper helped to hone my skills. "Are there different ones in the back?" I asked, trying to behave while finding the thought of sticking a colorful gnome in Chase's front lawn simply irresistible. It was either that or a pink flamingo. The well was adorable and might make a perfect centerpiece in the corner wild-flower patch in Mom's backyard.

"They are pretty much all the same. Which reminds me, I need to call Bill Perkins about wiring the security lights in the back lot."

"Don't tell me you have problems with crime?" Once more I perused the businesses along the street and the neighboring houses. Nothing bad or exciting ever happened here, at least not when I was growing up. For the sake of the elder citizens of New Hope, I prayed it was still true.

"Just the occasional teen looking for a little excitement as I'm sure you remember. They have yet to do any damage, but you never know. That's why I want Bill to install the lights."

"Right." I nodded. "Well, I should let you get back to work and get myself to the market."

"All right, Juli. I'll look for you at church on Sunday."

I felt the blood drain from my face. Church? That wasn't part of the plan. I might have returned home for my mother, but I wasn't replacing my mother. No one could.

"See you later, Harry." I waved a bit frantically and quickened my steps as the guilt began to rise. After what I did to David, there was no way I could set foot in a church.

My ticket to hell was non-refundable.

———

THE MARKET PROVED TO BE AS PLENTIFUL AS TESS HAD described. Since giving up meat years ago, I looked forward to fresh organic produce anytime I could find it. My shopping bag contained as much as I could carry while I made my way toward the antique shop.

When Mrs. Bailey told me Mom had done well for herself, that still didn't mean I wanted to inherit this place. I didn't like working there when I was younger, always wishing the place could be fun and full of spirit. While I knew more now and could appreciate fine antiques, I still didn't want to be a part of that world.

The familiar wooden sign reading "JB Antiques" hung above the door on a wrought iron hook. I balanced my bags while unlocking the door and stepped through. A cluster of silver bells tinkled above my head. They would be the first things to go.

Sorry, Mom.

After closing the door, I turned on some lights and found a notepad to take stock of the shop. Statues lined shelves, old pub signs hung on the walls and different colored glass pieces sat atop the many mismatched tables. A display case with finely detailed estate jewelry drew my attention. The delicate jeweled pieces had to be worth several thousand, from what I could tell through the glass.

The shop had the distinct smell of musty old items. Without further hesitation, I propped open the door with a brass umbrella stand. The place had potential, and the wheels in my mind began to turn. Fresh paint, a few air fresheners and maybe some brighter lights would be an easy place to start. I'd have to be sure to get Bill Perkins' number from Mr. Henderson.

With new-found excitement, I jotted notes and sketched my ideas within the pages of the tattered notebook. A cozy room off to the right with built-in shelves caught my eye. When I crossed the threshold, I knew exactly what I was going to put in there.

This would be the perfect spot for a health food nook!

I couldn't picture myself dabbling in old-fashioned merchandise like my mother, but as I looked around the main room, I could totally see it as an organic café. Yes, a place for people to relax, eat a healthy snack and purchase some wholesome ingredients.

I'd experimented with many different recipes over the years and with a rascally parrot and giant fluffball living on either side of me, I knew adding a line of pet treats would be perfect. The more I thought of the idea, the more I loved it. My dream could now become reality. Maybe it was time I put down roots. Doing business here would be a total Juli Butler experience!

I underlined a note to call some of my contacts in Boston and New York to buy out Mom's merchandise, keeping a few of the more usable pieces so I could have some of Mom still with me. I would consult some of my friends on an advertising plan and be in business in no time. Being home didn't seem so daunting now that I had a project.

"How's everything going?" Chase's voice came from out of nowhere, and I practically hugged him with excitement. He still wore his uniform and smelled of summer sunshine with a hint of his teakwood cologne.

"Perfect! This is all fantastic, and I can't wait to share my ideas for the shop with you."

"Ideas?" He eyed me wearily. "Wait. I figured you weren't sticking around. What are you up to?"

My chin elevated a notch at the sheer fact he assumed I wouldn't stay. "Adding my own flair to this old place, that's what. I've had a vision." I spread my hands to make a frame.

"This can't be good."

"Not good, but great. I'm going to rename the shop The Butler's Pantry." I swung my arms wide and scooted toward what would be my pet treat area, as a name popped into my brain. "And this is going to be called Petit Four Paws, my organic pet café and part of the pantry. Get it?"

"An organic pet café inside of an antique shop? No, I don't get it."

"No, let me explain. I'm selling most of the antiques, and I'm going to turn the place into a totally green health food store and café for humans and animals. It will focus on tofu and soy and homegrown organic ingredients. You know, make it a little more exciting and modern. And while people are here enjoying a healthy drink and snack, they can step inside Petit Four Paws with their pets and purchase some of my special organic treats. They take their animals for a walk, come right on in, and everyone is happy. Don't you just love it?" I bounced on the balls of my sneakers.

"A pet café. You can't be serious. You're going to have food and animals and people all under the same roof? Don't you think you're opening up a huge can of worms?"

"No." My smile slipped a little. I loved my idea and couldn't wait to see the looks on people's faces when they found out they could come with their pets.

"Well, I do." Chase walked toward the open door and looked out at the street. "You're going to have to apply for a license, check with the zoning board, and Lord knows what else, if you plan on serving animals. I don't think you've thought this through. The locals loved your mother's 'traditional' antique shop. New Hope is my town, and we don't need you turning her legacy into a farce with this urbanized idea."

"Urbanized? C'mon, Chase." I tagged along behind him, throwing my arms in the air. "I of all people know sometimes you just need to branch out and take risks. And the Butler's Pantry will be my risk, and a chance to show the people of New Hope something new and exciting."

"These people were born and raised on meat, potatoes, and good old-fashioned apple pie." Chase stopped walking and turned to face me. "I doubt you even know what you're doing. I thought maybe you were changing this to a wholesome old-fashioned food pantry, or something more useful to this town than a hoity toity, new-age doggie diner."

"As a matter of fact, I do know what I'm doing. Besides, it's a café for humans as well, and doggies aren't the only pets I'll serve. I don't think you give your citizens enough credit. There's no law telling me I can't open a café of any kind, now is there?" I waited, but he knew I had him. "I have a lot to do. Why don't you go back to your own job so I can do mine? I can have all this stuff shipped out tonight, get my foods on order and at least be open for samples in a couple of days."

"Just like that?" He crossed his arms.

"Just like that." I copied his actions.

"Okay, but it will be your loss. Give it time. You'll see. I bet I'm right. I smell trouble, big-time."

"I'll take that bet and happily prove you wrong." After a brief stare-down, I walked forward and firmly shoved him out the door. "Bye-bye, now." I waved through the glass.

Chase shook his head, and I could tell by the gleam in his eyes he wanted to say more on the subject, but the "good guy" inside wasn't about to let him. I smiled and turned away with a clap of my hands. I bet he played good-cop-bad-cop with his own conscience!

With Chase gone, I got right to work pulling empty boxes from the back room and starting to load up the smaller items for shipping. Thank God, Mom had a computer. My job became easier as I described each box via email and sometimes attached a picture. The local courier was going to love me tomorrow.

"Excuse me, Miss Butler," a soft male voice spoke, and I looked up into the face of Mark Walker. He smoothed a hand through his mussed-up hair. "I'd like to talk to you if you have a moment."

"I'm not officially open for business." I straightened and wiped my hands on my jeans. "What can I do for you?"

"I'm not here to buy anything. Actually, I wanted to talk to you about a job. If there's anything you need done, I can do it. The name's Mark Walker." He extended his hand, and I shook it, surprised by his strong grip.

"I appreciate that, Mark." I didn't let on that I knew who he was. "I can manage on my own for now. Thanks anyway."

"Your mother thought there might be a chance for work in the fall when shipments are due in. I'd appreciate it if you'd keep me in mind now that she's gone."

"I'm making a few changes to the shop, but I can do that." Knowing he was so down on his luck, I couldn't be mean to him even though my worry meter bumped up a notch over the underlying tone to his voice. Mom had her reasons for not offering him employment. Until I knew otherwise, I needed to err on the side of caution. "If you'll excuse me, I have to get back to my inventory."

Mark turned with a nod and smacked into a big burly man with a large gold hoop earring, wearing a black muscle shirt. The larger man growled and shoved Mark aside. I stepped back, not sure what was going to happen next.

"She's not hiring, Pete," Mark spat but kept his eyes on the floor.

"I ain't here to get a job, you idiot. Now out of my way and let me talk."

"Hey, you in on the poker game at Johnnie's this week?" Mark surprised me when he grabbed ahold of Pete's shirt, looking desperate, and I thought the big guy was going to rip him apart. "I want in this time. I'm good for it. I swear."

"Yeah, I'm in, but you're not," Pete snarled, and Mark's hands dropped to his side. "The whole town knows you ain't got money, Walker. You need to get some help for your problem," Pete said with a knowing glance in my direction, sending a rush of chills up my spine.

"I'll show you. I'll find the money," Mark mumbled to Pete as he scurried out the door.

"Can I help you?" I smiled stiffly as I placed my hands on the counter and tried not to stare overly long at his scary five o'clock shadow and dark bushy eyebrows.

"This here statue is one of them antiques." He pointed a tattooed hand about the room. "Here, take a look." He shoved the figurine in my face, and I dropped back a few steps, thinking I should keep the doors locked until I was ready for customers.

"Like I informed Mark, I'm not officially open for business. Besides, I'm not into antiques anymore. In a couple of days this place will be the Butler's Pantry Café and Petit Four Paws."

"Café ye say? That poses a little problem." He flicked at the gold hoop and then rubbed at the bristles on his chin, leaning over the counter when he said, "I don't like problems."

"Why is that my problem?" Bells were going off inside my body like a pinball machine on tilt, but I wasn't about to let him see. I could play his game.

"Your dearly departed mother promised me a deal when I brought the statue back." He slid it across the counter.

"Like I said, I'm not into antiques anymore." I gently eased the figure in his direction hoping he'd take the hint.

"A deal's a deal. Not my fault she croaked before I could come back here." He pushed it back towards me. "You going back on your poor mother's word?"

I bit my lip, choosing not to tangle with him over his poor choice of words. For a moment I wondered if the statue was stolen. This grey marble figurine of a mother and two children didn't look like something a guy like Pete would have in his own home. I studied the veins within the marble, knowing full well I couldn't go back on her word. Upon closer inspection, I saw a small crack along the baseline.

"What happened here?" I ran my finger along the seam, feeling a deep crevice as if someone had tried to repair the damage. For a split second, Pete looked alarmed.

"Not sure. That thing has been in my family for generations. My sister had it at her place. Maybe one of her kids broke it." He looked toward the door.

For reasons I would never know, my mother had agreed to do business with this man. I set the piece on the counter and made my offer. "I'll give you two hundred for it."

"That's it? It's a real antique, I'm telling ya." Pete flicked at his earring once more. "Sorry, but it would be worth more without the damage."

"Four hundred." He looked again at the door. My worry meter rose another notch.

"I said two," my voice was firm as I attempted my best poker face. "I'm doing you a favor."

"Fine," he huffed. "Can ya make it quick? I'm in a bit of a hurry."

I clenched my jaw and pulled the check binder and receipt book from under the cash register. Once Pete was out of here, I was going to close and lock the door. I didn't even care if I became asphyxiated from the musty smell.

"Last name?" I questioned with pen in hand.

"Cash is king, sister."

"And I need it for my records, in case there's a problem. Will there be a problem, Mister...."

"All right, the name's Seaver, Pete Seaver."

"Thank you, Mr. Seaver." I scrawled his name and signed the check.

Pete swiped the check from my hand, not even waiting for the ink to dry, and walked out the door without so much as a thank you. I closed the door on his heels happy to be rid of the bad juju. Back at the counter, I scrutinized my first unofficial-official sale, hoping it was the last that didn't have to do with organic food. I'd given him a fair price and would probably get at least half my money back when it sold with the rest of Mom's stuff.

The annoying bells above the door tinkled, and I muttered under my breath over forgetting to lock the door again. Mrs. Bailey appeared with a wicker basket which smelled like heaven, and I sighed in relief. My grimace turned into a genuine grin, and I greeted her with a big hug.

"Mrs. B what are you doing here?"

"I used to bring your mother dinner on occasion when she worked late like this. I noticed you hadn't come home, and Chase told me you were here getting organized for the disaster you planned to create. I take it he doesn't approve?"

"Chase approving of something I did? Not in this lifetime."

The man just couldn't stay out of my business. "He's just mad because I sent him away after he didn't like my ideas."

"Well, take a break and eat." The corners of her eyes crinkled when she smiled. "He's just watching out for you, Juli."

"No, he's just being a buttinski and trying to prove me wrong." I saw confusion glaze the older woman's face. "I just had my first transaction, and I'm not even officially open. I'd like to give him this ticket so he can choke on it. Don't know what I'm doing my—"

"Nothing changes with you two, now, does it?" She began to unload plastic containers from her basket, totally cutting off my rant. My stomach voiced its hunger. Vegetable soup with barley, one of my favorites, and she even had a zip lock baggie of fluffy biscuits. "Here, eat up, while I take a look around. What was your first purchase?"

"Mmm... it's that statue by the register," I said between mouthfuls. "Some deal Mom had started before she died. I don't really even want the thing. Soon as I sell it, I'll be off to a great start."

"Why don't I make it official?"

"What do you mean?" I set the spoon on an embroidered linen napkin.

"I will buy the statue. My daughter has a lovely house on the Cape, and this reminds me of her and my two granddaughters."

"Sold." With a satisfied grin I finished the transaction and watched Mrs. Bailey leave, the statue tucked safely inside her basket. Pride emanated from deep within and somehow in spite of the upcoming changes, I knew my mom would be just as proud. I was doing this on my own, and there was nothing that was going to stop me from becoming a success in my hometown. Nothing.

Even if my gut still felt funny.

Four

With one final turn of the screwdriver, I anchored my wooden chimes above the door. Stepping off the ladder, I closed the door and opened it to a sound more soothing than those darn silver bells. Sorry, Mom.

I'd come into the shop early to finish where I left off the night before. So far, eight people agreed to buy some of the antique merchandise, and I had a confirmation email that my new sign would ship by the end of the week. The appliances would be delivered this afternoon, and Bill Perkins was going to stop by with a quote on new light fixtures. Today was going to be a great day.

Not long after I'd put away the ladder and started dusting out the old armoire, the hollow wind chimes danced. I stepped from behind the giant doors to find Tess McDermott in a dusty blue dress and colorful apron, anxiously looking about the place. Her soft brown hair, free from a sun hat, showed very little signs of grey for a woman her age. My first thought was that she'd brought me some leftover produce or even a jar of her salsa.

"How are you, dear?" Her voice sounded a bit shaky. "Rumor has it you're opening a café for humans and pets."

"Yes, but I'm not officially open yet." I still couldn't figure out what was up. She didn't seem like the same put-together woman I'd seen yesterday.

"That's a shame. Fluffy, Cotton, and Steve came with me for a visit." She reached inside the bulging patchwork pockets of her apron to scoop out three tiny kittens.

"Oh, they are precious!" I took one from her and nestled the white-pawed baby in the palm of my hand.

"That's Steve." Tess pointed out and set the other two back into the depths of her pockets where they mewed their dissatisfaction. Steve purred, and I fell in love.

Still cuddling the content feline, I went into the office and came back with a plastic container filled with small circular snacks. "I made some special treats last night to get ready for my open house. These Kitty Krackers are made with all natural ingredients and dolphin safe tuna."

"Can I take some home for Fred?"

I pursed my lips in thought. "I'm making some fantastic herbal spreads and crackers for human consumption. If you come back tomorrow, you can try them."

"So, what's wrong with the tuna?" Tess squinted behind her glasses.

"Well, nothing. I had planned the treats for animals, but they are natural and healthy. If you'd like some to take home, you're more than welcome to do so." I pulled a small sandwich bag from under the counter and placed about a dozen snacks inside but not before slipping one to my furry friend, who meowed his approval. Tess stood next to the register with her change purse in hand.

"What do I owe you, dear?"

"Consider them a sample. No charge." I handed her the bag, and Steve. "Why don't you take Steve as payment? He seems to like you."

I looked down at the shiny black fur and white boots straddling the palm of my hand and blinked. Yes, he was adorable and his mini motor was on high speed, but I lived smack in the middle of a Scallywag and Major war zone.

"That is awfully sweet of you, but I can't," I responded. The woman looked disappointed, and I felt horrible. "With starting the business, I'm going to be working such crazy hours. It won't be fair to him." Giving Steve a kiss between his ears, I handed him back to Tess.

"Well okay, then. We'll be back tomorrow to say hello." And with that she was gone, Kitty Krackers and all.

As I watched her leave, a warm feeling touched my heart. The urban jungle had nothing on New Hope. I had only been here a few days, and already I felt a sense of community in the people I'd met and the old timers who remained. For years I'd tried so hard to get away from this place. Who knew growing up and coming home were exactly what I'd needed all along?

The wooden chimes clacked, and I looked up from cleaning the inside of the glass display case. Chase thought it was sacrilegious to store my new age treats in such a beautiful antique treasure. I thought it was a perfect mixture of Mom and me.

Two teenage boys walked around the shop with their hands buried deep in the pockets of their jeans. They appeared harmless enough, and I felt confident their curiosity was what had brought them in.

"Can I help you boys?"

"Yeah." The tall one spoke first, tossing his head to make the shaggy brown hair stay out of his eyes. "My brother Kyle and I want to trade in this gold watch." He pulled it from his pocket and held it in the air.

I was never going to whip this place into shape if people kept coming in trying to make deals with me, but I didn't dare put a closed sign on the door in case the delivery van showed up and I was in the back. Hopefully, they would be here soon so I could continue with my renovations. In the meantime, I'd have to deal with antique shop customers.

"I hate to disappoint you guys, but I'm not into buying antiques. That was my mom. I'm going to be opening a health food café for pets and humans." I motioned them toward the counter, holding my hand out for the watch. "What's your name?"

"Scott Iverson," he said with a quick look at his brother.

The watch appeared to be brand new. Then I saw the inscription on the back: Happy Birthday, Ben. I shifted my gaze to the boys, who didn't look nervous in the least, leading me to believe they didn't steal it. But they were up to no good just the same.

"Who's Ben?" I asked.

"Our dad," the younger one, Kyle, answered.

"And does your dad know you took his watch?" I rested my elbows on the counter, still holding the item.

"Not really." Kyle looked sheepishly at his feet.

"We planned on buying it back before he even knew it was gone," Scott spoke up, and I gave him a suspicious look. "The new Demon Slayer game comes out today, and he wouldn't give us our allowance early."

"And it's going to sell out," Kyle interjected with excitement.

"It's a really nice time piece, and a birthday present," I stated, wanting them to think about what they were doing. Since I had no intention of buying it, I had no doubt they'd hit the streets and sell it to someone else.

"It's from our dad's girlfriend, anyway. He has other watches." I sensed some dislike in Scott's voice.

"Are you sure you guys want to do this? If your dad wanted to sell it, he'd have done so and already given you the money."

"You're not going to take it?" Kyle flashed me a perfect puppy-dog face.

"I can't."

"That's great. I told you to let me do the talking, dummy." Scott swatted his brother on the back of the head.

"But I'll tell you what I will do." Both boys tossed hopeful expressions my way. "If you help me move some of these old antiques and heavy signs to the back room, I will pay you each forty dollars."

"That's enough to get our game!" Kyle pumped his fist.

One hour later, Karl and Scott headed to the game store eighty dollars richer. Yup, small towns were great for these feel-good moments. I couldn't help but remember some of the crazy things I'd done when I was their age.

Crazy was only the beginning.

The wooden chimes sounded again, and I started wondering if I shouldn't be installing a revolving door. Town gossip was making for some wonderful business, even if people were only settling their curiosity. This time it wasn't a sweet little old lady or brothers looking for some fun money.

Pete marched toward me with a wild look of panic in his eyes. "I need the statue back," he blurted.

I blinked and then frowned. "I'm sorry, I can't do that."

"What do you mean? I just sold it to ya last night. I made a mistake, and I need it back. I still have your check." He slapped it on the counter.

"I don't have the statue. I sold it before closing yesterday."

"Sold it?" he shouted. "You can't do that!"

"Yes, I can," I responded calmly, trying to defuse the situation. I'd dealt with all kinds of characters in the city, and I could smell trouble with this one. "This is my business."

"And you don't know what you're doing, lady. Don't you know anything?" He sounded like Chase, and I fisted my hands at my sides.

"Excuse me? I do know what I'm doing. My business sense is none of yours."

"There's a grace period. I have twenty-four hours to change my mind or buy it back. Everyone knows that." He tossed his arms in the air then stuck a fist in front of my face. "I want my statue."

I flinched slightly but held my ground. "I don't have it."

"Tell me who bought it. I'll give them the damn check."

"All sales are final and confidential." I thought of poor Mrs. Bailey having to deal with the likes of Pete Seaver.

"Listen, lady, you need to correct this or there's going to be trouble. Trouble I don't think a woman like you needs if you know what I mean."

Chase's words came back to haunt me. "I don't like what you're implying," I ground out, hating that Chase had been right. "I think you should leave before I call the police."

"Tell me who has my statue."

"No."

"You'll be sorry you screwed with me on this," Pete snarled, not backing down. "I'll find out myself."

I wasn't about to back down either, as I narrowed my eyes and placed my hands on my hips. "And you'll find your sorry self in the local jail if you don't leave right this minute. I'm done playing nice."

"I'm just getting started, Miss Butler, and I assure you there ain't nothin' nice about it." He cast an evil grin, swiped the check off the counter and flew through the door.

"Well, I'm not nice either, Mr. Seaver!"

"Outta my way, Vin!" He shoved a short man with slicked black hair out of his way. "Hey! Seaver! I need to talk to you!" The man pushed back at my door before it hit him in the face and whirled around, determined to follow Pete. I was right on their heels.

"I'm not talking to you, Minetti, unless you're the one who bought my damn statue." The men kept walking away as the hairs on the back of my neck twitched a warning. I wasn't about to let someone like him fluster me, or the gaping stares from the lingering townspeople on the street who'd heard more than they should have.

"And you stay away from sweet Mrs. Bailey, or you'll be the one who's sorry!" I yelled after them, then bit my lip, covering my hand over my mouth. I hadn't meant to say her name. Hopefully the gossip mill wouldn't spread the word about my little accounting error with Pete. The thought of Chase knowing he'd been right maxed out my blood pressure. Then again, as angry as Pete was, it wouldn't surprise me if he marched straight to Chase's office or even the town lawyer.

I wasn't going to let his negative energy upset me. Things always worked out the way they should, and this situation was no different. I suppose if I wanted to be really nice, I could talk to Mrs. Bailey and ask if she wouldn't mind purchasing something else from the leftover inventory for her daughter.

Before I left this morning, she'd stopped by with fresh muffins and mentioned going with her church knitting group to Lancaster and that she'd be home late. Hopefully tomorrow morning was soon enough to clear the air with Pete and do the right thing. I wanted New Hope to be a fresh start.

Lord knew I didn't need any more "real" trouble.

———

After a fitful sleep, I awoke with the vision of a gloating Chase Hargrave dancing in my head. The thought of his "goodie-goodness" finally wearing off on me made me shiver. Why else would I be so eager to get the statue back in Pete's hands?

"This calls for some serious coffee," I said while rubbing the lack of sleep from my eyes. Before I could reach my door, the sound of tapping and cackling made me stop. Slowly, I turned on the balls of my bare feet.

It couldn't be.

Charging to the window and flinging the yellow striped curtains back, I found myself face to face with Scallywag. The blue and gold parrot had escaped from Mrs. Bailey's house, probably when she came home last night. She would be worried sick if she woke up and found him gone.

"Mom," I spoke to the ceiling. "I don't know what has gotten into me since coming home, but you can stop laughing." Grabbing a sweatshirt off the floor, I pulled it over my head and then glared at the troublesome bird. "And yooou." I pointed. "You are in so much trouble." I heard Scallywag squawk when I scooted out my bedroom door.

I snatched a Chinese take-out container full of Sesame Peeps I'd made the night before, and then hit the button on the coffee maker. If I had to chase the mischievous parrot all around town, I didn't want to wait for the coffee when I returned. And I didn't want coffee with Officer-Goodie just in case Pete had reported me.

Going out the back door, I stood at the base of the oak tree underneath my bedroom window. I shook the box, and while the bird cocked his brightly plumed head toward the noise, he didn't move. The early morning air smelled of the coming rain as a breeze kicked up, ruffling his feathers, and blowing wisps of my hair across my cheek.

"Of all the parrots in the world, you must be the most stubborn," I ground out between my teeth and shook the box harder. Scallywag only stretched his wings as if I bored him. I scattered some crackers on the ground, hoping to coax the fowl down before Mother Nature decided to open her skies for a downpour. He still didn't budge. "Stupid bird," I grumbled, realizing what I would have to do in order to return him safe and undetected to Mrs. B.

Tossing the carton, I rolled my sleeves and shimmied up the tree like I had when I was seventeen. Only this time I didn't have Chase ready with a pillowcase to stuff him in.

Scallywag eyed me cautiously as I made my way from limb to limb. The climb didn't seem as easy as I remembered, and the crazy, stubborn parrot didn't appear threatened as I moved closer. Tree bark snagged the knees of my pajama bottoms as I crawled across a large branch. I was getting closer, and if he would just stay put, this would be a piece of cake.

Until Major bounced out of Chase's back door into the yard and started barking like crazy.

"Shhh...Major, quiet!" I whispered loudly, not really knowing why I whispered at all since Scallywag screeched back at the dog, which only made him bark even louder. "That's enough you two."

I crept closer to the annoying bird, feeling victory in sight. Just as I reached for him, Major put his paws on the fence, and Scallywag hopped to another branch. My grip slipped and I crashed to the ground. Aside from a few thorns poking through my clothes, my landing seemed softer than I'd expected.

I lay there for a moment looking up at the rascally parrot, who I swear was smiling at me. I scowled and the wicked bird cackled what sounded like a true laugh. Even the Major-pain-in-my-butt dog had stayed perched on his hind legs to peek over the fence and view my failed attempt.

"Real funny," I moaned since I'd just missed landing on Mom's award-winning apricot roses.

Something poked at my shoulder blades that didn't feel like a thorn. "Probably a stray branch, thanks to YOU!" I propped myself up on an elbow and shot Scallywag a death-look.

The bird whistled and Major barked. "Thanks for your help," I mumbled, then noticed a pair of legs sticking up between the blooms.

"Ahhh!" I yelled and scrambled to my feet.

My first thought was maybe Chase had seen me from his kitchen window, came out to help, and I'd flattened him. That would have served him right for being nosy. Upon further inspection, I saw silver tips on a pair of black leather boots, something I couldn't see Chase ever wearing in this lifetime.

"Oh, goodness, I'm so sorry." I stood mortified, thinking I had landed on a Good Samaritan. The wind stilled and whoever I landed on laid there motionless. "Are you okay?" I took a closer look and recognized the sideways number eight tattooed on the hand of Pete Seaver. What was he doing in my mother's roses?

Crouching down, I touched Pete's shoulder. The man didn't budge. A chill worked its way from my toes straight to my hairline.

Something wasn't right. Feeling a little weird, I bent even farther and turned my ear to check his breathing.

Nothing.

"Oh God," I gasped as the realization hit me. "Are you dead?" I asked, even though rationally I knew he couldn't answer, then I felt for the non-existent pulse.

"What have you done," screeched Scallywag from over my shoulder.

"Whaaat?" I screamed back, whipping around to face the blasted bird, who had positioned himself on a lower branch. "I didn't do anything." I stood for what seemed like an eternity, staring at the large bird who continued to taunt me as he flitted about.

Poor Pete was dead. I didn't have time to worry about a demented bird trying to point the finger at me. I needed to call the police. I rushed back in the house, grabbed the cordless phone—another small-town charm I was grateful for in this moment since I had no idea where I left my cell phone—and returned to Pete's side. With shaking fingers, I dialed the number.

"9-1-1 what is your emergency?"

"This is Juli Butler, and there's a dead body in my mother's rose garden!" I yelled, the hysteria finally kicking in at the same time the wind picked back up.

"Ma'am, can you tell me how it happened?" the operator asked in a calm voice when I was anything but.

"How should I know? I fell out of a tree, trying to catch a very naughty parrot, and landed on him. He's just, just lying there." Thunder rumbled overhead and I cringed, anticipating a streak of lightening. "The man, not the bird," I clarified for no other reason than I was freaking out.

"Okay, ma'am, we'll send an ambulance right away to your location. Please stay on the line."

"Juli? What's going on? Major has been barking like crazy." Chase appeared at the corner of the house, dressed in his uniform.

I stayed silent, not wanting to tell him. Not knowing how to tell him. "Juliana? What's the matter? Are you okay?"

"I'm fine," I said after a moment, then held up my phone. "Other than landing on a dead body."

"Dead?" Chase frowned, looking skeptical. "What are you talking about?" I watched him cock a trained ear toward the sound of distant sirens.

"It's Pete, from the shop. I found him here in Mom's garden. Trust me, the man is not breathing, not moving, no pulse, one hundred percent dead."

His eyes widened and mouth gaped as the reality of my words hit home. "Did you call the police?"

"You are the police, remember?" How did I not think to scream for Chase? "Anyway, yes, I'm on the phone with 9-1-1 right now."

I'd never been this close to a dead body before. I especially didn't like the looks Scallywag kept giving me. Nor did I appreciate the look Chase gave me when he shot through the arborvitaes like a baseball through Aunt Mae's kitchen window. Worry mixed with confusion morphed to anger then frustration. I didn't know why he was so upset. I was the one who found the body.

"What happened?" he questioned in his deep sheriff-like tone.

"Pete's dead, Pete's dead." Scallywag whistled and bobbed his head.

Chase stared at the bird, then at me, while all chaos erupted around us as emergency crews finally arrived.

"It's true." I pointed to where the EMT now crouched over the corpse. "What were you even doing out here and at this hour of the morning?"

"Scallywag escaped from Mrs. Bailey's, and I was trying to capture him."

"You should have called me. We—"

"I'm perfectly capable of catching a darn bird," I cut him off. "I don't need your help."

The EMT stood and motioned to his chunky partner who scurried past us with a back board and box of syringes. Chase grumbled something, and I couldn't quite read his expression when he decided to speak. "So why is Pete in your mother's rose garden?"

"Funny you should ask."

"Gonna get my money. Juuuuli." Scallywag opted for more cackles and whistles, which didn't seem to impress Chase at all. I, for one, was ready to strangle the evil bird.

"What money? Juli, what is this bird talking about?"

"I bought a statue from Pete the other day." I tried to smile proudly.

"You what?" Chase's brows disappeared beneath his hairline. "I thought you weren't opening the antique shop. What have you gotten yourself into now?"

"Before you get all worked up, just listen." I lifted my hand and then continued, "First, I bought the marble statue from Pete. Mrs. Bailey came in later that same day and bought the statue from me because it reminded her of her daughter. Then Pete came back the next day and said he changed his mind and threatened me when I wouldn't tell him who had purchased it."

Chase's continued stare of exasperation made me nervous. My off button refused to engage. "Pete was such a scary man. After thinking on it, I decided the best thing to do for everyone was to make it up to Pete by returning the statue. I know what you're thinking, I'm surprised at myself too. But that's what I was going to do once I talked to Mrs. Bailey this morning. Now Pete is dead, and I can't even do what I wanted to make it right. Which serves me right for trying to be a nice person. Sorry, Mom." I'd rambled so fast in one breath I had no idea if Chase had even understood me.

"Since when have you tried to make anything right," he grumbled, with hands on hips and shaking his head at the scene unfolding around us. "I'm surprised you didn't tell me any of this."

"Why would you need to know? It was my business transaction, not yours. I thought I could handle it."

"Not doing so well in that department now, are you? You've really done it this time, Juli." Chase walked away and stood next to a man taking pictures of Pete's lifeless body.

"What do you think, Tim? Cause of death?"

"Preliminary examination shows a trauma to the right side of his skull," the short balding man with wire-rimmed glasses said while continuing to shoot pictures. "He hasn't been dead very long, Chase. Maybe four hours max."

"You don't say." Chase turned to me. "Seems like you were here in the nick of time.

Did you notice anybody or anything out of the ordinary?"

"Of course not!" I waved my hand in Scallywag's direction. "I was trying to catch the blasted bird."

Scallywag wasn't about to be outdone. "You're a liar, leave me alone, what have I done?" Several more whistles echoed within the continuous rumbles of thunder, drowning out my gasp, but I could see the questions in Chase's eyes.

This was not looking good.

"Zip your beak, you naughty fowl," I growled as it struck me how guilty I was starting to look, and Scallywag wasn't helping.

"You said Pete threatened you. Did he show up at your house last night?" Chase asked. "No, well... I don't know. I was busy cooking for the open house." I looked down at the corpse. "Maybe he was lurking outside. I've got no other explanation as to why he would be here."

Chase jotted down something in a small notebook as fat droplets of rain splattered around us. "There's an explanation all right. The truth always comes out, one way or another." Chase's eyes were cloudy like the skies above, and I would have killed to get the mischief back.

"What exactly are you saying?" I swallowed hard, knowing I wasn't going to like the answer.

"We're going to have to take you down to the station for questioning."

"You can't be serious, Chase. I've told you everything."

"I hate to tell you this, but you can't leave town until this case is solved."

"Are you saying I'm a suspect?"

"It's Juli. Put that down. Pete's dead," the bird seemed to sing-song the words as he rocked in the tree.

Chase shook his head as if clearing it from the taunts of Scallywag. "It's procedure, Juli. I'm doing my job."

"Your job? This is ridiculous. You really think I killed Pete?"

"You're in trouble now!" Scallywag cried, then with a cackle, he spouted off, "Stupid Juli."

That's when I knew, out of all the messes I'd landed myself in, this was the biggest one yet.

$Five$

"Why did Pete want the statue back?" Chase asked from across his tidy wooden desk. Thankfully he'd given me time to change into a crisp pair of khaki shorts and white button-up blouse. The storm didn't last long but brought climbing humidity in its wake.

"How should I know? He pushed me into buying it from him like he was desperate for the money. I thought I was helping him out." I scooped my hair into a ponytail and fanned my neck.

"But then he came back." Chase flipped through his notes, not bothered by the heat one bit.

"Yes." I paused, remembering the fire in Pete's eyes when he'd demanded the statue and then a glimpse of what could have been called fear before he'd disguised it in anger when I'd told him the piece had been sold. Gazing around Chase's orderly office, I noticed certificates on his wall along with some framed rock band albums. "I guess he had a change of heart." I shrugged.

"Men like Pete don't have a change of heart." Chase scowled. "Did you ever know Pete Seaver?"

"How would I know him? I just came back to town."

"And I have a sinking suspicion you brought trouble with you."

"I moved away and tried to make a life of my own, so you're accusing me of murder?"

"I'm not accusing you of anything, Juli. Life in New Hope has been quiet and normal. You show up, and suddenly we have a dead body."

"And how is that my fault?"

"I'm not sure." He ran a hand along his clean-shaven chin.

"Chase!" I couldn't imagine him turning on me, even after all this time, but the puzzlement in his eyes had me worried. "I promise, I've never met that man until he set foot in my shop."

"Okay, so you never met him. Explain why he was dead in your mother's garden." "I don't know." I tossed my hands in the air. Then I sucked in a breath, bringing Chase's green eyes to my wide ones as I placed my fingers over my lips. "Mrs. Bailey."

"What about Mrs. Bailey?"

"Before Pete left my shop, I slipped up and told him to leave Mrs. Bailey alone. He knew she had the statue."

"You think he broke into her house?"

"Why else would he be in our neighborhood? Oh, Chase, what if Mrs. Bailey killed him in self-defense? Has anyone even checked on her? She must be so frightened."

"Of course, we checked on her. I'll talk to her again, but I highly doubt she could fend off someone like Pete."

"What about Scallywag? He could have distracted Pete enough for her to whack him over the head."

"I'd leave the bird out of this. Remember, he seems to be pointing the feather at you." Chase chuckled and I wished I could whack him.

"Not funny." I pinched my lips together. I had a feeling he was right about Mrs. Bailey. I couldn't imagine her hurting anyone, even someone as ill-tempered as Pete Seaver. "What are we going to do?"

"You aren't going to do anything." He met my gaze and held it, all traces of teasing gone. "My department will handle this and work with county officials to solve the case."

"So, I'm free to leave?"

"I'd say so." A man slightly shorter than Chase but equally muscular approached the desk. "I brought you some coffee, ma'am."

"Thank you," I said and smiled up at his sympathetic amber brown eyes and neatly cut sandy blond hair. While taking the Styrofoam cup he offered, I cleared my throat and added, "My name's Juli." The guy returned the smile with a nod. Our eyes locked for a brief moment before Chase muttered something inaudible. I blinked a couple times and focused back on Chase. Now was not the time for me to get distracted by anyone.

"Juli, this is Gary Maxwell. My deputy." Chase lifted his eyes toward his counterpart.

"Whoa! You mean this is Deputy Goo—"

"Where's my coffee?" Chase asked, thankfully cutting me off before I could totally embarrass myself. Gary was not a goober at all. I'd called that one all wrong.

"Coming right up, boss," Gary said, his eyes lingering on mine with a mixture of amusement and curiosity now.

Somehow, I could picture him spending summers at the beach. I bet he turned into a bronze god by the peak of summer; golden streaks in his hair and a tan to die for. I shook my head to stop the insane thoughts passing through my brain, blaming them on post-traumatic stress.

"You two need a moment?" Chase said with growing agitation.

"Uh, no sir, I'll grab that coffee." Gary turned away, and I pointed toward the black coffee in my cup.

"Bring back some cream for our guest," Chase called after him.

"That's right, because you don't have enough to hold me here." I raised my chin a notch. "And Gary said I could leave."

"Gary doesn't run this department, and I'm still thinking on that."

"Chase, you can't keep me here. I have a business to run. There's a lot that still needs to be done before my grand opening." Thanks to Pete's untimely death, my open house would have to be postponed.

"Oh, that's right, your pet café." He air-quoted the words before turning back to his notes.

"It's more than that, as I've explained to you before."

"Listen." He closed the book, setting the silver pen precisely centered on the cover. "I don't want you to get your feelings hurt or be disappointed if the town doesn't accept what you're doing. Many are still old-fashioned here and most likely don't even know what organic is, let alone eat it or feed it to their animals."

"I think you're wrong. Organic farming has been in the news for years now. More and more people are accepting it as a healthier way of eating and making positive changes to their lifestyle."

"If you say so." He hitched a shoulder then reached for the cup Gary held out when he returned.

"She's got a point, Chase." Gary once more flashed a smile in my direction. "There are farmers out on Route 64 who have gradually changed the way they feed their livestock and grow their crops."

I clapped my hands together. "This is perfect. I'd love to have their names and contact them about being a supplier for my shop."

"You just had to tell her that," Chase grumbled to Gary.

"I'll do more than give you names," Gary said to me, ignoring the scowl plastered on Chase's face. "How about I take you out there and introduce you to them? That way you can let them know what you're all about. I'd be interested to hear about your café, too. We also have a gentleman in town who sells organic honey, and O'Toole's Fish Market down by the marina."

"That would be great, Gary." I smiled sweetly at his thoughtfulness.

"Maybe you kids can stop for ice cream, while you're out." Chase's mocking tone killed the moment.

"Don't be such a sourpuss just because Gary is interested in my business, and you're too stubborn to be open-minded about it."

"I'm very open-minded," Chase contradicted.

"Since when? You are so by-the-book it hurts. I'm sure you consult a manual before you even decide to ask a girl out."

Gary laughed out loud. "She's got you there."

"Don't you have a job to do, Deputy?" Chase barked and Gary startled, sloshing coffee over the side of his cup. "Weren't you checking on the registrants for the Play Makers Game? Make sure there's no one we need to worry about."

"Right. My source told me Max Perez is supposed to be here. He's usually around bigger casinos and high roller kind of tournaments. What's in New Hope that would be a draw?"

"Nothing," I remarked, which garnered an unprofessional eye roll from Chase.

"Then I think you should look into it further, don't you?" He scribbled on a fresh piece of paper.

"Of course, I'll get right on it. It was nice meeting you, Juli."

I grabbed a post-it note off Chase's desk and scribbled my number on it. "Call me," I mouthed as I handed it to Gary. Once he'd left the room, it was my turn to interrogate Chase. "That wasn't very professional."

"What?" He sipped his coffee and re-opened his notebook.

"Why don't you kids go for ice cream," I mimicked him. "Who's the one being childish?"

He stopped pretending indifference and looked me square in the eye. "You two were practically drooling over each other."

I jumped to my feet in protest. "Face it, Chase Hargrave, you're jealous."

"Jealous of what?" he scoffed but couldn't quite meet my eyes.

"Any guy who ever gives me even a hint of attention. You've done this to me since we were kids."

He shrugged. "I don't know Gary very well. He's only been with us for about six months. I'm just looking out for your best interests."

I slapped my hand on his desk. "I'm a grown woman and I can make my own decisions about men and who I date. Not that I'm even planning on dating him. He has contacts, and I have a new business to launch. It's called networking."

"Suit yourself." Chase stood and tossed his now empty cup in the trash. "Shall we go?"

I sighed, giving up on trying to reason with him. "Depends on where you're taking me."

"Figured I'd drop you off at your shop on my way to go talk to Mrs. Bailey, unless you'd rather ride with Deputy Goober."

"Oh, we both know Gary is no goober," I walked past Chase, adding under my breath, "and you are definitely jealous." He caught my arm.

"Let's be serious a minute, shall we?" When his green eyes met mine, I stopped short. "Until we find some leads for who the real killer is, you are still under suspicion. Don't leave town and don't get into any more trouble, understood?"

"Understood." I slipped from his hold and continued out of his office.

"Hold up a minute." He paused, and I looked over my shoulder to see a thoughtful expression muddling his features. "I've got it!" He snapped his fingers and a mischievous twinkle flashed in his eyes as a huge grin made its way across his face.

"Got what?" I squinted. That look was trouble, and I knew from experience I wouldn't like it.

"Ohhh, this is perfect." He chuckled. With his thick, dark mustache, he could be the Devil's understudy if he grew a beard.

"Out with it." I planted my feet and held my palm against his chest so he couldn't get past. "What evil plan have you conspired to make my life miserable? Am I going to be your housekeeper for a month? Wash your car, run your errands, be your gardener for crying out loud?"

"None of the above, although the housekeeper and car washer sound pretty tempting." He winked.

"Spill it already," I groaned.

"You, Miss Scarlett, will be my dog walker."

"What?" I was already shaking my head and backing away from him. "Not a good idea, Chase. And stop calling me Scarlett. I'm grown up now."

"And still as feisty. Besides, you owe me." His tone was serious, and I cast a blank stare in his direction. "The ticket, or lack of one, remember?" he reminded me.

"You're really going to go there?"

"I am." His smile grew wider, if that were possible, and I wanted to pop him. I wondered if he pulled this stuff on all the town's rule breakers. "And so are you," he added. "It's either that or downtown."

He had to be joking, at least about the downtown part. Considering my crazy past, I already knew I was going straight to hell on a private jet. I didn't need a demon dog companion.

"Dog walking." I wilted against the wall. "I think I'd rather have the ticket, please."

"Listen. Valerie, my dog walker, went on vacation with her family. I've been so busy at work; I haven't found a replacement." Chase tossed his head and I followed him through a double door to where a very shaggy sheepdog waited in an empty cell. "This is Major. Consider it bonding time."

"What are you in for, big guy?" I asked as I set my cup on a nearby file cabinet to scrutinize the four-legged-criminal.

"WOOF!"

"You don't say...." I turned toward Chase. "He's not happy about this either."

"Then it's settled." He nailed me with a stubborn look.

I sighed, giving up. "Like I have a choice?"

"That's my girl." He patted my head as if I were the dog. "C'mon, let's go." He opened the cell door and the gigantic, overly happy bundle of fur barged out to greet me.

"WOOF-WOOF!"

I caught his leash and held out a hand to stop him from jumping on me. "Chase Hargrave, it's going to be your turn to owe me after this."

He left without comment, which must have been only the second time ever that he'd let me have the last word. My head wasn't the only thing held high as we walked out into the sunshine.

My worry meter had peaked, and it had nothing to do with Chase or Gary. While there wasn't enough evidence to hold me, I was still the prime suspect in the murder of Pete Seaver.

———

AFTER CHASE DROPPED US OFF, I SAT WITH MY FLUFF-ball companion among the boxes of Mom's antiques ready to be shipped off to the many buyers I'd procured online. No matter how hard I tried, I couldn't get the image of Pete's dead body out of my mid. A lot of people in New Hope had lost faith in me when I left town. By staying and opening my business, I'd wanted to show them I was a different person, a better person. How on earth were they ever going to trust me or want to do business with me if they believed I had dealings with a man like Pete, even if I didn't kill him?

While waiting for the IPS man to pick up the packages, I thought of ways to win the town over. I'd been planning a huge grand opening, but that was weeks away. In the meantime, I needed to slowly introduce them to my style and my treats. With an investigation hanging over my head, having an open house was out of the question, but it wouldn't hurt to give out some samples as people passed by on the street.

Hoping the heat wouldn't keep people inside, I set to work printing up postcard-sized flyers about the organic products I'd be selling. One column for people and one column for animals. Essentially, since there were only natural ingredients, the snacks could be eaten by anyone.

Next, I used some antique silver platters to display my Kitty Krackers, Sesame Peeps, and PB BisScottie. The clever shapes made me smile as I skillfully arranged the tiny fish shapes on one plate, the triangle peeps on another, and the hearty bone shapes on the third platter. Who wouldn't enjoy crunching on these delectable treats?

The town clock struck noon as I pulled a small table under the awning outside the door, with a fan blowing a refreshing breeze. Perfect timing to catch the lunch crowd. I left my drooling charge in the shop where it was cooler, not wanting all that fluff to become overheated. Not to mention I didn't quite trust him not to try and eat all my samples.

"You be a good boy, okay, Major? Auntie Juli will be right outside," I said in my best doggie-baby-talk, satisfied when he cocked his head in my direction. Most of the people of New Hope would remember me as a rebellious young girl, too eager to leave. I needed to show them I could follow in my mother's footsteps and be a profitable businesswoman.

Luckily, I didn't have to wait long.

"Hello, Miss Butler, I just wanted to see if you'd given any more thought to me helping you out." The meager voice belonged to Mark Walker. He didn't appear as disheveled as the last time I'd seen him, but he didn't seem relaxed, either.

"Hi, Mark, and please call me Juli. Honestly, I haven't had a moment to think about it, I'm sorry."

"Oh, yeah, considering Pete's murder and all. At least we won't have to worry about him anymore. Have no fear, I'm not listening to any gossip. You seem too nice of a lady to kill somebody, even if it was Pete Seaver."

"Right." I hesitated, wondering if Mark knew anything about who would want to kill Pete and why. Maybe if I shed some light on this case, the beloved town Sheriff would stop looking at me as a suspect and give me the credit and respect I deserved. "I wonder why someone would kill him." Mark's brown eyes grew wide over my words. "I mean, why not just beat him up?"

"I guess it was hardball time. Pete must have done something pretty bad."

"Hardball? Pete did seem pretty upset when he came in to buy his statue back."

"Pete owed a lot of money. Gambling does that to you. I mean, everyone pities me and my problem. Sure, I lost everything and now even my wife doesn't want me. But at least what I lost was mine and not someone else's."

"You mean like a loan?" My worry meter hummed to attention.

"Pete was deep in. I heard he owed like twenty G's."

"Twenty thousand dollars?" I croaked, and Mark nodded.

"He got roughed up a couple of times just before your mother died. I think that's why she made the deal with him. You know, she must have felt sorry for him."

"She always did believe everyone had good qualities."

"I don't think a mean-spirited man like Pete Seaver could have any goodness in him. He got his just reward." For the first time I noticed a darkness to Mark Walker. His jaw set and his eyes no longer held the gentleness I'd been comfortable with. Goose bumps worked their way up my arms even as the sun warmed the sky. When the police cruiser rolled around the corner, Mark buried his hands deep in his pockets.

"Everything all right here?" Gary asked from out the window, sharing an intense gaze with Mark.

I nodded.

"Here's the number where I'm staying," Mark spoke softly as not to be carried on the moist breeze of summer. "My brother-in-law owns Carson's Garage and he's letting me stay in the upstairs apartment while I work things out with Cynthia. Call me if you need a hand with anything. It doesn't have to be permanent."

"I will," I answered just as quiet. I slid the business card out of his calloused hand, noticing the front of the card had Bobby Carson's name in bold green letters. Mark sulked off down the street leaving me with an odd chill.

"Would you care for a sample of my crackers?" I happily changed the subject, leaving the curb with a small plate in my hand. Gary took two.

"Mmm...these are great." His amber eyes met mine. "But I'd rather have dinner."

"My, don't you move fast." I laughed and his smile widened. I had to admit, my stomach did a funny little flip.

"It's my job, ma'am. That's how we catch the bad guys." Before I could reply with a witty comeback, his cell phone rang. "Oops, it's the boss. Gotta take this."

I shook my head because even out of eyeshot, Chase could ruin my fun. Deputy Hot- Stuff nodded with a smile while answering the phone and slowly pulling away from the curb. I swear I caught him looking in his rearview mirror. Maybe things were finally looking up in New Hope.

"Juli Butler? My goodness you're all grown up!" A buxom woman with more salt than pepper in her hair and wearing a familiar canvas apron shuffled across the street. I recognized her right away.

"Mrs. Henderson!" I stepped around my table as she came closer, arms outstretched. She wrapped me in a bear hug so tight I could barely breathe. "It's so good to see you," I said when she finally released me.

"Oh, child, this town has been a bore since you went away. And call me Betty. I'm so sorry about your mama. I hope you know if there's anything you need, you just call on me and Harry, ya hear?"

Betty Henderson was the sweetest person, next to my mom, I'd ever met. She spoke with an accent she attributed to her Georgian roots when the truth was, she'd lived her entire life in the northeast. Betty swore by southern hospitality and endeared herself as a motherly figure to anyone she met. To think she hadn't changed in ten years made me appreciate her even more.

"Thank you, Betty, I appreciate that. I'm sure between the house and fixing up this place, I will be spending a lot of time at the hardware store."

"Make sure you take some time for yourself, now. I just finished a deep tissue massage and manicure over at Rita's." She flashed her freshly polished pink nails in front of my face. "You just call in what supplies you need, and Harry and I will have them delivered to you. You are much too busy to be running to the store all the time."

"Thanks, Betty. I'm enjoying my new venture. Would you like to try one of my organic treats?" I proudly motioned toward the trays on the table.

"Well, look at this. You've been busy. Is this your way of handling the grief, darlin,' because I'm here for you if you need to talk about anything." Betty scrutinized my snacks and for a moment, I questioned my ability to pull this off. She picked up a BisScottie, sniffed, and then bit into it. The moan of satisfaction and the light in her eyes told me I'd done well. Relief bubbled out in the form of a giggle, which was a lot better than a sob. It was getting easier to think about my mother thanks to old friends like these.

"No, I'm not doing this out of grief. I miss Mom so much, and I wish I'd been here with her. Cooking is something I love to do and I'm going to remodel the antique shop into the Butler's Pantry, my organic café for people and animals."

"You don't say." Her voice trailed off as she inspected the trays before her and then looked at the antique shop as if it were already disappearing. "We already have a diner in town, and a couple of restaurants heading out toward Redfield, not to mention the Sunflower Inn. Are you sure you won't be better off leaving things as they are? Your little run-in with Pete, God rest his soul, is the talk of the town."

"Change is good, and in this case it's also healthy and inclusive."

"Now, Juli Butler, you keep hold of that positive attitude. And remember, not everyone is going to think your changes are good ones." She reached over and snatched a couple of peeps. "These are delish!" Her pudgy fingers dipped toward the Kitty Krackers. "I've got to take some back for Harry!"

"Here, I have some sample boxes already made." I reached under the table where I had pre-packed my treats into custom made oriental food containers. They'd arrived at the house last night and I had been very satisfied by the cranberry-colored boxes with glossy B's centered on each panel and my contact information in smaller font underneath.

"What adorable packaging. You do have your mother's flair."

"Thanks, Betty, I'd like to think so." I smiled.

"Once you get up and operating, little Andie Evans would be the perfect helper."

"Who is Andie Evans?" The name didn't ring any bells.

"She's Jimmy and Tammy O'Toole's niece. It's a shame to have such a sweet young thing working at the fish market. Rumor has it she got herself into so much trouble in Chicago that she dropped out of school. Jimmy's sister couldn't do a blessed thing with that child, so they shipped her off here to work and finish her schooling. With a little luck, she'll be graduating next year."

Hmmm, troubled girl. Boy did that sound familiar. Was this Betty's way of telling me I could relate? I smiled, thinking of all the trouble I'd gotten into, not to mention my father's urge to find the adventure in life.

"I'm sure she'd much rather work in your trendy little café than be around smelly old fish all day." Betty pinched her nose.

"This town is so small, I'm sure you'll run into her. Pretty little blonde. She's got half the boys in this town smitten."

I noticed some pedestrians coming down the street. Keeping my ear on Betty's story, I prepared for a quick conversation to explain my crackers. Disappointment smacked me in the gut when they walked by without even looking at me or my table.

"Do you really think she did it?" I heard one of them whisper, my smile fading a little. "She's really making a name for herself if you ask me. Doesn't do much for her already tarnished reputation," the other responded.

"Don't pay them any mind," Betty said, coming to my rescue and lifting me out of the dark place I was headed.

"People really think I came back to kill Pete Seaver? I didn't even know the man. How on earth could I have a motive?"

"Why don't you tell me," Chase calmly stated and appeared from somewhere behind Betty.

"Stop giving this sweet girl such a hard time, Chase Hargrave," Betty scolded. "You let her go so you must think she didn't do it."

"I don't know what to think, Betty. I'm sure after ten years, Juli has a string of skeletons in her closet."

"That's not fair, Chase." I pressed my hands at my waist in defiance, hoping he didn't dig too deep. There was one skeleton in particular who needed to stay buried. "You're not giving me a chance."

"Just like you—"

"Like I what?" I cut him off and studied him, certain I could finish that particular sentence but I didn't. I wanted him to say it, only I knew he wouldn't.

"Never mind."

"I'll let you two catch up." Betty picked up her box of crackers. "I'll be sure to tell April you're back, she'll want to know. Maybe the three of you can hang out like you used to. Don't forget to make an appointment at Rita's. You won't regret it."

"Sure," I replied, never taking my eyes off the insufferable man before me. Just because he was the Sheriff didn't mean he owned this town, or me.

Betty walked away and I noticed Vinnie Minetti, the short man with jet-black hair who'd run into Pete the night of the murder, standing at the corner talking to a large man in a steel grey business suit. They seemed deep in conversation while Chase and I were stalled in an uncomfortable silence. Minutes ticked away before Vinnie slapped the guy on the shoulder and parted ways, and I remembered my conversation with Mark. This information would have to put me back in good graces with Sheriff Do-Gooder.

"I had an interesting conversation with Mark Walker."

"Oh really? Did he want to drive you out to the country, too?"

"What is wrong with you?" The man exasperated me.

"Just tell me about your conversation with Mark." Chase sounded tired, as if there were something weighing on his mind.

"If you're sure you want to hear about it. I think you should, because what he told me could be a major break-through."

"How so?" Chase squinted.

"Mark told me Pete was deep in debt with loan sharks. Apparently, they'd already beat him up a couple of times. I guess he still didn't pay so they took it to the next level."

"Sorry to burst your bubble, but that's old news. Pete was a notorious gambler and a drinker, not a very compatible combination for someone like him. He had some trouble around the time your mom died. I thought he had it settled."

"Apparently not. Do you remember who was around then? Maybe it's the same guys."

"Could be, but I doubt it." Chase hitched a shoulder. "Loan sharks like to mix things up a bit and keep you guessing so you pay up sooner."

"But it's still a shot, right? We could investigate the local loan sharks and anyone who's been accosted within the surrounding counties." I arched my fingertips on the edge of my table, feeling positive I'd found a solution.

"Wait a second, Juli, you're not investigating anything, got it?" He studied me with deep green eyes. "I think you know more than you're telling me."

Crossing my arms over my torso, I responded, "Everything I've told you has been the truth. I don't know what more I can say."

"You can fess up or remain silent, it's up to you." He pointed a finger in warning. "In either case, you need to stay out of this and tend to your own business."

Until I could make Chase believe me, this case had suddenly become my business.

Six

S ample day had been a huge success. I'd had mixed reactions from people, but I didn't let that detour me from my plan. They simply needed to be educated on the goodness of organic foods and I was just the person to do it.

Since I'd given away all my samples, I figured today was a good day to run errands. Tim, the IPS guy, delivered my new lights and sign. After calling Bill Perkins, I'd taken his last appointment of the day for him to install my new fixtures. With some free time on my hands, I decided the only way to find out who might have wanted Pete dead, or at least who had information on the loan sharks, was to do a little exploring.

Chase's words loomed in my head. I was doing this for him as much as I was for me. I knew he didn't always approve of the choices I'd made or things I'd done, but to doubt me just plain hurt. It meant he didn't trust me.

I locked up and headed straight for Ringo's Diner and Deli on the opposite end of town. The family run diner had been a staple in this community since Chase and I were kids. Everyone who worked there or ate there was either a family member or they treated you like one. The diner was the best place for gossip within ten miles.

I walked into Ringo's, and it was as if time stood still. Red vinyl stools lined the long counter with a full view of the kitchen and grill. Booths along the perimeter and center of the room remained the same worn, blue vinyl. The black and white checkered floor which I remembered as scuffed-up linoleum had been replaced by glossy ceramic tiles. An expensive upgrade but well worth it, in my opinion.

The corner booth brought back memories of extra-large milkshakes and thick cut steak fries. How many Friday nights had I spent with my friends here? Out of curiosity I sat in the booth, sliding across the seat, comforted that the sunken middle cushion hadn't been replaced. I couldn't help myself as I reached for the menu. Carefully I slid the tin napkin holder out of the way, and sure enough carved into the wood were the initials C.H. + J.B.

So long ago. Too many misunderstandings along with great memories. I quickly put things back in their rightful place before a boy came to take my order. I held in my laughter at his surprised face. It was Scott Iverson.

"Uh, can I take your order?"

"Sure. I'll take coffee—cream only—scrambled egg whites and a side of rye toast."

"Okay. Is there anything else?"

"How's the new video game?"

His eyes brightened. "Oh, it's awesome! Thanks so much for paying us to do chores for you."

"A lot better than pawning your dad's watch, huh?"

"Yeah." Scott's attention turned toward the tall girl who walked through the door. She headed straight for the counter, and I thought poor Scott's head was going to fall off from twisting it so far.

"Is that...." I thought I'd take a guess, but Scott finished for me.

"Andie Evans." His Adams apple bobbed when he swallowed. Oh, to be young, and crushing on someone from afar.

"She's very pretty." I watched her spin around on the counter stool and wait patiently. "Are you going to ask her out?" I couldn't help but smile at the horror on Scott's face when he turned around.

"I can't do that. She's out of my league now."

"Now?" I could smell a good story; the kind Ringo's was known for.

"We sort of grew up together. You know, hung out, did all the kid things here in town. She was my best friend." Scott paused and it was my turn to force a swallow. Maybe coming to the diner wasn't the smartest idea I'd had today. "Her family moved away a few years ago and she's only here because she got mixed up with some bad people in Chicago."

"What kind of bad people?" I leaned forward as if I was going to learn a secret about Andie Evans that would mimic my own.

"I didn't ask. Figure she'd tell me if she wanted to. Besides, she's got some boyfriend she met out there. He's older so I guess he's got money. I can't compete with someone like that." He took another look over his shoulder, and I saw his chest rise and fall.

"Don't be so sure. She may realize what she's missed someday." My own lungs released a sigh and Scott cleared his throat. His expression told me he had no idea what I was talking about.

"I'll bring your coffee right out." Scott turned away and I saw him hand a To-Go bag to Andie. They exchanged smiles before she left. I shook the whole young love scenario out of my head, very much in need of breakfast, and started reading the Farmer's Almanac quotes on my paper placemat.

"Hey, Juli! Aunt Betty told me you were in town." I looked up to see the petite figure of April Henderson striding toward my table, her blonde hair bouncing with each step.

"Hi, April. How have you been?" I had to admit she looked great. She might have been a few pounds heavier through the hips than I remembered, but she carried it well. A pang of something unexplainable clenched in my gut, and I wondered if there was truth to what Harry had hinted at. Were Chase and April an item?

"Doing great. I teach photography at the Community College, and I have my own studio at my house. You'll have to come by sometime and see my work."

"I'll have to do that," I mused, sizing her up because I wasn't feeling her sincerity. The evil part of me wanted to bring up the new photographer in town, but I decided to wait and hold judgement on my suspicions about her sincerity, trying hard not to let her get on my nerves. Scott brought my coffee, and I nodded a smile of thanks.

"I'm terribly sorry about your mother. She was always such a giving person." Without invitation, April slid into the booth.

"Thank you."

"You must have been traveling, right? Is that why you couldn't get here in time for the funeral?"

Boy, did she know how to verbally sucker punch.

"I, uh…I was right in the middle of something and couldn't get away." There was no way I'd be telling Suzie-Sunshine about my not-so-perfect life. I'd left New Hope with big dreams. No one needed to know just what a failure I'd been on my own.

"That's too bad. At least you're here now and can take care of your mom's business. Have you seen Chase yet?" I opened my mouth to reply, but April continued to speak as if she hadn't even asked me a question. "Of course, you have! Silly me, he lives right next door now. I'm sure you two have been living up old times, haven't you?"

This time she paused long enough where I could tell she was fishing. Oh, I could have toyed with her, but there was no point. Chase was Chase and he'd do whatever he wanted to do as long as it was appropriate. And I was turning over a new leaf in honor of my mom.

"We've talked some, yes."

"I heard he basically bailed you out of jail after the whole Pete-thing. Then again, he is the sheriff, so I guess you could say you're in protective custody or is it house arrest?"

"Bailed me out?" I choked on my coffee, then took a moment to regain my composure. I refused to let her get to me. "No, and there is no house arrest, April. They had to let me go, there was no proof. Not that there would be any proof since I didn't kill Pete Seaver." I said the last words a bit too loud, and several diner patrons turned their heads in my direction, the clatter of silverware scraping against dishes ceasing along with their conversations. After a moment, everything resumed once more.

"Hmm, maybe I heard wrong." April shrugged. "Glad I asked. I would have been so embarrassed if I'd gotten my facts mixed up. I'm hoping to have dinner with Chase later in the week. I've been sewing some potholders and the cutest little ragdolls to sell at the school's next craft fair, and I can't wait to show him."

"I bet." I nailed her with a sly look. She was up to something. "Not that Chase would be discussing the investigation with you because that would be unethical since it's still an open case."

"Oh, of course! I would never ask him to break his code of conduct." She placed a hand over her heart.

"And you know he wouldn't. For anyone," I added with some emphasis on the word.

"Of course," April repeated and stood, setting her hand on my shoulder. "It's been great catching up. We need to do this more often while you're here. Maybe you can join Chase and me some night for drinks at my place."

Did she just insinuate they were a couple? Did Chase know this?

"We'll see," I said, returning her fake smile. April and I were social friends. We'd all hung out in the same group, but the only thing she and I had in common was Chase Hargrave. She'd basically been telling me to stay away from him now that I was home. Little did she realize that's exactly what I had planned to do, only a dead body in my mother's garden had made that next to impossible.

"Here's your eggs and toast, Miss Butler," Scott said after April vanished out the door. He stared at her with a disapproving frown, and I knew I had at least one true ally in this town.

"Thanks, Scott." I smiled at him.

"I don't care what they say, I know you couldn't have killed Mr. Seaver. You're just too nice of a person."

"Aww, Scott, that is so sweet of you. But until the police find out who might have done it, I guess I still look guilty to everyone else. Unfortunately, no one seems to know anything about him." I pushed the food around my plate, not really feeling hungry anymore.

"There's not much to know, really. My dad said Mr. Seaver inherited his house after his mom passed away eight years ago. He didn't even come to New Hope right away. Kept to himself mostly unless he was playing cards. He tried to get a loan from my dad at the bank, but I guess he didn't have a job, only his inherited money."

"A loan, huh? But if he had money, why did he need the loan? He told me he had a sister. Didn't she inherit any money?" I added jam to my toast, not wanting Scott to feel bad that I wasn't eating.

"I don't know." Scott shrugged, and then shook his head to move his shaggy hair out of his eyes. "We always thought he didn't have any other family, at least that's what my dad said."

"You don't happen to know where his house is, do you?"

"Nah, me and my brother stayed clear of him. Every time he came into the diner, he ate up at the counter. He always seemed pissed off." Someone from the kitchen called for a pick up, and Scott excused himself from our conversation. I didn't have all day to wait for his dad to come into the diner, but what I did have was the perfect painting in need of a safe deposit box.

———

I SPENT THE EARLY PART OF THE AFTERNOON PICKING out paint and flooring for Petit Four Paws. After finding a white tile bordered in tiny black paw prints, I fell in love and had the store special order it along with a matching wallpaper border in black and brown. The white beadboard and trim would be delivered tomorrow along with the two gallons of paint in rich milk chocolate. I picked up two pairs of white wooden shutters for the interior of the windows and some material to sew a window valance for the top.

Thrilled with my purchase and orders, I headed back to the café to meet Bill Perkins. Ben Iverson, at the bank, had been most helpful in securing me a safe deposit box for my valuables. What I didn't receive was pertinent information regarding Pete Seaver. With time to spare before Bill's arrival, I started to install my shutter. A couple of turns into the first mount, I heard a tiny "meow."

"What in the world?" I set the screwdriver down and listened. After a few moments of silence, I heard it again. "Where are you? Here kitty-kitty." I stood and slowly walked around the Four Paws area.

"Meow."

"You're not in here, are you?" I cocked my head and listened once more. The sound came from the main room. It took me several loops around the room before I found it. I opened the antique pie cupboard to find the tiny kitten.

"Steve?" I recognized the stark white boots of the kitten Tess McDermott had tried to give me. "How on earth did you get in here?" The door had been locked since I'd left this morning, and it had been locked when I returned. I didn't think anyone else had a key, but this made me want to replace the locks.

Tess was a sweet old lady and the last thing I needed was more trouble. The kitten squirmed in my hand, so I cuddled him close to my neck. The poor thing was probably starving if he'd been in that empty pie cupboard all day.

Bill Perkins walked through the door right on schedule. A

gentle looking man in his fifties with a full head of silver hair and pale blue eyes, he carried his large toolbox with ease as well as balancing the boxes containing my new lights. Years of carpentry work had wielded a strong, healthy man. Sandy Perkins was one lucky woman, even though Mrs. Bailey insisted she was evil.

"Where would you like me to start?"

"The smaller lights will go on either side of the Four Paws entry." I pointed to the wall. "The ceiling fan with the wide blades will go in the pet café, and the other two will go in the main room as well as the new black lacquer globes for the outside of the building."

"Great. Why don't I work the small stuff first?"

"That's fine. I'm just fixing Steve here a bowl of almond milk. I'll be right in to finish the shutters." I brought Steve, and the small China bowl I'd snatched from a box of mismatched dishes headed to the Rescue Mission, into the Four Paws café to find Bill hard at work. Setting the kitten at my feet, I went back to installing my decorative shutters.

"How does it feel to be back in New Hope?" he asked.

"Fine, but different without my mom." My screwing ceased as I held back a sob. If I let myself linger, the tears would come and while I'm sure people expected it, I just didn't want to cry in front of anyone. I took a deep breath and releasedt. "I'm taking one day at a time. That's about all I can do."

"You've got a lot of support here, Juli. This town loved your mother, and they will love you too."

"I hope so, Bill. I'm just not sure what Pete's murder is going to do to me."

"Eh, I wouldn't pay too much mind to what people say. I didn't know Pete Seaver all that well, but from what I heard, he was a rotten, gambling drunk. He took what he wanted and didn't care whose life he ruined." Bill opened boxes and kept working as he talked. Easy for him to be so nonchalant about it, his life wasn't in jeopardy of being ruined.

"Sounds like Pete had a lot of enemies around here between his drinking and gambling. Did many people in town lose money to him?" I couldn't imagine nice Bill Perkins losing big money to Pete, but you never knew. The poor man had to answer to evil Sandy, which I'm sure wasn't pretty.

"Oh, I'm not too sure of that. I know Mark Walker had some dealings with him. Those two were at odds quite a bit. Jimmy O'Toole who owns the fish market is a big card player. I think the two of them even got into a fist fight once or twice. There may be others. I never really cared about his comings and goings, but when people take advantage of this town's hospitality it really makes me angry." He ripped open another box with more force than he had the others.

"I can understand that," I said, feeling like Bill and I were kindred spirits. "I firmly believe in karma, and that's what happened to Pete in the end."

"I couldn't have said it better myself." He shook his head in frustration. "Now you've come home to deal with the passing of your mother, and do right by her, and Pete strikes again. Only this time he's dead, and they think you have something to do with it. It's just wrong, Juli. That's what gets me all fired up."

"You and me too, Bill." I stepped back and eyed the shutters to make sure they looked level. "Try telling the good sheriff that, would ya?"

"What's going on with Chase?" Bill stopped laying out the fan blades on the floor.

"He's one who thinks I had something to do with it."

"He does? Now...what would give him that idea?" Bill didn't miss a beat as he returned to the directions, making note of each rod and screw as he set them outside of the box, multi-tasking better than half the women I knew.

"Chase and I grew up together. There's not much he doesn't know about me. Therefore, he holds the fact that I left New Hope against me every chance he gets and seems to think I've brought trouble with me by coming home. Silly, I know, but that's just Chase."

"Not silly at all. Our sheriff has a stubborn streak, that's for sure. He's always been gracious to Sandy and me. I've had the privilege of playing in a charity golf tournament with him. You get no mulligans, not even for charity." Bill chuckled fondly.

I laughed along with him, finding the time spent with Bill Perkins to be very enjoyable. Sandy better watch out, or someone would steal him right out from under her. Time flew by while we worked. Bill finished with the final ceiling fan just as the grandfather clock—that I just couldn't part with—chimed five times.

"Quitting time." He grinned and flexed his fingers after setting his tools neatly back into the toolbox. "Better not dally or Sandy will have my hide."

"I appreciate you stopping by so quickly today. This is going to speed things along toward my grand opening."

"Not a problem at all, glad I could help. Summer tends to be slow for me with folks going away on vacation. I've been thinking it might be a good time to take Sandy on that tropical getaway she's always wanted."

"Dually noted," I said, pointing my finger toward the slowly spinning ceiling fan. "I will be sure to give you more notice. I bet I will find wiring issues once we start remodeling the kitchen area."

"Any time, Juli, any time. Will we see you in church on Sunday?" He stood and gathered his things.

What was it with these people and church? My mouth became dry, and my palms started to sweat. I'd probably incinerate the minute I stepped through the doors. Well, if I did, it would be their fault, but maybe church was the way to win the town over.

"I...guess so?" I squeaked with a shrug, not sure he even noticed because he was headed toward the door.

"I'll let Sandy know. If you want to meet some of the people in town, my Sandy is the one to talk to. You'll know the old timers, but this town has grown over the last five years. You might make a lot of new friends."

"Tell Sandy I look forward to meeting her. I hear she gave my mom a run for her money in the baking department."

"Ohhh, I wouldn't be bringing that up. It's still a sore spot with my better half." Bill chuckled then scooped up Steve before he could sneak out the door. "Better watch out or you'll be missing a kitten." He stretched his arm to hand me Steve.

"He's not my kitten. Mrs. McDermott is determined to make him mine, though." I scratched Steve between the ears. "It's not that I don't think he's adorable, because he is and I'm a huge animal lover. It's just I've got so much to do here, and I don't want to leave him alone at home what with Chase's big lug of a dog on one side and Scallywag on the other."

"Ah, I see what you mean."

"Would you mind dropping him off to her?"

"Not at all. C'mon, Steve, let's get you home."

I closed the café right behind Mr. Perkins and headed to the serenity of my house. There was a veggie burger with my name on it, and I had a growing list of people to mull over who might lead me to Pete's real killer.

Seven

"Juli! Are you up?" Chase's voice yelled as he pounded on my front door. I ran from the kitchen with my half-eaten bagel still in my hand and tossed open the door.

"For goodness sakes, what?"

"You're shirking your dog-walking duties." He stood there, in yet another crisply pressed uniform which hugged his muscles in ways that were anything but professional, with his hands on his hips.

"What?" I tilted my head, my messy morning hair flopping over my shoulder.

"Dog walking, remember, that's our deal instead of giving you a ticket?"

"That was your deal, and I did walk him." Once or twice, but it was his dog, not mine. "I've done my time, officer." I took a bite from my bagel.

"Not until my regular walker comes back, Juli. I worked late last night and came home to a disaster, thanks to you." Chase held up a wad of shredded newspaper. "This is just a small piece of the havoc he wreaked."

"Oops." I'd been so busy at the café and then gathering information about Pete, I'd totally forgotten about Major.

"Oops, nothing. I'm going to have to spend my day off cleaning up the mess." He raised the paper in emphasis.

"What does that have to do with me?" I mumbled with a mouth full of food, as I continued to hold the door open.

"You're going to spend the day with Major. Keep him happy. Wear him out."

"He's your dog."

"Would you rather clean my house?" Chase rocked back on his heels and crossed his arms.

"No. I'm not your maid service."

"See you in a few minutes." Chase snatched the last bite out of my fingers, turned, and hopped off my porch.

I frowned. "He's going to have to come back to the café with me. I planned on painting Four Paws and refinishing some of the cabinets."

"Good. Coffee is on, why don't you bring over the rest of breakfast? I like more cream cheese on my bagel," he said, as he squeezed between the Arborvitaes.

The infuriating man had no consideration for what I was doing. Rules, rules, rules. I swear he made them up just to annoy me. Maybe if I played by the book, he'd let me off early for good behavior. I ran upstairs and threw on my favorite pair of capri yoga pants and matching racer-back tank. Working my hair into a messy bun, I headed to the kitchen to prepare his bagel.

"Not too much cream cheese, I hope," I said moments later when I set the bagel on his counter, an angelic smile painted on my face.

"Perfect." He eyed me with suspicion as he motioned for me to sit and headed for the coffee pot.

"So, you worked late, huh?" I added cream to the steaming cup of coffee he handed me.

"That's not unusual. I am the man in charge you know." He sat on a barstool next to me.

"Any new leads on the Seaver case?"

"The Seaver case? Do you have P.I. on your list of odd jobs?" He squinted over the rim of his cup as he took a sip of his dark brew.

"No, but isn't that how you refer to it?"

"Yes." He grinned, polishing off the rest of his bagel.

"So...do you have any more information?" I puckered up and blew across the top of my cup before taking a sip. Major stretched on the floor, his fur fluffing up in front of the air conditioner vent.

Chase cleared his throat. "I can't discuss it with you, and you know that."

"C'mon, we're old friends. You've trusted me with your deepest secrets, we've committed small town pranks together, surely you can fill me in."

"It's the law, and you're still implicated in this." His teasing smile vanished, signaling our playdate was officially over.

"You honestly believe that?" I held the mug to my lips.

"Until proven otherwise, I have to. It doesn't matter what I believe. Wouldn't you agree?"

"No." My coffee suddenly tasted bad. Chase was throwing the book at our lifelong friendship. I pushed the mug away. "I'll let you get to your housework. C'mon, Major."

"Sorry, Juli, I know that's not what you wanted to hear," Chase said, leading the way to the front door. "I wish it were different."

"Do you?" I challenged, trying to hide the hurt of his betrayal.

"Of course," he replied while grabbing the leash off the hook on the wall and attaching it to the dog's collar. "Why would you even ask?"

"Oh, I don't know. Maybe because you've been condemning me since the day you pulled me over."

"I'm upholding the law and trying to stay objective. You don't make it easy."

"Because God forbid you cut someone a little slack."

"What's that supposed to mean?"

"That's your job to figure it out, lawman. Mine, is apparently dog walker and nothing more." I tugged the leash from his hand and marched Major out of the house. Amazing how Chase could still get under my skin. All I wanted was a little inside information, and he couldn't stop being his goodie-goodie self long enough to help me.

Major pranced by my side, his long, shaggy fur a mass of bouncing silken waves. Birds chirped from high in the trees and an occasional squirrel skirted across the sidewalk as we made our way into town. We passed Ringo's on the opposite side of the street, and I couldn't help notice Vinnie Minetti, the owner, standing outside in a heated argument with a man in a navy blue business suit. I pulled back on Major's leash to slow his pace, hoping to hear a little of their conversation.

"I told you to be careful," Vinnie's thick Italian accent yelled.

"I'm sorry, Vinnie. What was I supposed to do when the guy wouldn't listen to me?" the other man whined.

"Why did you have to hit him? If anyone finds out, we will be in a lot of trouble."

Hit him? Did they have something to do with Pete's murder? What if Vinnie ordered a hit on him and this guy was the hitman who'd whacked Pete over the head and killed him? In the quiet of the morning their voices carried and even though there were others out and about, I seemed to be the only one paying attention.

Suddenly Major pulled hard to the left and barked. Vinnie and the stranger whipped their heads in our direction. Vinnie's eyes turned to slits and his mouth hardened in a frown as he stared me down.

"Good morning, gentlemen!" I called and waved, trying hard not to let my voice quiver. Yanking the leash I mumbled, "Bad dog." Major whimpered then quickened his pace as Harry Henderson set up his weekend displays along the sidewalk. "Good morning, Harry," I said with a huff when we approached.

"Well, hello!" He smiled as broad as his waistline and reached into his apron for a dog biscuit. "Here you go, boy."

"Crazy dog, I thought he was going to take my arm off to get to you. Bad, bad, dog," I reprimanded.

"Oh, he's a good boy, aren't you Major?" Harry ruffled the dog's mop of a head and Major barked approval.

"Chase says he's been acting up in the house," I pointed out in my defense. Major might be adorable, but he was most definitely mischievous.

"Hmm, maybe he should take him to see Lily Johnson. She's the local vet. Nice girl."

"I'll be sure to tell him when I bring Major back later. I'm off to do some painting at the café, and Major is going to keep me company."

"Need any supplies while you're here?" I shook my head as the big dog started walking. "Keep us in mind if you do! See you tomorrow."

"Tomorrow?" I twisted around until I was walking backwards.

"Church, of course, it's pancake breakfast Sunday. Sandy organized it to benefit the local SPCA."

"Oh," I stammered and almost tripped. "I'll be there. Have a nice day!" I waved and spun back around, coming to terms with my fate of attending Sunday Service. Glancing at the clear blue sky, I couldn't help but smile. "See Mom? I'm even going to church and the sky hasn't fallen yet." I'd also have the opportunity to meet the illustrious Sandy Perkins.

A couple more blocks and we were standing in front of my café, complete with my new Butler's Pantry sign hanging above the door. Pride swelled in my chest. I reached down to massage Major's huge fuzzy neck and kiss the top of his fat head.

"Let's get to work. C'mon you big lug head."

I pulled out my key but before I could slip it into the lock, the door opened as if pushed by a breeze. I glanced around to see if anyone was nearby. The dog and I were the only ones. I opened the door slowly and peered inside.

"Is anyone here?" Stupid question, I know, because if a thief was dumb enough to answer me, then I deserved to be robbed or even shot. The main room remained silent, so I left the door open and walked farther inside. This wasn't Boston. There was no need to disturb Chase on his day off.

"Meow."

"No way."

"Woof."

"I thought you'd agree," I said to Major, unhooking his leash and returning to close the door. "That explains how Tess keeps getting in. Apparently, I need some new, sturdier locks. Find the kitty, boy!" I pointed around the room, hoping the dog would take the lead and find Steve.

"Meow."

"Woof!"

Major sniffed every nook and cranny, barking every time the kitten cried. When he stopped in front of the corner-cabinet hutch, I knew he'd found Steve. The bottom doors to the hutch had beautiful, screened doors with detailed burned wood frames. When I opened the door, there was Steve sitting inside a small wicker basket.

On my way home I'd be sure to ask Harry if he could return Steve to his rightful owner. If Tess was able to come in, then what was to stop someone else? I'd also have to ask Harry for the name of the town locksmith. Smart move on my part with a murderer on the loose.

———

Church.

Summer of my senior year was the last time I'd set foot in any holy institution, unless you count the steps of St. Patrick's Cathedral in New York City. Maybe this wouldn't be so bad after all? Morning sun filtered through the stained-glass windows lining the walls on both sides, and so far, lightening hadn't struck. The altar was decorated with summer flowers in memory of deceased loved ones while the choir sang softly. I felt all eyes on me as I walked with Mrs. B down the aisle to take a seat in the pew behind Chase and the Hendersons.

Of course, April was sitting right beside him, in her purple polka dot sundress with matching cardigan. I'm not sure why that aggravated me, but it did. Chase hadn't been home when I returned Major, and I didn't remember seeing him leave this morning either which made me think he'd spent the night at April's. Must be he had a little dessert with his dinner invitation. I smirked at my own clever deduction.

"Don't be thinking that way in church, my dear," Mrs. Bailey whispered and patted my knee.

Was I that transparent? "She's just so obviously putting on a show because I'm here." I nodded toward the way April scooted closer to Chase. "I should stick my head between them and tell them I don't care."

"Now, now. You do care or you wouldn't have said that." Mrs. Bailey smoothed her simple navy-blue pant suit.

The wise old woman was correct. I cared. Unlike Chase Hargrave, I valued our friendship, and I didn't want to see him get into a relationship with someone like April. She came from a wonderful family, but there was a selfish, mean streak in that girl, I could feel it.

After the service, everyone went into the basement of St. Mary's for the pancake breakfast. I waved to the Iverson boys who stood as tall as their father, and even he waved back with a smile. I helped Mrs. Bailey to a table and offered to get her a plate.

"Glad you got yourself to church, darlin.'" Betty Henderson

waddled toward our table with a wide smile across her face. "Would you mind if we sit with y'all?"

"Please, Betty, sit down," Mrs. Bailey said. "I've missed so many historical society meetings, you must catch me up."

"Sure thing, but aren't you going to eat? We don't want you wasting away now!"

"Juli is being a dear and going to fix me a plate. I'm not a fan of Sandy's pancakes, but my tea and toast this morning didn't last long."

"Maybe someone else is in charge of the kitchen?" I asked, and both women burst out laughing.

"Darlin' that's one area Sandy won't give up. When she plans an event it's her event, no ifs, ands, or buts."

"Your mother tried for years to help, and Sandy shot her down every time. It's her recipe or no breakfast," Mrs. Bailey harrumphed.

"She hasn't met Justine Butler's daughter, now, has she?" I pretended to roll up non-existent sleeves on my pale-yellow dress and tapped my yellow-sandaled foot on the linoleum floor.

"Good luck, sweet pea. Chuck Sanders is with the Ambulance Corp. He's the skinny bald man over by the coffee if you need assistance after Sandy's done with your butt-whooping," Betty chided, and Mrs. Bailey chuckled.

"Thanks for your support, ladies." I laughed along with their teasing. I'd come across worse than Sandy Perkins over the years. She couldn't be that bad, could she?

Through the half wall cut-out, I had a clear view of the kitchen area. Sandy's pristine, platinum blonde head reigned supreme over the members of the congregation who were mixing batter and preparing various griddles and pans of bacon. She even had Bill working!

"Hi Juli!" Bill stopped stirring and waved. I returned the gesture. "Hey, come around and meet my wife."

Perfect.

I followed the direction he pointed and entered the kitchen. Bill handed over his mixing duties and steered me toward Sandy.

"Sandy, darling," he said softly as not to startle her while tapping her on the shoulder.

"What? Bill, is there a problem?" Her blue eyes registered immediate concern.

"No, sweetheart, I'd like to introduce you to someone."

"Is she here to help?"

"Not exactly," I added, and she cast a curious glance in my direction.

"This is Juli Butler, Justine's daughter. I told you about her yesterday and that I installed a bunch of new lights for her."

"Justine's daughter?" Her platinum brow arched in surprise. "It's nice to meet you, Juli. Your mother will be sorely missed in this town." Sandy seemed preoccupied with more than just the breakfast at hand as I caught a mix of sincerity and something else buried in the tone of her voice.

"Thank you. Although I'm sure now you'll have the county fair bake-off all to yourself." I couldn't help myself, and I could almost see her bristle.

"Excuse me?"

"I'm sorry, but my mother used to tell me you two had quite the competition going every year." I grinned in spite of myself.

"Yes, we did. Like I said, she will be missed." Sandy's faraway expression told me she had retreated to obvious memories of my mother. "I would have finally liked to beat her fair and square, not because she up and died. No offense."

"None taken," I replied. Sandy was classy, that's for sure. She kept her demeanor even though I was sure she would have lambasted me if most of the town hadn't been present.

"I told Juli you would be the perfect person for her to work with if she wants to get to know some of the folks around town," Bill interjected.

"I would love any opportunity to work some charity events

with you. I'm hoping to spread the word about my café, the Butler's Pantry. I make organic treats for both humans and animals."

"Organic treats? That's an interesting concept." Sandy placed a flawlessly manicured finger against her lips. The bright shade of pink was a perfect match with her lipstick.

"I think my mom would be proud of the changes I'm making." My heart filled with love thinking of Mom's approval.

"I'm on several town committees as well as the church group. Why don't I call you when I'm arranging the next event? I can always use an extra hand."

"That would be great." I smiled brightly. "Maybe I can lighten your load by taking over one of the committees; you know, add my own flair and maybe spotlight some of my organic products? I would be more than happy to help out if you and Bill take that trip."

Sandy's complexion blended with her platinum locks. Crystal blue eyes grew as round as fresh batter spreading on the griddle. I hoped Bill was ready to catch her because I feared she would faint.

"Trip? No, no, no, that won't be necessary," Sandy gasped and then shared a look with Bill as she pulled herself together. "I've always handled things. While I appreciate your enthusiasm, there's a certain way things are done around here. I hope you understand."

"Of course." Not sure what else to say, I decided it would be best to end on a good note with Mrs. Perkins. "Everything smells and looks delicious. I will let you get back to what you do best."

"I'll be in touch." Sandy kissed Bill on the cheek and returned to supervising the kitchen. Bill shot me a thumbs up and an "I think that went well" expression before trailing after his wife and taking over at a neighboring griddle.

"Juli!" I turned around to see the smiling face of Father O'Malley. If the church were going to collapse, now would be the time. "It was so nice to see you back in church today."

"It was nice to be back." I pasted on a smile. Watch yourself, Juli...

"We missed you for your mother's funeral. Such a loss to this church and the community." He cupped my elbow with his hand, and I felt beads of guilt, in the form of sweat, dot my forehead. "Having you here is like having a little piece of Justine."

"Excuse me, Father, but I promised a plate of food to Mrs. Bailey."

"Of course, we'll talk soon." He released my elbow and smiled. "See you next week?"

"I wouldn't miss it." I waved and turned away before Father O'Malley called me out in the church basement, no less.

I took two plates of pancakes and bacon and set them at my table. Betty and Mrs. Bailey looked surprised to see me emerge unscathed. April and Chase broke from their lighthearted conversation to stare at me as well.

"She's not that bad," I said to Mrs. Bailey.

"She's luring you in by making you feel comfortable. She did that with your mother, too." The old lady's eyes twinkled right before she winked, and this time I laughed.

"I didn't know you were here," Chase said, sounding surprised. He looked so handsome in his khaki pants and mallard blue golf shirt which accented his green eyes. April latched on to Chase's bicep as if staking her claim.

"Is that a problem?" I asked, directing my question more to April than Chase.

"Nope, not at all," he said, sounding too cheerful. I lost my appetite when April gave his arm a squeeze.

"What perfect timing!" Betty's excitement was undeniable as she waved a hand to flag someone over to our table. "Juli, I want to introduce you to Simon Banks. He's new in town, staying at the Sunflower Inn."

"Ah, yes, we sort of met the other night when I was on my porch with Mrs. Bailey." I watched him scan the table behind his dark sunglasses, my eyes being the last he met, giving me an opportunity to study his tall, lean build and wavy blond hair. He even had his camera strapped around his neck. Freelance journalist would have been my guess. "Juli Butler. It's a pleasure to meet you up close." I extended my hand, and he gave it a firm, all business, shake.

"Likewise." He kept his lips together when he smiled, and I withdrew my hand when an uncomfortable shiver resonated within my stomach. Thankfully, Betty saved the day by clapping us both on the shoulder, still full of enthusiasm.

"Simon is a food blogger, and boy is he at the right place with the way Misty cooks!"

"You just passing through?" Chase stood and shook the man's hand, never breakingeye contact, even though Simon didn't remove his glasses. "As the town sheriff, I like to know who's coming and going.

My worry meter hummed as I wondered if Mr. Banks had any connection to Pete. "No worries here." Simon turned his neck toward Chase and then me. "My house is being built a couple of towns over. While passing through to check on the progress, I fell in love with the charm here."

"Which is very easy to do, darlin'. We citizens of New Hope pride ourselves on hospitality. Don't we, Sheriff Hargrave?" Betty sent him a stern expression while her voice held that sweet southern warning everyone knew not to ignore. Including Chase.

"Yes, we do." Chase nodded with a smile in Betty's direction. "I'm sure you'll enjoy your stay at the Sunflower Inn. It's been in the Shepard family for generations. Misty has made some amazing upgrades to the place."

"While maintaining the historical character," Simon said, exchanging an almost knowing smile with Chase. "I've had the pleasure of her company over breakfast the past couple mornings. She has big plans for the place."

"Is that so?" Chase's brow arched in unsaid question.

"And Mrs. Henderson is spot on about her cooking."

"Oh, please call me Betty. Mrs. Henderson was my mother-in-law. God rest her soul."

"Betty," Simon enunciated, "is spot on." Misty's dishes are to die for. Now if you'll excuse me, Sheriff, I hear these pancakes come in a close second and I'd like to eat them while they're still warm. You all enjoy the rest of your day." With a general nod to our group, he moved to sit by himself in a corner with his breakfast and a magazine, still not removing his glasses.

"Now he's an interesting character," Chase mused as he sat back down next to April.

"He seemed nice enough." April shrugged, returning to her clingy self by rubbing Chase's back. "I know that look, Chase, and I don't think you have anything to worry about."

I'd seen that look more times than I could count. There was something off with Simon Banks and Chase felt it too. Speaking of being off, I had to take advantage of every opportunity to find Pete's killer and clear my name, and that opportunity was knocking now.

"You know, I think I saw Mark Walker down the street on one of the benches. I'm going to take a plate and see if he's still there." I could see the wheels turning in Chase's head as he tried to figure out what I was up to. Not wanting to give anything away because I could certainly do this on my own, I turned to Mrs. Bailey. "Will you be okay for a moment, Mrs. B?"

"Bless your heart, Juli," Betty said, and I swear she got all teary-eyed. "I was just telling Ida about our Historical Society meetings. I offered to take her to the museum on our way home."

"Thanks Betty, I'll see you later, Mrs. B."

"Be sure to grab him a carton of milk. Mark always liked his milk," Mrs. Bailey called after me.

I nodded my goodbyes and took a plate of pancakes plus a pint of milk. After my brief conversation with Mark the other day, I wondered if there wasn't more he could offer up about Pete Seaver.

From what Bill told me last night, Pete had a history with quite a few people around town. People who might have wanted to see him dead.

Luckily Mark was still on the bench when I walked out of St. Mary's basement door.

He was dressed in a pair of jeans and a plain white t-shirt. I checked to see if Chase had followed me, thankful when I didn't see him. I was sure April was keeping him occupied. Before I crossed the street, I looked up at the church steeple and thanked April for doing something nice for me, for once. Add that to the fact the church didn't crumble, then I guess miracles could happen after all.

"Hi Mark, thought you might be hungry," I said holding out the plate and milk.

"I really appreciate this, Juli." Mark eagerly took the food, and I sat down when he began to shovel the thick flapjacks into his mouth. "Sandy's recipe no doubt. She makes the best pancakes."

"You'd be right." I paused for a moment, wondering if I should be direct with my questions. What did I have to lose? Chase wasn't any closer to finding Pete's killer, and I couldn't afford not to try. Mark finished the plate and rose to throw everything in the nearest trash can.

"Thanks again. Not many people in town are very nice to me now that Cindy and the kids are gone."

"Well, I'm sure things will change for you soon. Everyone occasionally goes through a bad spell."

"I guess. This one has lasted a long time, and I can't seem to get out of the mess I'm in." His gaze wandered anxiously up and down the quiet street.

"Is it the gambling? There are programs for that. I'm sure your family would support you if you went for help."

"I tried. It didn't work."

"Maybe because the temptation was still around."

"Are you saying now that Pete's dead, I'd be cured?"

"I don't know about that, but it's one less card game you'd have to worry about."

"Maybe. I know I'm sitting outside a church, and this might not be very Christian of me, but I'm glad Pete's dead. He bullied so many people it was only a matter of time before someone offed him."

"Did you two have a lot of disagreements?" I watched him closely, mentally taking notes. I might not always be a good judge of people, but I felt confident in my ability to read their body language.

"All the time. He kept taking advantage of my misfortune and then made me a laughing stock when I would fail. I just got tired of it." Mark closed his eyes and shook his head. His posture crumpled a little, displaying his emotional fatigue. "This is my last chance."

"Mark, the night Pete was in my shop and you wanted to get into the card game, did he let you in?"

"You heard him." Mark laughed harshly. "He didn't want me anywhere near their card game. Not because he was afraid I'd finally win, but because he considered me bad luck." Mark looked me in the eyes. "I did go to Jimmy's. He's got some space above his store that's perfect for card games. Even Jimmy wouldn't let me in. Pete shoved me away from the door, and I fell on the upper deck, which is how I ripped the knee of these jeans. He made me so angry that night." Mark stared at the ground in shame and embarrassment and something I couldn't quite identify. "I only wanted another chance to change my luck."

"What happened after that?" I asked gently. "Did you wait for him outside? Did you follow him?"

"That's just it, I don't remember. Jimmy tossed me a six-pack and a bottle of Jack and told me to go cool off somewhere. I did, and I think I blacked out. Story of my life unfortunately." Mark's eyes widened with genuine fear, and I didn't know what to say to him.

I heard April's trilling laughter and glanced across the street in time to see her with Chase getting into her convertible. I couldn't let him catch me still talking to Mark.

"I'm sure everything will work out," I blurted, for lack of anything better to say. "Look at the time! It's been nice talking with you, but I've got to run. More work to do at the café and I need to stop at home first."

"Let me know if I can help. I'm a pretty good handy man."

"I will." One last peek toward the church and I could see April's bright blue car still sitting in the parking lot. Good, easier for me to make my getaway. I wasn't lying to Mark. I did need to run home and change my clothes before diving back into painting and staining at the café.

I also needed to compare my new intel. Chase might not offer up information, but he might be interested in hearing what I'd been able to find out. Mark couldn't remember what happened which meant he most likely had been drunk.

And angry enough to commit murder.

Eight

I spent Sunday evening mixing and baking more Sesame Peeps and BisScottie, as well as experimenting with a recipe for Cinnamon Sugar Snaps. I'd been so focused on my baking, I hadn't given Pete Seaver another thought. I had to believe Chase would prove me innocent and trust that he didn't believe I was guilty. With positive thoughts in my head Monday morning, I dropped some Peeps off for Scallywag, stopped to pick up the demon dog who'd managed to destroy one of Chase's pillows, and headed into work.

It felt good to say I was going to work even though I still wasn't officially open.

Thanks to my evening bake-a-thon, there was enough product in my canvas tote for people to sample if they stopped by. Giving out free samples seemed to be working as a perfect opportunity for them to get to know me. Harry turned out to be the town locksmith, and I had a confirmation email that my appliances were being delivered today. What a perfect start to my week.

Major inspected every area of the café as if he expected to find Steve again.

Thankfully, no stray kittens were hidden. I stood in the doorway of Petit Four Paws with an eagerness I hadn't felt in a very long time bubbling within me.

I was really doing this.

I'd fit a dozen tables within the sunny space. There was a scratching post in the corner for feline friends, and I even put a large fifty-gallon glass aquarium by the window for owners of iguanas and other lizards who wanted to stop by. A representative from the pet store had filled the tank with sand, warming rocks and a bowl for water. Overall, Four Paws already had a pet-friendly feel. I couldn't wait to have my first real paying customers. In another week once the flooring and tile were installed, I would have my grand opening.

The wooden chimes about the door clacked their hollow welcome. I spun around to find Tess McDermott and her basket. I wondered if she had kittens or produce this time.

"Hello, Mrs. McDermott. You're in luck today. I brought more Sesame Peeps, and I even have some new Cinnamon Sugar Snaps you can bring home to Fred."

"I need you to help me." Tess sounded frightened, and my worry meter started to rise. "Of course, what is it?" I placed my hand on her frail shoulder and escorted her to a table by the window.

"You have to save him from that monster," she said in such a shock-ridden voice, I wanted to grab the phone and call 9-1-1.

"Save who? Mr. McDermott? Where is he?" I started to rise, ready for action when she pulled my hand to stop me.

"No, no, Fred is home. You need to save Steve." Tess reached into her basket and pulled out my adorable little friend. "I've told him over and over to stay put, but he keeps coming back home somehow. Something bad is going to happen."

Guilt stabbed at my heart. "I'm sorry, but I keep sending him back," I admitted. "I just can't have him here during all of this construction." The sadness in her old eyes and quiver of her lips broke my heart. "This is a pet café, not a pet store. I'm afraid if you want to sell the kittens, you should maybe see if Harry will put up some flyers.

"But that horrible man is threatening to drown my babies in the nearest river! We can't let that happen. You must take him." She tried to hand Steve off to me, but I was more worried about what she'd just said than the kitten.

Horrible man? I studied Tess curiously as she rambled on and on about how the kittens were in danger. She seemed disoriented, which could have been from all her worrying.

"Who is trying to drown the kittens?" I relieved Steve from her shaking hand.

"That Pete Seaver that's who!" Tess declared, peeking into her basket for Fluffy and Cotton.

"But Tess, Pete—"

"Is going to kill them, I tell you. He found them romping in his flowerbed and tossed them on my porch telling me if he caught them on his property one more time, he'd drown them. We can't let that happen, Juli." She grabbed at my arm with surprising strength.

I held Steve close and kept my eye on the frail woman sitting next to me. Something in her behavior seemed very off, and it wasn't just her concern for the kittens. Was it possible Tess didn't even know Pete was dead?

"Tess, I'm not sure if you know this, but Pete Seaver was murdered."

"What? Who would do such a thing?" Her violet eyes grew wide. Amid their surprise I thought I recognized a glimmer of satisfaction.

"The police are still investigating," I said carefully. "Pete's body was found in my mother's rose garden. Someone hit him in the head and killed him."

"He had that beautiful statue, too. It's a shame he never got to sell it."

"How do you know about the statue?" My worry meter simmered as Tess's rambling took on a whole new meaning. What if she killed Pete in an insane rage over his threats to the kittens and didn't remember because she suffered dementia?

Before Tess could answer, the chimes above my door clanked softly again. I excused myself and went to see who it was. Deputy Gary Maxwell stood in the doorway, hands on hips, surveying the café. I couldn't tell by his expression if he was here to arrest Tess or not. I found myself standing between him and Four Paws until I found out for sure.

"Hi, Gary, what brings you by the café?"

"I've heard about the progress you've been making here, so I wanted to stop and see for myself. Very impressive work you've done."

"Thanks." I tried to keep my emotions in check. Until I found out how much poor Tess remembered, I didn't want to hand her over to the police.

"Is something wrong? You seem a little distracted." Gary walked closer, and I met him halfway so he wouldn't get a peek at Tess.

"Nothing is wrong. I just have a lot on my mind. I was up baking half the night and packaging more treats. Once my appliances come in, I will be able to do it all here."

"Well, you're doing a fine job from what I can see." Gary nodded his approval and shot me a make-your-knees-weak smile. "If I can be blatantly honest with you, I have an ulterior motive for stopping by."

"You do?" I rocked on my heels in surprise. Maybe he wasn't here to arrest Tess after all. Gary was the perfect package of personality and good looks. If he were going to ask me out, I'd be forever grateful to the dating gods. Forget what I said earlier, I could use a distraction right about now.

"I haven't been able to get you off my mind from the moment I met you. I haven't asked Chase about this, but I'd really like to get to know you better." Gary's words snapped me back to the conversation at hand.

"You would?" Hallelujah. I could have a man in my life who didn't annoy me! Through my inner delight I recalled his words. "Wait a minute. What does Chase have to do with this?"

"He's my boss, and well, it appears you two have some history. It's only proper to check with him first.

"Whoa. I must have misunderstood. Are you saying you're going to get his permission?" Please, please let him say no.

"I have to. It's Bro Code." His adorable dimples lit up his face. Unbelievable.

"You can't be serious?" I gazed into unwavering amber eyes, knowing his answer before he even spoke.

"Dead serious. Chase and I work closely together, and I wouldn't want things to get awkward at the office, if you know what I mean."

Unfortunately, I knew all too well.

Gary, I'm an adult. We are all adults. What Chase thinks about you asking me out is irrelevant. He certainly didn't ask me if he could date April." I blinked. Where had that come from? I forced myself to focus and continued, "The only person you should be concerned about is me. And I'd like to get to know you, too, but if you're going to constantly be deferring to Chase, then I'll stop you right now because it's not going to work."

"Wow. Chase told me you could be a handful, and now I see what he meant." Gary leaned back, creating a neutral space.

"Gary."

"I'm sorry, Juli. But he'd mentioned you the day after you came back to town."

"Uh-huh." I pursed my lips in thought, wondering if it were ever going to be possible for me to date someone in New Hope without Sheriff Buttinski involved. Then I remembered Tess in the other room and decided it best to change the subject. "Do you guys have any leads to who might have killed Pete?"

He looked surprised, but he rolled with it. "We're ruling out some of the local gamblers who might have had a vendetta with Pete but that's about it. Why?"

"Tess McDermott is in the other room and she's talking a whole bunch of crazy, including how threatening Pete was to her."

"Unfortunately, we've been out there before because he scared her half to death in a drunken rage. She just heard him yelling and banging around in his yard. He never actually hurt her."

"She says he threatened to kill her kittens. When I told her he was dead, she mentioned the statue. I think it's the same one he sold to me that I sold to Mrs. Bailey."

"We didn't find a statue in Ida's house. Do you think Tess knows who stole it?" Gary rubbed his jawline in thought. "I could call Marty at the station, or Chase, and have one of them see if the statue is in or around Tess's house." He pulled his phone from his back pocket.

"She wasn't in the shop when he came in to sell it, so how could she know about it? Unless ...You don't think she took matters into her own hands do you?"

"And killed Pete?" Gary stayed silent for a moment. "I don't think she'd do it." He shook his head. "She'd be too afraid of him."

"Go in and see for yourself." I pointed toward the Four Paws door. "She isn't acting like herself."

Gary walked into the sunlit room, and I followed. Tess had the lid flipped open on her basket, cooing softly to the kittens. The poor old woman was in her own world, making me believe even more that she could have done something drastic to protect the helpless creatures she considered her babies.

"Mrs. McDermott, how are you today?" Gary approached and sat down, setting his phone on the table.

"I'm just fine, Sheriff, how are you?"

"I'm well, Ma'am. Juli says you need to protect your kittens. Is everything all right?" He scooted the chair closer, placed his elbows on the table and folded his hands.

"It is now that that horrible monster Pete Seaver is dead. Thank goodness my babies can play in peace around the yard."

"Do you know what happened to him?" Gary asked, reaching to stroke Fluffy's orange head, and I moved to stand behind Tess.

"No. Juli told me he's dead. That's all I need to know."

"Why don't I give you a ride home?" He stood and offered her an arm, gazing at her like a devoted grandson, and my heart melted.

"That would be very nice." She closed the basket lid and smiled when Gary helped her stand. "Fred will be worried if I'm gone for too long." As they walked toward the door Gary's eyes met mine, and I knew he'd take good care of her and her babies. Her husband shouldn't let her wander about on her own like this.

"Juli, be a dear and take Steve. He misses you." Tess started to open the lid, and I heard the tiny meows inside.

"Tess, I can't. I still have a lot of construction going on. Maybe another time." I grinned over her persistence in making me a cat owner. Maybe someday but not now.

"He will just have to be happy playing with Cotton and Fluffy. I'll give the new cookies to Fred. He loves cinnamon."

"I'll call you this week for dinner," Gary said while opening the door for Tess. A doorbell sound chimed across the room. "Oh, that's my phone. It's back at the table."

"I'll go grab it," I said and headed back into Four Paws. I snatched the phone off the table and as the notification sound went off again, I looked down at the partial message on the screen.

Mark: It's diamonds.

I tripped on my own feet as I immediately thought of Mark Walker and suddenly wondered why Mark would be texting local law enforcement. I handed the phone to Gary, feeling guilty for even looking.

"I didn't mean to look but it lit up in my hand." I handed him the sleek black device. "Someone named Mark says it's diamonds."

Gary's eyes registered surprise before he replied. "My brother-in-law. We had a bet on what birthstone is April. He didn't believe me when I said it was diamonds. My sister's birthday is in April, and he wanted to buy her a birthstone necklace. He was hoping she wouldn't have the most expensive birthstone."

"How much did he lose?"

"He buys drinks next time I'm in town, but I might have pity on him." He winked. "He still has to buy that necklace."

I watched them leave in Gary's squad car. I'd landed a potential dinner date and suspect all in one day. Now if I could only make heads or tails from all of this. I'd be one step closer to solving Pete's murder and clearing my name.

———

True to her word, Sandy dropped off information on upcoming events through St. Mary's. First up was a charity Texan Hold Em tournament held in the lower level of Nailed It!, Rita's salon. I called the number and Rita Davis seemed incredibly happy to welcome a newcomer to the game. Fifty dollars to play, one third of which went toward Lily Johnson's veterinary practice to help feed the stray or abandoned animals people would drop off. Rita told me that every month they played for a different charity in town or to support a family who needed help. The remaining two-thirds of the entry fee would be split between the church and the winner.

At first, I thought the fifty-dollar fee was a bit steep since I had no shot of winning. I never really understood the game. From my conversation with Rita, this monthly game happened even if they didn't have a charity to play for. What better way for me to gather information than from the women's side of things while also playing a part in the generosity of our community.

I was able to bake more snacks before heading to Rita's. I even brought some carob- drizzled graham squares and whole grain with sun-dried tomato crackers. No harm in using these ladies as my guinea pigs. There were still a lot of people in town who hadn't stopped by for free samples. Hopefully, that would change once I had my grand opening.

All the lights were on at Mrs. Bailey's, and I could hear Scallywag squawking. Chase never told me how his talk went, and I could only hope he was as gentle with her as Gary had been with Tess. I had a little time and decided I'd check in with Chase and see if he might finally give me insight into Pete's case. He didn't have to give me exact names, only let me know if he and his office were getting close. That darn bird made me seem guilty and unless they found a viable suspect soon, I'd hate to think I'd be sentenced for a crime I didn't commit. I'd no sooner squeezed between the hedges when April's voice startled me from the porch.

"Juli? What are you up to?" She eyed my cartons of organic snacks as she smoothed the front of her paisley skirt. "Chase invited me over for dinner and a movie on cable."

"That's nice." I stifled my urge to say anything negative, reminding myself that turning over a new leaf wasn't easy. "I'm sure you guys will have a great night." I turned to walk away from the dizzying design of her skirt when Chase opened the door.

"Juli?" He shot an almost nervous look from me to April. "What are you doing here?" He shoved his hands into the pockets of his jeans and leaned against the door.

"I was on my way out and remembered something I wanted to tell you but no worries, it can wait."

"Dinner is just about ready, garlic shrimp over linguini. I've got plenty if you'd like to come in." Now it was April's turn to be surprised, only the expression she nailed me with was more of a warning glare.

"I'd be intruding on your evening," I said and April visibly relaxed. "It can wait, really. I'll catch up with you tomorrow."

"Where are you off to? You're not working late, are you?"

Chase took a step down his porch followed by April who wasn't about to miss any of our conversation.

"Actually, I'm off to play some cards at Rita's. Sandy dropped by with a list of community events. I'm taking some samples with me." I held up the containers. "I want the townspeople to get to know me and this is for a good cause, too."

"That's right, Lily's animal hospital. She works hard to find abandoned animals a home. Nice girl, Lily."

"That's what Rita told me."

"Maybe you'll come home with a furry friend?" April chimed in and hung off Chase's bicep. Inwardly I chuckled. Garlic was never a friend to Chase. She'd better enjoy the contact now, because she wouldn't be snuggling up to him during movie time.

"I don't think so. Poor Tess McDermott keeps trying to make me adopt one of her kittens. I've had to keep explaining I can't do it right now."

"That crazy old lady? Her family needs to come take care of her," April stated. "One of these days she's going to hurt herself or someone else."

"April, c'mon, she's a sweet old lady. She's probably just lonely." Chase slipped out of April's death grip.

"I suppose, but she rattles on so much about things that don't make sense." April placed her hand on Chase's back, moving in closer. He seemed to tense up but then relaxed before I looked away.

"I like her. I just can't adopt Steve."

"Steve?" both April and Chase said in unison.

"The kitten," I corrected and glanced at my watch. "I really need to get going. Rita has plans to introduce me to some of the women I haven't met yet. I'll let you get back to your date night."

"It's just dinner and a movie," Chase called behind me, as I grinned all the way to my truck and all the way to Rita's.

I rang the back doorbell and could hear a group of women talking and laughing. Moments later an athletically built woman wearing yoga pants and a bright orange tank opened the door. Her silky black ponytail draped over one shoulder. Rita was a knockout.

"You must be Juli?" she questioned in a friendly voice. I nodded. "We're so excited to have someone new join in. C'mon, let me introduce you." Rita led me by the arm into a lower- level game room. "Don't mind the mess, it's still a bit under construction." She pointed at a corner loaded with carpet scraps and pieces of molding. "Not only do I own the hair and nail salon, but I teach Zumba at the gym. One of these days I'm going to teach from here and part of this will be my studio."

"That's great." If I could Zumba my way to a body like Rita's, I'd be her number one customer. "I brought snacks."

"Perfect! Come right this way." We moved to the center of the room, and there must have been two dozen women there. "Everyone, this is Juli Butler, Justine's daughter. She's the one who's turning the antique shop into an organic café."

"Oh, I've heard!" One woman said. "It sounds interesting."

"Thank you. I even brought some samples if any of you would like to try." I held up my containers.

"How wonderful!" A perky blonde extended her hand. "I'm Tammy O'Toole. My husband Jimmy and I own the fish market down by the marina."

"I don't remember a fish market being there."

"It used to be the old bait shop, only we bought it and fixed it up. We've been there for five years now. You'll have to stop by sometime."

"I most definitely will. I could use some fresh tuna for my Kitty Krackers." Not to mention Jimmy could be the Jimmy from the card game Pete went to the night of his murder.

"Tammy, how did Jimmy make out the other night? Bobby said he heard him and Pete fighting after the game," a young woman with short, brown, curly hair wearing cut offs and a purple tank top said, confirming my suspicions.

"Thanks for asking, Wendy. I stayed up worrying half the night when he didn't come home or answer his phone. Jimmy didn't roll in 'til about 4:00 that morning. Said he'd followed Pete around trying to convince him to give everyone their money back on the count of they all knew he cheated that last hand. Of course, that ornery Pete Seaver wouldn't listen. He told Jimmy he had big plans for that money. I'm sure Bobby wasn't the only one who heard them fighting."

"Bobby said he's tried to ask Jim about it, but Jim won't talk." Wendy shook her springy ringlets. "So much pressure on these guys with the Play Makers Game coming up. They all want in, and they all want to win."

"That's not the first time Jim has lost big in a card game. Depends on how many drinks he's had." Tammy laughed. "This one with Pete really got under his skin. He told me there's no place for greedy people like Pete in this world. He knows how I feel when he dips into our vacation fund. To make it up to me, he brought me home the most precious statue."

Statue?

My ears perked while I faded out of the conversation I'd been having with Rita and a couple others. These women had to know Pete was dead by now. New Hope was a small enough town and heck, Chase knew everyone. They had to have questioned the men from the card game. If Jimmy O'Toole didn't want to talk to his own friend about the incident with Pete, he sure wouldn't want to talk to the police if it meant he could be a suspect.

"You got yourself a good one, Tam," Rita said from where she stood organizing the table of snacks.

"I sure do. If only that were true for his niece. You'd never know they come from the same gene pool."

"You just have to give her time," Wendy offered up as she poured the wine. "She helped me out at the counter and was as friendly as can be."

"You must have caught her on a good day. Most of the time

that girl is a sassy glass of hormones. Poor Jim doesn't know what to do with her either, which means Andie and I butt heads constantly. Watch out girls, I need to let loose tonight." Everyone laughed and raised a glass.

"Is she staying 'til the end of summer? Maybe she needs to be involved more with the community?" Rita began to shuffle the cards, and we all took our seats around the table.

"Unfortunately, we have her until she graduates next year. Jimmy's sister wants her to complete her education, and she can't do that with all the temptation in the school she's at in Chicago. Kids here still know her from when they used to live here. If she can get unstuck from her boyfriend long enough to reconnect, she'll be fine."

"Long distance romance, that's tough. I can totally relate there." Rita delt the cards.

"You're an adult. Andie is seventeen and involved with someone old enough to buy his own booze! He's twenty-four and she won't even show us pictures of him. She says he's very private and doesn't like social media. I think there's something shady going on."

"She's your niece, not your daughter. You're just going to have to trust her mother, and support her," Wendy said and patted Tammy's forearm.

"Don't be trying to look at my hand Wendy!

Two hours at Rita's flew by. So much fun and laughter made me think of how much I'd missed by moving away. Quickly dismissing the regret, I blamed my itch to travel on my father. While I didn't have a chance to speak with everyone, the women I did talk to were very friendly and open to my idea of the organic café. They loved how they would be able to bring their pets, and that's all I needed to know. I said my good-byes and promised I'd play in the next game even though I didn't win one hand tonight.

While I wanted to let Chase know what Tammy O'Toole had said, I also wanted to make sure my facts were straight. Tammy seemed like such a good person, and I could use the fresh seafood. I didn't want to upset either one of them by falsely accusing Jimmy. Even so, what if Jimmy O'Toole killed Pete out of revenge, used the money to replenish their vacation fund and then gave his wife the statue? Not many people saw Pete bring the statue into my shop, and even fewer people knew Mrs. Bailey bought it.

Tammy could be married to Pete's murderer!

$$\mathcal{N}ine$$

"**C**ome here, Major. Bring Auntie Juli the wooden spoon." Not that I would do anything with it now that it was covered in dog slobber, but this evil dog needed to know it was bad to destroy things that weren't his—or Chases for that matter. The fuzzy four-legged mop stared at me with his butt in the air. I knew he wanted to play, but I had a million things to do still to prepare this space for my grand opening. I was eager to test out my newly installed ovens and had whipped up another batch of cinnamon snaps until my furry friend jumped up and snatched the spoon.

"You won't get a treat if you don't behave," I reprimanded, holding the bone-shaped cookie. I knew I had his full attention when his butt hit the floor. "You know you want one. Look at the BisScottie, yum-yum-yum." Major cocked his head and dropped the spoon, in an almost too easy victory. Of course, the second I moved, he lurched forward and raced past me leaving the spoon behind. "Now what?" I picked up the spoon and power walked to where he stood in the kitchen.

Looking guilty?

I stared matter-of-factly at him trying to figure out what was up. Then I noticed something protruding from the corner of his mouth. He'd been inside with me all afternoon so I couldn't imagine what he'd gotten into. Then again, he'd so deftly grabbed the spoon it wouldn't surprise me if he'd put his fat, furry mitts on my desk and somehow pulled down a receipt.

"Show me what you've got?" Not wanting the receipt to be ripped and ruined, I slowly walked to my counter and opened a glass jar full of my new strawberry-banana BisScottie.

Holding the bone-shaped treat high in the air, I called him over again. "C'mere Major. Who's my good boy now?"

Major bounded in my direction and thankfully dropped the paper at my feet. I knelt to give him the treat, patted his fluffy head, and straightened the crinkled paper against my thigh. I stared in shock at what wasn't a receipt at all, but a pieced-together-ransom-looking note:

I KNOW WHAT YOU ARE DOING. YOU NEED TO COME CLEAN BEFORE SOMEONE GETS HURT.

"Juli, we need to talk," Chase's deep timbre startled me from behind. "Why are you on the floor?"

"Sure, we can talk. I've wanted to talk to you too." I couldn't let him see this note until I knew who sent it and what it meant. Keeping my hands close to the ground, I crumbled the note into my fist and then picked up some crumbs left over by Major. "I gave your dog a treat and he's a very messy eater." I stood and walked to the small waste basket, brushing the crumbs from my hand and tucking the note safely in my front pocket. "Reminds me of you." I grinned, proud of my little jab.

"Very funny. See what you'll be getting yourself into by opening this up to animals? Humans are messy enough. Now you'll have crumbs, dirty footprints and drool."

"I'm ready for it. This is exciting and I'm watching my dreams come true." I paused, hoping I didn't seem too anxious, like I was hiding something. When he didn't apologize for not really supporting my dreams, I asked on a sigh, "What do you want to talk about?"

"You first. I only stopped by to pick up Major and make sure you were both behaving." He grinned and motioned for the dog to come to his side.

"Me? Misbehaving? He's the one you need to worry about." I pointed a finger and the fluffball whined. "I'm working like mad to make sure everything is set up, and at the same time basically dog-sitting because we can't leave him alone. He even stole one of my wooden spoons earlier."

"I know you, remember?" He crossed his arms over his broad chest. "I'm sure you don't feel like we're doing enough to figure out who Pete's real murderer is. I just don't want you trying to take matters into your own hands. It could be dangerous."

"I would never do anything like that."

"Is that so? How come when I talked to Mark Walker, he happened to tell me about the conversation you two had? He was surprised since we're neighbors and old friends that you hadn't told me about it already."

"Oh, that." I flicked my wrist like I'd seen Mrs. B and Betty do. "I was going to, but I've been busy and keep forgetting. Sorry." I lifted my shoulder and smiled sheepishly.

"Mmm hmm. Anything else?" Those green eyes stared knowingly at me, and I tried not to squirm. He was correct, as usual. He did know me too well.

"As a matter of fact, there is." I raised a brow, and he mirrored me exactly. "I haven't even had a chance to sit down with Mrs. Bailey to make sure you didn't come down too hard on her."

"Did she tell you I pushed her around?" he said, and I gasped, causing him to laugh. "Everything is fine with Mrs. B," he reassured me with a gentle hand on my shoulder. "She couldn't give me much more information than what you provided. She didn't hear a thing, not even Scallywag sneaking out."

"Good." I nodded.

"No, not good. Pete's statue is missing from Mrs. Bailey's house, which leads me to believe Pete did steal it, left the window open for Scallywag to fly out and someone killed him to either get the statue back or sell it for money."

"It's not worth much due to a break at the base which someone poorly repaired," I offered, watching determination swirl in Chase's eyes as he smoothed his mustache in thought.

"So maybe Pete originally stole it from someone else?" He raised a finger at his obvious deduction.

"He said it belonged to his family and it had gotten broken at his sister's house."

"A sister? Based on Pete's past, I feel confident that's not true."

"Scott Iverson mentioned he didn't think Pete had a sister, either."

"And why were you talking to Scott Iverson about Pete?" His brow arched so high I thought for sure the hairs would fall out due to the tension on his skin.

"I swear I didn't start it. He said how he didn't think I killed Pete because I'm too nice."

"Okay...and...."

"I may have mentioned the statue and the sister, but I didn't ask specifically for information. You'll still check it out, right?" I asked, and Chase nodded, not taking the discussion further. "If Pete lied, then why was he in such a hurry to sell and then get the statue back?"

"We're still looking into the loan shark angle."

My thoughts immediately flew to the statue Jimmy O'Toole gave to Tammy. What if my assumption was correct after all? I could have this mystery solved and with no help from the police.

"What's going on in that pretty little head of yours?" Chase stepped closer, and I snapped to attention. I couldn't give anything away, not until I was sure.

"Nothing, just following your by-the-book-logic. You're very good. Did Mark give you any new information? I also think you should check out Tess McDermott."

"Tess? Is this what you wanted to tell me the other night when April was over?"

"Yes. I wanted to share what I'd found out from talking to Tess and Mark. Now you already know about Mark."

"I'm looking into his story, not sure if I'm buying his whole bit about not remembering. He used to be such a good citizen." Chase swiped his hand across the top of his head. "I hope when this is over, he finds help and turns his life around."

"Yeah...." I knew all about wanting to turn your life around, and one day I wanted Chase to understand. Today was not that day. "I was wondering about Mark too. Every time we talk, he seems so anxious. It's like he's afraid someone is going to spot him or beat him up. But Tess could seriously have motive, and I think she could have killed Pete."

"You've said so yourself, she's a sweet old lady. How in God's name do you see her killing someone like Pete Seaver?"

"Because Tess hysterically told me Pete had threatened to kill her kittens, that's how. She could be surprisingly stronger than she looks. You should have seen her. That fire in her eyes spoke volumes. Chase, if she were defending those adorable creatures, she very well could have clubbed him over the head and have no recollection because I think she suffers from dementia."

"When did you become a physician?" He leaned his elbow on the counter, all casual and ready to listen.

"I'm just saying April is right." I caught the smirk and pointed my finger at the tip of his nose. "Watch it. This is probably the only time I will ever admit that."

"How is April right?" His smirk transitioned to a full-blown grin.

"Tess rambles on and on, and sometimes what she's saying doesn't add up." I continued as not to give him the advantage. "I think she forgets where she is and what year it is. Why would Fred let her leave the house alone? He should at least be with her, but she's always by herself."

"Juli." Chase's face grew emotionless.

"She could seriously get hurt or even lost. What if she somehow ended up in the next county?" I persisted, hoping he'd understand what I was getting at. "He's not a very attentive husband, if you ask me."

"Juli, Fred has been dead for two years."

"But she talks about going home to cook for him and that he's waiting for her." I felt a sob stick in the back of my throat. Poor, poor, Tess, she really was lonely. "Then those kittens are all she has." I gulped down the sob. "Oh, Chase, do you really think she could have killed Pete?" I didn't want to think I'd been right, not about Tess.

Chase pulled me in his arms and gave me a hug. "I don't know. Gary and I will have to check it out. I'll keep you posted on what we find."

"Thank you." I stepped back, not comfortable with how the warmth of his embrace affected my insides.

"Not so fast," he said, snapping me out of my awkward state. "I still think you're up to something."

I fluttered my lashes innocently. The crinkled note in my pocket burned like a juicy secret to be told. Only I couldn't tell him about that either, not yet. Knowing Chase, he'd lock me in a jail cell for my own safety, and then I wouldn't be able to help at all. I knew in my heart Tess McDermott couldn't be Pete's killer, which meant I had to step up my search.

The only way to do that was to check out the fish market and the O'Toole's house.

———

I WAITED UNTIL NIGHTFALL BEFORE VENTURING OUT TO the fish market. After leaving some lights on in my own house and my truck in the driveway, I donned my black yoga pants, purple sweatshirt, and black neoprene driving gloves and pulled my hair back into a messy bun. I'd rummaged through the garage until I found a couple different screwdrivers, some clothesline, and a small flashlight. The clothesline was a last-minute grab, but it seemed like something I would want to have, in case of an emergency. Didn't all thieves have a backup plan?

Only I wasn't stealing anything. I was investigating a lead and searching for evidence which would link Jimmy O'Toole to the murder of Pete Seaver. The O'Toole's had a gorgeous two-story house right on the water. Lucky for me, the fish market was two blocks down by the dock and marina. The sky was clear, and the full moon guided my way like a mystical spotlight.

There was no car in their driveway and no lights were on inside. I looked up at the stars and said a little prayer to Mom that no one was home. I started toward the house when I heard foot-steps approaching fast. Knowing I appeared ridiculously out of place, I dove into the thickest part of their landscaping and held my breath. Lily Johnson, the vet I'd met at the card game, jogged by with Rita. To my surprise they stopped directly in front of my hiding spot.

"I didn't mean for this to happen, you know. It was completely an accident." Lily placed her fingers on her neck and stared at her watch.

"What are you going to do now?" Rita asked, barely out of breath, making me think more about taking her Zumba classes.

"I'm not sure. Don't tell anyone, okay? If this gets out, it will stir up all kinds of trouble. I can't handle it, not now. I need more time."

"Don't worry, your secret is safe with me. C'mon, we're at the last mile."

The women jogged out of sight, and I didn't move until I felt sure they were long gone.

Like I'd seen people do in the movies, I stuck close to the house so as not to be noticed and worked my way through the Weigela to the back. With the clothesline looped diagonally across my body, I used an old paperclip trick one of my New York friends had taught me when we worked the locks at the gallery. The O'Toole's lock clicked then turned and I pushed the door open.

Moonlight reflected off the water and shone throughout the house so there was no need to use my flashlight. I tip-toed around, making sure I didn't touch anything but also keeping my eyes open for something that might look suspicious. Disappointment weighed on my chest as there was no statue resembling the one Pete had anywhere on the first floor.

"Hi," a soft, feminine voice said.

I froze, thinking I'd been caught by the cleaning crew or someone, but why wouldn't they turn lights on? Through the doorframe I could see a thin silhouette on the window seat and the dim light of a cell phone screen.

Andie.

"I miss you." Andie's lovestruck voice said softly, and I wilted against the wall. There was silence as she listened to the reply. "No, no one suspects anything. I'm doing what you told me to do, and they are giving me more freedom." She released a breath before answering again. "I'm working on it. You know I don't like this. They went out tonight, and I'm meeting up with some old friends later. Yes, there will be guys. You're the only one I want. You know I'll do it. Tell me you're coming soon." She giggled and I felt like I was intruding on their secret. "Tell me when and I'll meet you there. I love you." I watched Andie's shadow hop from the window seat and slip the phone in her back pocket. Then I heard the front door click shut.

Now I was completely alone.

Moving to the second level I peeked in each room but still didn't see the porcelain woman and daughter statue. Jimmy must have taken it from Pete when he killed him. Why else would he have been out until early that morning and then bring it home to his wife so she wouldn't suspect anything? Then again, he could have told her the truth about what happened, and they hid the statue together.

Once inside their master bedroom, I scanned the perimeter. There had to be something here that I could take to Chase and show him I'd found the real killer. I dropped to my knees and shined the light under the bed.

Tick, tick, tick, came a tapping noise against the window.

I froze with my body half under the bed and my butt in the air. Maybe it was just a branch from the neighboring tree? I held my breath and waited a moment, then I heard it again.

Tick, tick, tick.

Slowly I backed out and stood. Turning toward the window, a flurry of blue and gold feathers flapped before my eyes against the glass. Had that crazy bird followed me?

"Juuuli." The parrot lit on a branch, cocked its plumed head, and clicked its beak several times as if taunting me.

"Scallywag," I ground from between my teeth. "Get out of here!" I shooed my hand toward the window, but the bird didn't even flinch.

"Where's the money? What's that!" he mimicked, and I wondered if those were Jimmy's words.

I opened the window and was about to scare him away when I heard car doors close. My head snapped in Scallywag's direction while his head bobbed up and down as he danced along the branch.

"Oh no, what have I done!" he squawked. "Watch it! Someone's coming. Baaaad Juli!"

"What? No, you rotten bird!" I raised the window wider and reached for his taloned toes. "C'mere you!" Scallywag only clicked and squealed inches from my reach. From the driveway I heard Tammy's tinkling laughter followed by Jimmy's hearty belch.

"Uh-oh, Juuuli. Bad Juli." If that bird didn't shut up, they would surely find me.

"No, Juli good, Juli good." I moved my palms up and down in a calming motion while a burst of panic shot through my system like a harpoon through a blue fin tuna. Then I remembered the cracker in my pocket. "I have treats, now shush before you blow my cover." I reached into my pocket and pulled out the last Sesame Peeps. I didn't have a cover to blow, but Chase would have a field day if I were caught in the O'Toole's master bedroom.

"Hurry, Jimmy! I'll crank up the Jacuzzi tub." Tammy called from somewhere downstairs. I scooted away from the window, ducking and dodging about the room in search of a place to hide. One glance at my feathered friend told me there would be no safe hiding place as long as he remained within earshot.

"I've got to get out of here," I said, gazing at my only way out. The window.

I tied a slip knot with the clothesline and lassoed the nearest sturdy branch, praying it would hold. Scallywag continued to make clicking noises and cock his head from one side to the other. Once I pulled the knot tight, I grabbed hold and slid to the ground. Scallywag swooped from the limb and circled me like a vulture.

"Go home," I ordered as I headed for the street. Trying to find clues had become more stressful than I'd imagined as my heart drummed within my chest.

"Pete's dead! Pete's dead!" Scallywag squawked and flew away with an almost demonic chuckle. I silently prayed Tess's mama cat was out hunting and would bring home a vibrant feast.

"Juli?" a car pulled along the curb startling me from my vengeful thoughts. Gary's sandy blond head leaned out the squad car window. "What are you doing out at this hour?"

"Oh, hey Gary." I stretched my arms high over my head in a stretch and transitioned to some torso-twists. "I couldn't fall asleep so I thought an evening jog would do the trick." I jogged in place, but his eyes studied me as though he didn't quite believe it."

"Dressed in black? That's not very safe."

"I hadn't planned on going far, maybe just around the block." I caught a glimpse of blue in a distant tree. "Then I noticed Mrs. Bailey's parrot had escaped again so I started chasing him."

"In the dark?"

"Well, it is nighttime," I stated, forgetting he was a deputy. "And I know how much Mrs. B. loves that rotten bird," I emphasized, knowing full well Scallywag could hear me. Gary's brows became lost under his thick golden hair. "Sorry."

"Why don't I give you a ride home? You seem a little stressed." He motioned me toward the car.

"What about Scallywag?" And my clothesline, I thought.

"If he found his way out, I'm pretty sure he can find his way back in."

"I guess you're right." As I opened the door, a flash of blue and gold passed over the car.

"I've got to get out of here. What have I done? Stuuuuupid Juuuuli."

I plopped into the passenger seat, tossed Gary a weak smile and shrugged. "Stupid bird?"

Ten

"Woof."

At first, I thought I might still be dreaming. The sound was airy and soft and barely broke through my consciousness. I rolled over, snuggling into the sheets, not quite ready to face the day. Only I had a strange feeling someone was staring at me. The second I cracked open an eye, a white fluffy head lunged forward and licked the entire side of my face.

"Woof."

"Aww, yuck." I scrambled to sit up, jumped out of bed and straight to the bathroom to wash the slobber off my skin. "What in the world are you doing here?"

Images of Scallywag taunting me from the tree made me wonder what I'd done now to be terrorized by the other obnoxious animal in my life. As I dried my face and glanced up from the towel, I had to admit Major's big brown eyes full of anticipation were adorable. That still didn't explain how he had gotten into my house.

"Chase?" I called, expecting him to appear. My house remained quiet except for Major's heavy breathing. "And here I thought I was the one breaking and entering." I patted Major's head. "C'mon, let's go have breakfast."

Once in the kitchen, I noticed a thermos with a bright yellow note on my counter. There was still no sign of Chase. I looked down at the sheepdog happily sniffing the new chew toy I'd picked up for him at the Hardware Store and then at the scrawling script of Chase's handwriting.

Heard about your late night "jog" so I brought you coffee. Stop by my office when you decide to wake up and remember to lock your front door. ~ Chase

"Who does he think he is, my father?" I asked Major who paid no attention to me. "You can thank me for the toy by being a good boy." Although the big oaf of a dog seemed to behave better for me than Chase these days. A semi-evil smirk formed on my face knowing I had one-upped Chief-Goodie-Good with his own animal.

"Sorry, Mom," I said while looking up. "You know how I am." And so did Chase, I reminded myself while pouring the coffee. For as easily as he could drive me nuts—and I swear he enjoyed every minute— had to admit I liked having him close again. My departure from New Hope ten years ago hadn't left us on good terms, so the fact that he even talked to me now was a good sign I hadn't destroyed our friendship.

A couple hours later, Major and I headed for work with my tote bag full of goodies to put in the display case. First, I would have to make the detour to Chase's office and find out why he wanted to see me. Major tried to pull me in the direction of the hardware store, our usual route, but I had to rein him in.

"No cookie today, big guy. Your master left us orders." I paused beside a parked car and checked my reflection in its window. By the off chance Gary was in the office, I wanted to make sure I looked good. I walked through the door a little disappointed when there was no Gary in sight.

"Well, if it isn't Sleeping Beauty and her beast," Chase kidded as he walked out of his office. "Hey, there, buddy!" He roughed up Major's head and patted the dog's wide back.

"Woof."

"Thanks for the coffee," I said.

"I'd planned on drinking it with you, but when I called the office Gary said he'd run into you late last night when you were out jogging so I figured you wouldn't be up early." His voice was smooth, but his eyes were those of a trained man of the law waiting for me to screw up.

"You would be right on that call. I was wiped out from all that exercise." I didn't dare let him know what I was really doing, or he'd lock me up for sure.

"Since when do you jog? Last I knew you hated any form of physical activity." He extended his hand toward his office.

"There's a lot you don't know about me now." I sat in the chair he offered. "For your information I was talking to Rita about her Zumba classes, and it really made me want to become more fit."

"Not buying it." He returned to the chair behind his desk, and Major sat beside him like the dutiful canine deputy.

"Plus, I couldn't sleep. What started out as a simple walk turned into an all-out jog."

"Still not buying it." He raised his eyes and shook his head.

"Maybe you should. It was quite refreshing."

"Maybe you should think about what time of day you decide to engage in your new fitness hobby. Oh, and lock your doors for crying out loud. I walked right in this morning without a problem."

I slapped my palms on the arms of the chair. "I'm not in Boston anymore. This is New Hope. Nothing ever happens here."

"Then what do you call Pete Seaver's dead body?" He quirked a brow.

"Murder," I stated matter-of-factly. "But need I remind you that things like this normally don't happen here."

"Exactly, at least not until you came back to town."

"I don't like what you're implying." I crossed my arms and leaned back against the grey tweed fabric.

"And I don't like to see you put yourself in danger." He pointed at me from across his desk.

"Aww, so you really do care," I said with a tilt of my head and fluttering lashes as I perfected my posture.

"Would you be serious?" Chase didn't smile and his green eyes darkened like a tumultuous sea. "You could have gotten yourself hurt being out that late at night. Jogging, my ass. What were you really doing wandering around at eleven o'clock at night?"

"None of your business. I'm twenty-eight years old and capable of protecting myself. I guess I didn't realize you set a curfew in this town, Sheriff."

"Listen, Juli, all respectable people are home by that hour. The only ones I expect to find out that late are the young, crazy kids looking for something to do."

"Like we used to be?" I pointed out. "Do you hear yourself? You sound like some old fuddy-duddy who's about ready to retire. God Chase, you're my age! Live a little and enjoy life." I flung my arms wide for emphasis and Major perked his ears.

"I live just fine, thanks. Maybe you should live a little less so people wouldn't have to worry about you," he grumbled.

"Wait, did you just say you worry about me?"

"The same way I worry about every citizen in this town."

"Uh-huh," I replied with a smirk which told him I knew he was lying.

"There's a murderer on the loose. Until I find out if your mother's rose garden was a deliberate location or not, I need you to be smart and stay safe. I just wish we'd found the murder weapon by now."

"Maybe the killer tossed the statue. It could be long gone."

"Who said the murder weapon was the statue?" Chase leveled his stare at me. "I never said anything about a statue."

"Well, um, I remember that EMT guy saying something about a blunt object."

"Could have been a rock, a tree limb."

"And the statue is missing from Mrs. Bailey's house!" I pointed my finger at him having a fake ah-ha moment to cover up my mistake.

"We knew that, remember? Which put Pete at the scene of the crime because he was going to steal the statue back, but then someone killed him for it, escaping with said statue. We need to know who else wanted the statue, why they killed him for it, and what they used to hit him on the head. All my leads have been dead ends."

Oh, boy, did I want to tell him Jimmy O'Toole wanted that statue as payment to replace all the money Pete had cheated them out of. Jimmy was a big guy, and if he didn't kill Pete with the statue, he surely could have pummeled him with his meat-hook of a fist. The only problem was I hadn't found the statue in their house which led me to believe he'd either sold it already or hid it.

"What did you find out about Tess McDermott and Mark Walker?" I asked instead of relaying my suspicions about Jimmy.

"Gary's been working the night shift and found Mark passed out drunk on the other side of town around four that morning. He dropped him off at his brother-in-law's around four- twenty."

"Oh. What about Tess? She's not crazy enough to kill, is she?"

"No." Chase shook his head, and I relaxed. "Doc Peterson confirmed Tess had a reaction to her medication that evening and spent all night in the ER. They are still working on correcting her dosage."

"That's good, I guess." I couldn't help to be relieved for Tess and Mark, but concerned now that maybe my thoughts about Jimmy O'Toole were correct. Part of me wanted to mention it to Chase but the curious side of me wanted to find out on my own and not send him on another dead-end lead. Also, if Gary had picked up Mark, then the man obviously had an alibi. Knowing that, why was he still so keyed up and nervous?

"You okay?" Chase moved to take the chair next to mine and placed his hand on my arm, obviously concerned with my silence. "Don't worry, I'll find the real killer." Again, we shared that comfortable connection, and I knew deep in my gut he'd have my back no matter what.

"It's not that. I mean, I know you will." Our eyes met and held.

"Tell me what you're thinking?" His hand moved from my arm to my thigh as he waited patiently for my answer. Now would be a good time for me to tell him. I ran through the notes in my head, took a deep breath but never had the chance to speak.

"Chase! Oh, my goodness, I'm so glad you're still here," April sounded out of breath as she rushed through the door. She threw me a quick glance to let me know she saw me and flung herself straight into Chase, who'd stood immediately upon her whirlwind entry. She plastered herself against his chest and leaned her head on his shoulder. I felt my morning coffee curdle in my stomach from the drama.

"Hey, easy now. What's going on?" Chase took a step back, placed his hands on her shoulders and gazed into her eyes. April blinked several times, then I caught her peeking at me out the corner of her eye. She blinked again and I noticed the glimmer of a tear.

Unbelievable.

"I feel so silly now." She covered her mouth with her hot pink polished fingers. "I really shouldn't bother you at work."

"You're here now, so tell me what's the matter?" Chase stayed calm and by the book. I almost laughed out loud because even the drama queen couldn't get a rise out of him.

"I locked myself out of my flat and I knew you had my other key." April cast a wicked glance I knew was for my benefit. I chewed my cheek to keep from saying something I shouldn't as she took both of his hands in hers. "I don't want you to be a stranger, so why don't you come over for dinner again tonight?" Chase slipped his hands free, appearing a bit uncomfortable.

"I'll have to call you later on that, okay? Let's walk outside, and I'll give you the key." He motioned for April to lead the way, and I couldn't resist a jab.

"Looks like Detective Do-Good does know how to live."

"Not now, Juli," he whispered as he passed by, sounding annoyed.

"That's all right," I said to his back while wagging my finger at the chunky blonde's backside, "you just go get 'em tiger! Grooowwl! Me and the Major will slip out the back like we were never here."

I'm sure that's how April Henderson wanted it. I always knew she had feelings for Chase, I just never knew how threatened she felt by me. Or maybe, I'd always been so nonchalant about my relationship with Chase, I never noticed.

So why did her drama and attention to Chase suddenly make me want to rip the hair off her head and scratch her eyes out?

———

VINNIE MINETTI HAD TO BE IN HIS MID TO LATE thirties and judging by the amount of gold around his neck and on his hands, Ringo's Diner profited well. I'd caught Scott Iverson on his way in to work the breakfast shift and asked if he wouldn't mind watching Major for me while I ran in for a coffee and muffin to go. While I sat patiently at the counter for the waitress tobring me my order, I couldn't help but overhear the short Italian man talking on his cell while scrutinizing the workings of his kitchen.

"Did you get it?" he asked the person on the other end. "Don't worry, I'll be there on time." He paused as if listening intently to what was said and then responded, "Yeah, I'll bring the money and a few other surprises." He slipped the phone into his pocket and disappeared farther into the kitchen.

I remember Mom telling me he took over the family business after his father died and that his wife, Connie, was a shrew and refused to help. He seemed all business, yet nice enough as he joked with his employees. A smile formed on my lips at the sound of his deep laughter, and I glanced down to skim the morning paper someone had left on the counter.

"Well, good morning, Miss Butler. We meet again." The gentle voice beside me belonged to Simon Banks.

"Good morning." I smiled even though my worry meter began to hum. The man still had his sunglasses on. "Are you here for breakfast? Ringo's has the best frittatas."

"That's what Misty said. She left some fruit and muffins because she had to go help a friend for most of the day so I'm on my own for breakfast and lunch. She highly recommended the diner, so here I am. And you?"

"Too lazy to cook," I admitted. "Coffee and a muffin to go."

"That's right, you're opening your café soon. How's that coming?" His interest in my business tripped the first spike in my meter.

"It's fine." Was all I had a chance to say before Vinnie approached the counter. "Here you go sir. Frittata special with a honey-glazed bear claw."

"Thank you." He took the covered plastic container and paper bag from Vinnie and lifted them in my direction. "See you around."

"You bet," I responded weaker than I'd intended, but something seemed off with him and Vinnie was glaring from across the counter.

"And you! I suppose you're here to scope out your competition?" A white paper bag dropped onto the newspaper.

"I'm sorry, what did you say?" I slowly straightened my spine, thankful that Simon Banks had cleared the door out of earshot. I didn't need a stranger believing I was capable of murder, too. Must be Vinnie saved his niceness for the employees when he should be using it on his patrons.

"Listen, I know your kind," he continued while puffing up his chest. "You think you can waltz in this town making all kinds of crazy changes when you know nothing of the history here."

"History? Vinnie, I'm not changing anything about New Hope. I grew up here and now I'm starting my own business that—"

"I know exactly what you started. A war, that's what. You and your organic this and that." Vinnie waved his hands in the air as he spoke. "You jump right in without any thought to anyone else's livelihood."

"The antique shop was every bit my mother, and the Butler's Pantry is who I am. My idea is unique. The storefront is mine to do as I choose and I'm not violating any town or county codes." On that I made sure. The last thing I wanted was Sheriff Do-Good riding my butt because I wasn't up to code. The man gave me enough grief without one more thing to set him off.

"I'm not talking about codes," Vinnie grumbled. "I'm talking about you trying to steal my customers with your fancy-schmancy organic crap. I'll have you know I make my pastries from scratch. There are fresh blueberries in this muffin." He snatched the bag and shook it in front of my face.

"I'm not doubting you." I took the bag from his hand. "I'm not out to steal your customers, either. There is plenty of room in this town for both of us to be profitable." My eyes were drawn to the three gold chains around his neck.

"Funny, your mother said the same thing when I accused her of trying to lure folks to her shop by selling homemade pies."

"My mother?"

"Sweetest lady ever, may she rest in peace, but she was out to ruin me, too. She had no business selling pies at her shop." His mustache twitched. Vinnie Minetti, for as well as his business was doing, seemed insecure and jealous. Total opposite of the outside appearance he put on. The fact that he'd had this almost exact conversation with my mother sent chills vibrating higher than my worry meter.

Along with the glass jars lined on a shelf sporting labels that read The V-Hive! "Y-You grow your own honey?" I stammered.

"Got a couple colonies out back, why? You gonna take that idea, too?"

His words fell on deaf ears. Mom died from a bee sting. She'd always been so careful and never went anywhere without her EpiPen. Mrs. Bailey confirmed Mom had hung her sheets on the line like she'd always done. Her death had been a freak accident...or was it?

Maybe Vinnie and his bees had something to do with it. He'd taken her out, and now he planned on getting rid of me before my business could even get started. Did he feel so threatened by my organic products he'd resort to murder just to set me up? Those jars of amber sweetness represented my first official connection.

I'd not only discovered my mother might have been murdered but possibly Pete's killer too. Vinnie could have been stalking my house when Pete showed up to break into Mrs. Bailey's. Pete wanted the statue, not me. I needed to confirm Vinnie's whereabouts the night Pete Seaver died and then I'd be able to prove my theory.

"Here's your coffee." Vinnie set the foam cup in front of me and adjusted the jars on the shelf, pulling me from my analysis.

"Wait!" I needed more information. "I hear a lot of the guys in town lost big money at one of the card games not too long ago."

"What's that got to do with you stealing my customers or my bees?" He eyed me suspiciously.

"Nothing. I, I, just noticed your chains and rings and thought you might have been the big winner, that's all. I have some friends back in Boston who share similar taste and I wanted to ask where you bought them." I prayed Vinnie didn't pick up on how lame my excuse sounded.

"Riiight," he said as if he were on to me.

"Maybe I can get in on a game sometime. It could be fun."

"Fun?" Vinnie laughed and this time it was almost sinister. "There's nothing fun about it. A pretty woman like you wouldn't last twenty minutes with those sharks. Besides, they don't allow women anyway."

"They might change their mind if I showed up one night. Could you tell me where the games are played?"

"No."

"It never hurts to ask," I replied as my nerves were replaced by persistence.

"You can keep asking, but I'm not telling. Your coffee's getting cold." Vinnie nodded toward my cup before disappearing into the kitchen.

My coffee might be lukewarm, but my suspect list was just heating up.

Eleven

"**M**ajor! You naughty dog, put that down right now!" I dropped my new wooden spoon and charged at the woolly mammoth who chomped on a linen napkin in the middle of the café.

"Woof!" His butt bounced up while his front paws held the napkin firmly between the floor and his drooling mouth. He let loose a playful growl and his butt wiggled.

"I don't have time for this." I leveled him with a firm stare.

The next step I made forced the sheepdog to run with the napkin still in his teeth. I followed behind trying to catch him as he weaved in and out of the tables. The moment I thought he was close enough to grab, he'd juke in the opposite direction.

"That's it. I'm done." I stopped and folded my arms. Enough was enough and I was through playing his game. "I don't know what has gotten into you, but it stops now."

Trying for a little reverse psychology, I turned and marched back to the kitchen and my wooden spoon. I was dying to look at him, but I didn't dare. It wasn't long before I heard a big, heavy sigh.

"Glad you're seeing things my way." I glanced away from my oatmeal carob cookies and into his huge chocolate brown eyes.

"Woof."

"Don't give me any lip." I continued to stir.

"Woof-Woof."

"Unbelievable." Major had dropped the napkin but now playfully held a small bag of sesame seeds between his teeth. "How did you get those?"

He shook the bag and the sesame seeds rattled within the cellophane wrapping. Those brown eyes of his brewed with mischief. I didn't even have to move before he dropped the bag and bolted through the café.

"Major!" I yelled, wondering what the big lug was going to get into next. I hadn't figured out the first note he'd magically found, I prayed he wouldn't find anything else. I followed him around, corner to corner until he worked his way back to the front door. He sniffed around like a hound dog moving in for the kill, then raised his eyes to mine with the sweetest tilt of his head.

"Woof."

"You're kidding. All of this for a walk?" I snatched his leash off the hook by the door. Major's body wiggled and bucked with excitement. "This is crazy," I said as I latched the leash to his collar. "I think we need to call in a professional."

The day was hot, but not so humid. An occasional katydid buzzed from high in the trees while Major kept his nose to the sidewalk during our entire walk across town. It was as if he were on a mission, and I knew exactly how he felt. Chase had been telling me how the dog was misbehaving at home, and after this morning in my shop I was beginning to think even I wasn't immune. My only problem was, I needed to find Pete's killer, not play puppy-psychologist.

"You takin' that there pup to the vet?" Betty Henderson asked from behind me, making me jump. "He's okay, isn't he?"

"He's fine, Betty." I glanced to where she pointed at the etched glass window, not realizing I'd stopped in front of the veterinary clinic. "Major has been acting up lately with both Chase and me. I have no idea why."

"Lily will know. She has such a way with those animals, even Ida's Scallywag! I'm so glad she set up shop here in New Hope. Everyone loves her."

"You don't say." Thanks to the big mischievous fur ball, I now had the perfect excuse to scope out the lovely lady vet. I'd been thinking about a manicure with Rita to see if she would hint to their late-night conversation but that could wait. "I wonder if she has any openings today?"

"When are you going to open your café? Everyone I talk to loves your goodies and treats you've been handing out."

"They do?" I don't know why I was surprised. My products were all natural and healthy. I'd wanted so much to make a fresh start here with my own identity, but with the murder of Pete Seaver hanging over my head I hadn't taken the time to notice the town's reaction. While everyone seemed nice enough, I had assumed they were quietly judging me.

"Of course, they do, sugar! You're the spitting image of your mama and just as nice. Sure, there are some stick-in-the-muds all set in their ways, but don't you worry about them. They will come around." She stopped talking to look at the town clock above the fire hall. "Oh, my, look at the time! I've got to relieve Harold this afternoon. He's finally getting that aching tooth taken care of. You take care, now." Betty waved and her polyester capris swished as she power walked toward the hardware store.

"Thanks, Betty!" I called after her and chuckled at her bright pink backside as it swayed down the street. "C'mon you big lug, let's see the doctor." I tugged on Major's leash, and he whimpered. We passed through the door in time to hear part of Lily's phone conversation.

"Let's just come clean. It will be okay." The pretty brunette pinched the bridge of her nose, too intent on her conversation to notice us standing there. She sighed. "Fine. I don't want to keep this secret much longer, so please make it work." She looked up as if finally feeling two pairs of eyes on her. "Oh! I've got to go, we'll talk later." Lily hung up the phone and smiled from behind the glossy black reception desk. "Juli, right?"

"Yes." I returned the smile, happy she remembered me from the card game at Rita's. "Do you have time to take a look at Major?"

"My receptionist called in sick, so I'm kind of a one-woman show." Lily clicked a couple computer keys and stared at the screen. "Thank goodness my appointments are spaced out today, and you're in luck because my one o'clock cancelled. Why don't you bring him back?"

"Perfect." I followed Lily to a small exam room, papered with classic paw prints and complete with posters about fleas, ticks and heartworms. She took down Major's weight, peeked into his ears, and opened his mouth to inspect his teeth.

"What seems to be going on with him?" Lily crouched and looked as though she were massaging a fluffy white bear as she worked her hands from behind his ears, down his back to under his legs and stomach.

"I've been taking care of him for Chase since his regular dog walker is on vacation. Everything has been fine until the last couple days. Chase said he's destroying things in his house, and today he started misbehaving with me. I don't know what is making him do this."

"Hmm." Lily pursed her rosy lips and stood. "He seems to be in great shape. His weight is where it should be, and I didn't feel anything out of the ordinary. Has anything changed at home?"

"I beg your pardon?" How would I know what the drool machine's home life was like?

"Animals can be reactive to change the same way children and some adults are. Additions to the family, moving or a change in rules or routine might be enough to throw him off."

"No kidding. I'd never thought of that. I guess I always assumed animals adapted."

"Most do." She ruffled his shaggy head. "Sometimes they act out when they are trying to tell you something."

"Come to think of it, Chase has been very busy working on the Pete Seaver case. He's been getting home late, leaving early. Even I've been preoccupied by it and trying to have my grand opening soon."

"That could be it. He wants more attention."

"Are you feeling neglected, big fella?" I asked the dog, surprising myself by dropping to my knees and holding his fat, fuzzy head in my hands. Major's wet nose touched mine, and I barely escaped a lip-lick.

"I guess there's your answer."

"What does the eight stand for?" When I stood, I pointed to the tattoo I'd noticed on the inside of Lily's wrist. Pete had one on his hand, too, the night he came in and sold the statue.

"It's an infinity symbol." She marked some notes on a file for Major.

"Is it popular?"

"I guess, no more so than anything else." She rubbed it with her other hand as if me bringing it up brought back a not so good memory.

"I only asked because Pete Seaver had one just like it on his hand. It seems odd for a man."

"We had them done together." Her eyes seemed sad, but there was something else in them I couldn't put my finger on. "Are they any closer to finding his killer?"

"Not yet. Were you two friends?" I had to ask but found it hard to believe. She totally didn't look like the nasty man's type.

"We dated for a while. That's why I came to New Hope. I really loved him, or at least I thought I did."

"Oh, really?" I said, trying to hide my surprise.

"You think he was too old for me, right?" she replied. All of my friends said so, but it didn't matter. Love has no age limit. Love is never-ending. That's why we chose the infinity symbol."

Lily's blank expression told me she was in a place I couldn't even imagine, reliving pieces of her relationship I would never be privy to. I couldn't picture her with that man no matter how hard I tried.

"Are you okay?" I asked, concerned she was zoning out too far. "Do the police know?"

"Police?" She snapped out of her trance. "Our relationship was never a secret, Juli. Our breakup was just as public. He broke my heart, and I can never forgive him for that. He made me promises, shattered my dreams, and then had the nerve to come begging me for money. I'm glad he's gone, and I wish I'd never gotten this tattoo."

"I'm sorry. I didn't mean to—"

"No, I'm the one who's sorry." Lily took a deep breath and composed herself to the sweet veterinarian the town so obviously loved despite her misguided affections. "I know better than to mix business with my personal issues. Let me know if Major continues to act up, but I think finding a little more time to focus on him will be all that he needs."

"Will do. Oh, and send Chase the bill. This is on his dime, not mine."

I left with Major leading the way all the while thinking I now had another serious suspect. Between Vinnie and Lily, they both had reasons to want Pete out of the picture. But who could be capable of murder?

———

I'D DECIDED TO WORK FROM HOME THE REST OF THE day. Major seemed to like it better than hanging around the café. He chewed his new toy, and I took an occasional break to throw a ball with him in the backyard. Chase called to say his meeting with the mayor had run late. He had some paperwork to finish up at the office and would stop to pick up the dog as soon as he could.

I couldn't wait to explain to Chase the information Lily Johnson gave me regarding the dog's poor behavior. As I watched the shaggy dog prance around in the grass, she was dead on with her prognosis. Unfortunately, I had a feeling she was somehow involved with the death of her ex-boyfriend, Pete. I was eager to fill Chase in on that, too.

Hopefully I wouldn't have to wait much longer. I left Major rolling around in the late afternoon sun and stepped back into my bright country kitchen to begin working on dinner. The white-washed cupboards with glass panes and white enameled knobs were the perfect backdrop to the pale peach walls and white wain-scoting. With the dog happily enjoying the backyard, I had time to multitask with my laptop on the counter, putting the finishing touches on my menus. Burgundy paw prints and comic sans font accented the crisp white menu of Petite Four Paws, while the opposite was true for the Butler's Pantry. I chose clean, block char-acters in a narrow gothic font.

Everything was coming together, and I would submit my file through the printer's website before the day was done. The only thing keeping me from being on top of the world was that a killer was still on the loose. Only when Pete Seaver's killer was found could I relax and enjoy my venture into entrepreneurship.

No sooner had I flipped the tofu on the grill when the doorbell rang. I closed the cover and walked through the house to the front door with Major at my heels. Chase's silhouette shadowed the sheer white curtain.

"Hi. Rough day at the office?" I asked as I opened the door to let him in, noticing right away the weariness in his eyes and the part of his shirt that was untucked at his waist.

"Don't even get me started." Chase passed through the threshold and patted Major, who sat close to my leg.

"Sorry." I stood with my hand on the doorknob, the summer

breeze flowing into the house like a current. "Anything new about the case?"

"You know I can't tell you that." He wiped a hand down his weary face. "I just came to pick up Major and get home. I'm beat."

"I wouldn't be me if I didn't ask, right?" I smiled, attempting to perk him up a bit, only it didn't work. "If you have a minute, I'd like to tell you what Lily Johnson said about Major."

"You didn't have to take him to the vet."

"I wanted to. Not only was he acting up at home, but he started giving me problems at the café. I figured there was something going on."

"And is there?"

"As a matter of fact, yes." I guided Chase into the living room and shut the door. "You're ignoring him."

"What?" Chase's eyes grew large, and his jaw unhinged. "I am not ignoring him."

"No, I'm not ignoring him. Anymore," I corrected, and the big fur ball sighed. "Face it, Chase, we all get busy. But animals need attention, too. Major made me aware the last couple of days, and it appears he's been trying to tell you for a while."

"Give me a break. How much did Lily charge you for this priceless advice?"

"She's sending the bill to you in the mail." I put my hands protectively over the dog's ears. "He knows when you're agitated you know. You need to be more sympathetic to his feelings."

"His feelings?" Chase's chin dropped as he cocked a brow, giving me his you've got to be kidding expression.

"Yes. Dogs are very sensitive. If you're stressed out, then he will be too."

"I'm not stressed out," Chase countered, and we shared a look which confirmed otherwise. "Yeah, okay, I'm stressed out. I have good reason to be."

"Then let's figure out a way so you won't be."

"What did you have in mind?" He broadcast a devilish expression which made me laugh.

"I've got tofu on the grill and wine chilling. Why don't you stay for dinner? I have some other things I need to tell you about." I left Chase and Major by the front door, knowing he wouldn't turn down a free meal, and returned to the back patio and my delicious smelling grill. "Mmm, almost done."

"Tofu? You don't really expect me to eat that, do you?" He appeared behind me, scoping out the grill over my shoulder and sniffing.

"Would you stop being so skeptical and give it a chance. You might discover you like something new. Remember, step out of your comfort zone."

"I'm perfectly fine with it, which is why it's called a comfort zone." He tweaked my nose. "It does smell pretty good."

"Ha!" I jabbed his chest. "Go grab the salad from the fridge and an extra plate. We'll eat outside tonight."

Chase disappeared into my kitchen, and I smiled at his retreating backside. More and more I liked having him back in my life. Sure, we'd given each other attitude when we were younger, but that history was the glue sticking us together. If I were truthful with myself, I'd have to admit I really missed him over the last ten years.

"Is this everything?" Chase stood in the doorway balancing the plates and silverware atop the salad bowl, two wine glasses between his fingers and the bottle of wine in the crook of his arm. He looked adorable.

"Yes, thanks." I turned the grill off and rushed to help him before something hit the ground. We both set the table and lit my decorative citronella candles to keep the bugs away.

"Why don't you serve it up since I have no idea how to eat tofu. I'll pour the wine."

We sat down with our plates loaded with field greens and fresh vegetables. I cubed the grilled tofu and set it on top of the bed of greens. The protein had been seasoned with different spices, so we didn't need dressing. I watched as Chase stabbed a chunk of tofu with his fork and carefully inspected it, smelled it, then added some greens. He chewed in slow motion as if trying to decide.

"Well?" I set my fork down and sipped some wine. "You have to admit it's not bad, right?"

"No, it's not bad. I'm not sure of the consistency, but the flavor is great." Warmth spread through me. "Thanks, it's my own secret seasonings."

"My compliments to the chef," Chase said and raised his glass.

"So back to Major," I said between forkfuls. "He needs some of your time, Chase."

"I know, the poor fella. Things have gotten so busy at work. I thought we'd be pulling in some new officers, but that's not going to happen any time soon according to the mayor.

Gary hasn't been here very long, and I feel like I'm overworking him by constantly asking him to take over the night shift."

"He's low man on the totem pole, right, so he should expect it."

"I guess. Then you have Marty who's probably got another year before he retires. I can't ask him to pull late hours so that leaves me." He sipped some wine before adding, "Budget cuts suck."

"Listen, it's been proven animals are good therapy. Promise me you'll make better use of the free time you have."

"You're right, and I'm glad I have him to come home to. That old house tends to get lonely."

"I thought you were spending a lot of time at April's place. Isn't that why she gave you a key?" I couldn't help adding.

His gaze locked on mine. "You jealous?"

"No!" I scoffed and slapped his bicep. Even if I was, which I clearly wasn't, I'd never ever admit it to him.

"Not buying it." He laughed.

"It's true," I clarified, but he kept the smug expression on his face as he poured us both another glass of wine. "Thanks."

"Don't mention it. If we run out, I think I have another bottle at the house."

"Speaking of houses...." I couldn't believe I was going there, but it was on the tip of my tongue, and I had to know. "Fess up. What's the deal with you and April Henderson?"

He paused for a moment. "There is no deal."

"I don't believe you."

"Let's just say, it's complicated." He took a drink.

"Hmmm...now that, I would believe." I grinned over the rim of my glass and took another sip. "I know something else that's complicated."

"What's that?"

"This Pete Seaver case."

"Don't tell me you've been snooping around because if you are, I'll have to seriously detain you." He paused to swirl the wine in his glass, smell it, then take a sip. "I've recently come into possession of some rope. You wouldn't happen to know anything about why it was in Tammy O'Toole's tree, would you?"

"That was totally by accident," I said, putting my hand to my lips when I realized I'd spoken out loud thanks to my second glass of wine.

"What was an accident? Juli, you're making me nervous." He eyed me carefully.

"There's nothing to be nervous about." I decided to steer the conversation away from the rope I'd left behind in my haste that night, and back to what Chase really needed to know. "It's something the Vet told me, that's all."

"You already told me what she said about Major. What does that have to do with Pete Seaver?"

"They used to date you know, Lily and Pete." I leaned closer and whispered, "They have the same tattoo."

"That's old news, sister. The whole town knew. Trust me,

Gary and I intercepted a couple domestic disputes after their breakup, too."

"You mean he got violent with her?" I sat ramrod straight at the thought of nasty Pete laying a hand on such a nice person. Then again, if he hurt her, she'd want revenge. "She said he was the one who broke things off."

"They never became violent. Their disputes were mostly yelling and screaming at each other." Chase stabbed a forkful of lettuce. "Disturbing everyone's peace would be a better representation."

"Lily told me the night Pete died, he'd come back begging her for money."

"I didn't know this." Chase set the fork on the edge of his plate and froze with his hand on the wine glass.

"He did. Lily didn't give it to him, but she wouldn't admit where she was, either, only that she was furious with him for even thinking she'd give it to him after he dumped her." I set my hand on his forearm and looked him in the eye. "Chase, I'm thinking Lily Johnson could be Pete's killer."

"You think this was a crime of passion?" He lifted his glass to take a drink.

"Why not? She has enough motive." I moved my hand and fiddled with the napkin in my lap. "He broke her heart. She's desperate and angry. Then he comes along asking for money but with no intention of getting back together with her." I paused for a moment and then tapped my finger on the table. "That's what put her over the edge. If you would have seen her face, you'd be thinking the same thing."

"We've already questioned her, and her alibi checked out." Chase took another sip of wine and set the glass down. "It might be worth speaking with her again. I tell you what, I will look into this tomorrow, but I don't want you to do anything else, understand?"

"Stop trying to be my father and telling me what to do." I raised my palm to let him know I didn't want to hear it.

He took my hand and lowered it to the table, his voice soft and sincere when he spoke, "I don't want you to get hurt or in any more trouble than you already are. You're still a suspect, remember?"

"I haven't done anything wrong, officer." My frustration meter started to rise, regardless of the fact I knew he was trying to help. "I didn't force that information out of her, she offered it up. It's not my fault."

"Mmm-hmm. Just keep your nose clean." He reached out to flick the tip of my nose with his finger.

"Of course," I replied but couldn't resist a devilish grin of my own.

"I mean it." Chase helped me pick up the dishes and bring them inside. "Thanks for the dinner, or should I say snack." He rubbed his stomach. "I may be foraging in my cupboards later."

"Later? It's already late enough. Your body will never digest something heavier by morning. Are you admitting you like my cooking?"

"It was okay. I don't think I'd want it all the time, but I could definitely handle it once in a while, for lunch maybe."

"Watch it, or I'll be experimenting with other foods."

"Don't count on it." He whistled for Major, who trotted over with his tail wagging. "C'mon boy, let's head home. Thanks again, Juli. This was nice."

"Yeah, it was." I watched him squeeze between the hedges and up onto his porch. We both waved and then I closed the door with a contented sigh.

I knew deep down, Chase of all people understood me. I couldn't rest until this case was solved. Either he'd give me the freedom to do my own thing, or he'd have to let me work with him. Regardless, keeping my nose clean wasn't going to happen until I made sure my clues pointed to a killer.

$$Twelve$$

Who knew two glasses of wine would make me sleep like a rock? I stretched my arms above my head and trudged to the shower. I couldn't wait to follow up with Chase later.

Hopefully, he'd have better luck pulling details from Lily Johnson about the case than I did. After leaving my hair to air dry, throwing on a pair of cut offs and a white tank top, I made my way downstairs. I still needed to investigate the fish market and talk to Jimmy O'Toole, but I'd need to do that without Major. I didn't want to think about the trouble he'd get into with all that raw fish around. There wasn't much on my to-do list other than to stop by the local paper and place the ad announcing my grand opening.

When I stepped off the last stair, I froze at the destruction that used to be my living room. Cushions were upended, and papers lay haphazardly around the room as if someone had thrown them like confetti. There was nothing in my house that hadn't been trashed.

I thought I'd locked the door after Chase left. Thanks to my wine-induced sleep of the dead, I couldn't remember. My mouth hung open as I followed the mess from room to room. This had all the makings of a bad dream.

"Who would do this?" My shocked voice echoed in the quiet of the morning.

The answer to that question became very clear when I crossed into the kitchen. My take-out containers littered the counters and floor. Tied to a wooden spoon was a small doll with brown curly hair. It resembled a voodoo doll in that it was constructed of material and had a paring knife—not a pin—shoved into its body. That doll represented me, and somebody apparently wanted me dead.

I never screamed so loud in my life.

The next thing I knew someone was pounding and banging on my door. I screamed louder, thinking the perpetrator had returned to finish the job. The voice which filtered through my hysterical brain belonged to Chase.

"Juli! Are you okay?" By the time I rushed to the door, he'd pushed it open and I fell into his arms. "What the hell's going on? You're shaking."

"Someone was here." I backed away exposing the living room.

"What on earth?" Chase moved protectively in front of me.

"They're gone. It's worse in the kitchen." I weaved my fingers through his, needing the calm of that simple touch, and led him toward the back of the house. I picked up the wooden spoon with my fingers and held it out as if it were contaminated. "Why would someone do this?"

"This is obviously a warning, Juli."

"For what? Starting my business, moving back to New Hope?" Being close to you? I swore I'd never cry in front of Chase, but I couldn't control the tears any longer.

"They were looking for something. I'll need you to take a good look around and let me know if anything is missing." In a flash, Mr. By-the-Book was back on the job. "It could very well be the loan sharks who were after Pete Seaver. They must think you still have the statue."

"The statue?"

How could he be sheriff and not see the real connection here?

Betty Henderson held tight to her southern roots. There was no doubt in my mind this was April's handiwork. She was sending a message all right, and I intended to formulate a reply of my own.

"I don't think it's a good idea for you to stay here alone."

I shook my head to disagree. I could handle April. "I'll be fine."

"What happens if they don't stay on the main floor next time?" He leveled his gaze to mine, and I felt an icy chill sweep across my skin. "My instincts tell me they won't. The threats will continue until you're out of town, or dead. Is that what you want?"

"No," I barely squeaked out when the reality of his words hit home. If I was wrong, and this wasn't April's doing, then this was far worse than any summer thunderstorm.

"You're not going to like this, but you don't get a choice this time." He picked up the voodoo doll and studied it closely. "You're moving in with me and Major until the case is solved."

"Chase, I—" There was someone else who wasn't going to like this either.

"It's for your own safety."

"Okay," I agreed and watched the shock register across his face. "Okay?"

"Yes, you're right. Let me get my things together."

"Glad you're seeing this my way. Excuse me but I've got to call this in."

He punched numbers into his phone, and I went upstairs to pack. I wasn't thrilled with the idea of moving in with him, especially since I believed April was behind all of this. Until I could prove it and her instability, I needed Chase to protect me. Being under his roof would certainly keep her at bay.

April Henderson wasn't about to tarnish her perfect reputation no matter how much she wanted me gone. If she were going to slip up, then Chase would have a front row seat.

<hr>

"Stay put," Chase said later that morning as he pointed a finger at me. "I don't even want you going to work today. Stay here and lay low."

"Don't you think someone is going to figure out I'm over here?"

Chase wanted to keep this morning's events on the down low. No police scene tape on the door, and he told Gary to be discreet when going in and out of my house. He even went as far as to explain to Mrs. Bailey I'd be staying at his house while I had the exterminator spray for spiders.

"I'm sure they will, but we don't have to make it easy for them."

"Whatever helps you sleep at night, lawman."

"Still seeing things my way? Gee, have I finally rubbed off on you?"

"No, I'm just stressed out and I have to admit a little scared." In a show of strength and friendship that suddenly seemed to knock my socks off, Chase took my hand and squeezed.

"That's why I'm here and I won't let anything happen to you, ever."

Tears welled behind my eyes for a different reason now as the increasing pressure of his hand worked magic on my insides. Sheriff Do-Good had never looked sexier than he did at this moment. My rational side argued I was lonely and with everything coming to a head, any man would probably look good right about now.

"I'm going into the office for a while. You've got the dog and you've got my number. Call if you need me."

"I will."

"I'll check on you later." He kissed my cheek, winked, and walked out the door. He knew all too well being rational was not my forte.

With Chase gone, I needed a distraction to stop myself from worrying. For as much as I wanted to do more investigating, the thought of stepping outside made me realize how vulnerable I'd be. April could be stalking me at this very moment, waiting for me to leave the safety of Chase's house. I wasn't about to give her the satisfaction.

I wandered around his house, allowing myself to replay memories I'd kept locked up for over a decade. Leaving New Hope had been something I had to do. Chase and I would always be friends no matter where our lives took us. In an act of defiance, I had pushed him away and into the waiting arms of my nemesis. An ache formed in my chest at the thought of him loving April Henderson.

"Idiot," I chastised myself. "There is way too much brown in this house." I swiped my cheeks and headed for the back door. "C'mon, you oversized dust bunny." I motioned for the dog, who was already on my heels.

Leaving him in the back yard, I snuck out of the gate and back into my house. Running into one of the guest rooms, I snatched some colorful pillows to replace the ugly, masculine brown and white ones—that reminded me of cow spots—currently on Chase's sofa. Happy with my choice of a burnt orange and beige geometric print, I shot back across the yard to snip some bright blossoms from Mom's garden, then got to work.

"What's all this?" Chase's deep voice startled me then warmed me through and through. "I'm gone for four hours and you've practically redecorated."

"I had to do something. How do you live with all this brown?"

"What's wrong with brown? I happen to like it." He laughed.

"It's like living in a chocolate factory, with a splatter of cow."

"Oh, really?"

"Yes, really. C'mon, you must admit the room pops now." I added some 'jazz hands' for emphasis.

He rolled his eyes. "It's colorful, I'll admit that."

"If you don't like it, I will take them back home when I leave. They were just extras."

"No, I like them." He picked up a pillow and set it back down. "You left the house after I told you to stay put?"

"Did you honestly think I wouldn't?"

"I kind of hoped you'd learned your lesson."

"I was going stir crazy and all this brown wasn't helping." I shrugged, trying for an innocent demeanor that didn't work with him at all.

"Well, if you're so inclined to venture out then let's take Major to Miller Park. They built a dog park in the middle. He can socialize and we can...."

"We can what?" I squinted, not sure how to read the strange expression on his face. "Talk, we can talk," he said, leaving me to grab Major's leash by the front door.

"Does this mean you have information on the case? Oh my gosh, did Lily give you the details?"

"Let's go."

We didn't say much while we walked, and I wondered what he was thinking. We reached the park which had been built a couple of blocks from the high school. The park had become quite popular, judging by the number of people there during lunch hour. This was a good sign that Petite Four Paws would be a welcome addition to my café.

"You okay?" Chase asked when I stopped just short of the park gate.

"What if the person who left the voodoo doll is here? What if they followed us?"

"I kept my eyes and ears open along the way. You're safe with me." He put his arm across my shoulders and led me to a bench under a huge oak tree. Before we sat down, he unclipped Major's leash and the dog bounded about the fenced-in park happy to be free and exploring.

"Oh, look, there's Rita Davis," I said and waved across the park. "I didn't know she had a dog?"

"She dog-sits her boyfriend's rotti," Chase replied while

keeping his eyes on her and not the dog. I jabbed him in the ribs. "Hey!" He rubbed his side. "She's got a rockin' body. I'm only human."

"Uh-huh." I elbowed him again for good measure.

"You should see the muscles on her boyfriend."

Ahh, I take it they make the perfect couple?"

"I kid you not, movie star quality."

"Nice. So, he's not from around here?"

"Jefferson County." Chase picked up a stick and thumped it against his thigh. "I guess he's in some form of sales and travels quite a bit." He launched the stick and Major raced after it. "She's tried to convince him to move here, but he doesn't want to live out in the country."

"Hmm, sounds familiar."

"I want to know something." His voice held a serious edge which put me on guard.

"What's that?"

"I want you to be straight with me."

"I only switched pillows, really. I wanted to do more, but you came home." I grinned, trying to lighten the mood.

"I don't care about the damn pillows. This is serious, Juli. I need to know what the hell you've been involved with in Boston and New York and Atlantic City. You seem to have spent ten years moving around the east coast apparently making enemies."

"I, I—" I blinked repeatedly trying to form a coherent thought.

"This case is becoming an intricate weave of deceit. Something's not right."

"Deceit? What are you talking about?" My heart dropped, realizing he truly doubted my innocence. "I didn't kill him, Chase."

"Then why is someone now after you? You can't take that break-in lightly."

"I'm not." The teasing note was gone from my voice as I tried to harden my heart and remain all business from now on.

"Then explain to me what you've done all these years."

"Atlantic City was short term. One summer on the Jersey shore dealing cards. I had acquaintances only, my bosses at the casino and some other dealers. Honestly, I don't even remember their names." I kept my face blank.

"Okay, I'll buy into that one."

"I'm surprised you haven't run a background check."

"Oh, trust me, I have. I just want to make sure what I found out matches what you're telling me."

"You're testing me?" I launched to my feet, hands on my hips, professionalism gone. Chase had always brought about a flurry of emotions within me. I guess he still did, which was why his lack of trust hurt so much.

"Sit down," he ordered, and I did. "Tell me about New York?"

"I spent five or so years there working odd jobs. I had a pretty good gig as a personal shopper for people on the Upper East Side, um, a short stint as a dog walker." His brows shot up and he nodded toward Major. "Yeah, I know, I gave you a hard time with that one. Trust me, one dog is easy. I only lasted a week in So-Ho because I couldn't walk three or more dogs at once."

"Continue."

"Well, I worked for a catering company which is how I ended up at the art gallery in Boston." I hoped he was satisfied because the thought of going into detail about David, our relationship and our ultimate parting was making me break out in a nervous sweat.

"Is there more?" Chase didn't take his eyes off me when I wiped my hands on the tops of my shorts.

"That's the gist of it. Why the interrogation on my past? I really thought you believed me."

"I want to believe you. Part of me does, but the mayor was on me again this morning about closing this case. I don't have anything new to tell him and the threat to you—"

"Incriminates me even more." I leaned back on the hard bench with a sigh, placing my hands over my face. "What can I say to you?"

"Tell me what you're hiding."

"I've done some really stupid things, things that aren't worth repeating."

"Juli." Chase used a warning tone which convinced me even more not to utter a word about David or the painting. My Ex had no idea where my hometown was. There was no way David would be here trying to kill me, and he surely didn't run in the same circles as Pete Seaver.

"I'm not going to embarrass myself in front of you, I don't care how well you know me. You and Gary are going to have to work harder or let me help out."

"That's not happening."

"Then I guess this conversation is over."

"I guess it is."

We gathered up Major and walked home in a tension-filled silence. I'd prove to Chase once and for all I could handle things on my own and that I wasn't the screw up he still thought I was. We were back to square one, and the only way for my name to be cleared was for me to go it alone.

Thirteen

hase and I had called a truce of sorts. He continued to investigate the Seaver case, and I continued to stay out of his way by checking into leads of my own. What the good Sheriff didn't know wouldn't hurt him.

Since I hadn't gone to work yesterday, I decided to leave Major at home and check on the café. The final arrangements for my grand opening were almost complete, and I felt like a slacker staying away for even a day.

On my way down the street, I caught Vinnie peering into my storefront windows while he spoke with the same, large man in a business suit I'd seen him with before. They exchanged envelopes and shook hands. The man in the suit left and Vinnie hung around, suspiciously taking in every detail through my windows. I quickened my pace wondering what Vinnie thought he'd find inside my café. When he snapped his head from side to side glancing up and down the street, I crouched behind a parked car so as not to be spotted.

In the twenty-four hours since my break-in, I'd convinced myself April was behind everything because of her jealousy. Watching Vinnie suddenly made me doubt myself. He was up to something, and it might very well be staging a break-in at the Butler's Pantry. What if Vinnie had been responsible for the note, the doll and Pete's murder? His anger issues certainly made him a candidate for murder. What if Vinnie and April were in on it together?

I didn't know what to think anymore.

My thoughts became interrupted when an SUV with dark tinted windows pulled up. Vinnie continued his surveillance of the street before stepping closer to the door. A petite, female hand caressed his cheek then motioned for him to climb inside. I needed to know if that hand belonged to April Henderson.

Or maybe it belongs to Vinnie's wife, I reprimanded myself.

My paranoia was beginning to get the better of me. With my truck parked at home, I needed a way to follow the SUV. Jogging down the street I slipped into the hardware store. What better way to go un-noticed than to tail April in her aunt's car.

"Hi, Betty," I said, sneaking up on the woman and making her jump a mile.

"My gracious, Juli, you scared the dickens out of me!" She fanned her face for effect.

"I'm sorry, but I'm kind of in a bind, and I was hoping you could help me."

"Sure thing, doll, what do you need?"

"Can I borrow your car for a little bit? I promised I would check out the Billings Farm for some of my ingredients. I seem to have lost track of time and now I don't have time to run home for my truck." I leaned back on my heels, peeking through the door at the SUV still idling in front of my café.

"I don't see why not. There's probably enough gas to get you to Billings' and back." She fished around in her big apron pocket for a hoop-style key ring. After finding the correct key, she held it up and handed the entire key ring to me. "I've been procrastinating putting gas in the tank. Don't tell Harry."

"Don't worry, I won't, and thank you! I owe you one," I called and dashed out of the hardware store praying the SUV was still there.

The vehicle pulled away from the curb as I started the engine to Betty's small car. Perfect, I'd be able to stay back and not look obvious. Luckily, I didn't have to follow them far. They pulled into Pepper's Motel on the edge of town.

I parked several spaces down and slid low behind the wheel. As uncomfortable as it was, I had the perfect view. Vinnie stepped out of the SUV and opened the driver's side door. This was the moment of truth. With a shaking hand, I grabbed my cell phone to snap a picture of the criminals.

When they rounded the front of their vehicle, Vinnie had his arm tightly around her. She wore a baggy sweatshirt with the hood covering her head. Dark sunglasses covered her eyes. The only thing I could tell by the form-fitting jeans she wore was that backside did not belong to April Henderson. I tossed my phone in the passenger seat, sat up and rested my head and hands over the steering wheel. Vinnie wasn't a criminal. He was a jerk cheating on his wife.

April had now moved her way to the top of my suspect list. The only thing left to do was confront the woman. At this point I was desperate and had Chase on speed dial if she tried anything crazy.

Betty's key slid into the ignition when a black sports car rumbled through the lot. A tall man wearing a red ball cap, sunglasses, and a nicely fitting t-shirt stepped out of the car first.

He proceeded to walk to the passenger side to assist his female companion, who I immediately recognized as Andie Evans! Her golden tresses sat atop her head in a messy bun, while her four-inch stilettos and figure-hugging sun dress left nothing to the imagination. Her entire ensemble created the illusion of a young adult, not a rising high school senior.

"This must be the secret boyfriend," I whispered, alone in the car, as my mind returned to the pieces of her phone conversation from the night I broke into the O'Toole house. She didn't appear as if she was being pressured to do anything. She seemed quite eager and willing to be with him. When he dropped the black leather duffle in front of the motel room door and pulled her hard against him for a kiss that curled my toes all the way across the parking lot, I chalked up her conversation as young love drama.

I felt like I was watching a younger version of myself. They were still deep into their kiss as he opened the door, kicked the duffle inside and closed the door without breaking lip lock. "Girl, I hope you know what you're doing." Because all these years later, I still didn't have a clue. By the looks of things happening at Pepper's Motel, I didn't have a clue here either that would help me catch Pete's killer.

Feeling frustrated over another dead end, I pulled away to put gas in the tank and return Betty's car. It was the least I could do for her after letting me borrow it. Moments later, I was on my way to April's studio when Sandy and Bill Perkins walked toward the Hardware store. Bill waved and I returned the gesture. They really made a striking couple, both tall and fit for their age. Sandy with her perfect platinum bob and Bill with a full head of silver hair.

"Juli, wait, I have something for you," Sandy called as she held a paper high in her hand. Her heels clicked along the sidewalk as she rushed to meet me half-way.

"What's this?" I took the flyer from her brightly polished nails.

"Flyers for the New Hope High School fundraiser I'm putting together. You said you wanted to help, is that still true?"

"Of course," I replied while scanning the information and noticed April's name at the bottom as the event photographer. This would be one event New Hope's little sweetheart wouldn't be at if she were held up in a jail cell.

"Do you like the flyer? April and I put it together yesterday." Sandy wrinkled her nose as if she wasn't sure about it. "Poor girl, she seemed a bit frazzled, not her usual self, so I was concerned this wasn't her best work."

"It looks great." I tried to sound chipper. Of course, April had been frazzled. She'd trashed my house. "Let me know what you need, and I will do it."

"I was hoping you'd say that. It's going to be an auction. If you have any leftover antiques from your mother's shop or even items from home, in good condition of course, they will work too."

"Let me see what I can find. I sold most of Mom's antiques, but there may be some interesting trinkets in the attic."

"Perfect! Why don't you make up some gift baskets from your café? You're all the buzz around town lately." Her affirmation gave me more joy than the thought of April in an orange jumpsuit.

"What a great idea, Sandy, thank you."

"You know, Juli, your mother and I were fierce competitors right up until she passed."

"Yes, I know."

"Justine was a wonderful person, practically a saint in everyone's eyes. We had our moments of congeniality when no one was looking. I never wished her ill will, and I would love to see your café a success." I felt myself tearing up at her words. Even though they'd been arch enemies, it had all been for show.

"Thank you, that means a lot." I sniffed.

"Don't mention it. I mean, really, don't mention it." She patted my arm. "I have a reputation you know. Call if you have questions. C'mon, Bill, we have more flyers to deliver, and I must stop by Rita's to fix this chipped nail."

Sandy and Bill continued their mission, and I felt more inspired toward mine. April and I would never be amicable toward each other, not after this. I was calling her out and there was nowhere for her to hide.

———

TWENTY MINUTES LATER I WALKED INTO APRIL's studio. As I browsed the photos on the walls, I had to admit she was a very good photographer. The girl had the proper cover, that was for sure. No one would suspect she was so evil underneath that sweet exterior. Only I knew better.

"Juli?" April's eyes widened when she saw me. "What are you doing here?"

"Don't sound so surprised. You had to know I'd figure it out sooner or later. You would have preferred the latter, once your plan to run me out of town succeeded." I kept my voice neutral like I'd seen crime fighting women do on TV.

"What are you talking about? I would never run you out of town."

"Everyone has been glad I returned to New Hope, except you. You have done nothing but flaunt your attraction to Chase at every possible moment. After all these years you're still jealous of my friendship with him." I took a couple of steps closer, surprised when she stood her ground.

"Have you been drinking?"

"You can't stand the thought of Chase and me still being close. It's eaten at you to the point where you will stop at nothing, even murder, to get me out of the picture." There, I'd said it. And by the horrific expression on her face, I'd struck a nerve.

"How dare you!"

"No, how dare you." I pointed at her face, letting the surge of adrenaline take me where it may. "We were all friends. I've never done anything to give you a reason to do this. To stoop to such a heinous act is unforgivable." I stood there, mesmerized by the change in April's features. They seemed to alter between shock and anger. She stepped toward me, and I raised my hands, ready to defend myself. This was our moment of truth.

"You have some nerve, Julianna Butler. You come into my place of business citing all kinds of crazy. I don't know what heinous act you are talking about."

"The doll! You broke into my house, trashed it, and left that voodoo doll with a knife stuck in it, a doll that distinctly resembles me.”

“A voodoo doll?” She laughed. “You must be on something. Where do you think I would get a voodoo doll? Or are you crazy enough to think I make them in my spare time?”

“Your Aunt Betty has southern roots. She could have picked one up for you, or for all I know you DO concoct them! So much for making ragdolls for the craft fair. That was just your front.”

“Oh, my, Juli, you should really seek professional help.” April placed her hands in front of her as if to keep me at bay. “You need to grieve the loss of your mother in a way other than lashing out at those who care.”

I glared at her, and the softness faded from her features. She wasn’t going to wear me down. I knew exactly what she was capable of whether she would admit to it or not. I had the proof with the doll. All I had to do was get it all to stick, and I’d find my own pin if I had to.

“Chase saw the doll, April. It’s only a matter of time before he figures out his sweet little girlfriend is a lying, deceitful, murderer.”

“You stay away from Chase,” she ordered. “It took me years once you were gone to help him over the anger and hurt of you leaving. Years, Juli, of being there for him in any way he needed me.”

Her words gave me pause. Had he really thought of me for years? I tried to focus. “I bet you were. Once we started dating, I noticed how you always hung back in the shadows waiting, no, wishing for us to fall apart.” I walked a circle around her, stopping when I faced her once more. “You must be thrilled to finally have what you always wanted.”

“I love Chase. You never did, and he knows it. He was finally starting to see me the way I always dreamed he would. Then you came back to town, and he’s all messed up like he used to be.”

“Bingo, there’s your motive. You all but admitted to breaking into my house.”

"Why would I break into your house, knowing the end result would be you moving in with Chase?" I noticed the hysteria creeping into her voice. She was about to crack like the bad egg she was.

"To be the supportive friend and lover, of course, until he discovers the truth about you."

"You are way off base, Juli. I've been trying to convince him to stay away from you and let the past remain in the past. I will always be a supportive friend and look out for his best interests. What Chase and I do behind closed doors is none of your business now. You gave up that right a long time ago."

I nodded, trying to get a read on her before I dropped the bomb. "So instead, you murdered Pete Seaver to set me up, figuring a prison sentence would keep me away long enough for you to become Mrs. Chase Hargrave."

"What?" Fury transformed her face.

"You heard me."

April lunged at me. I blocked her attack, but we both fell to the floor. She slapped my face, and I turned my head from the sting of contact. I raised my knee to her hip, grabbed her shoulders and rolled until she lay flat on her back.

"Get off me!" she yelled.

"Not until you admit everything you've done." I straddled her, pinning her shoulders to the floor while she attempted to grab the few hairs hanging around my face.

"I didn't do anything! Let me go, you lunatic!"

"Juli?" Chase's voice questioned from the doorway.

"Oh, hey, Chase," I flicked a nod in his direction then leveled my gaze back to April. "You're just the person I wanted to see."

"I dropped in to take April to lunch and find you on top of her," he said in a dazed and confused voice.

"Oh, my gosh, Chase! Get her off me, the woman is crazy!" April shoved me to the side and scrambled to her feet screaming, "Juli attacked me!" She rushed into his arms and buried her face against his chest. I shook my head and rolled my eyes at her shaking and quivering form wrapped in his arms.

"I did no such thing. You attacked me. I was merely defending myself."

"What the hell is going on?" He cradled April closer, turning slightly as if to put himself between the two of us while at the same time casting daggers toward me which ripped through my armor. I could see it in his eyes.

He believed her over me.

"She stormed in here accusing me of all sorts of horrible things. Things I would never do, Chase." April sniffed and wiped her eyes. "She thinks I broke into her house and that Ikilled Pete Seaver!"

"What?" His green eyes burned into what was left of my soul.

"Chase, I—" His infuriated expression cut off the rest of my oxygen. By the increasing redness of his face, I knew the seriousness of this offense.

"Go back to the house, Juli," he said while rubbing April's back and soothing her with shushing sounds which made me want to do crazy things like tackle them both to the ground.

"Wait a minute." I raised my palm and stepped forward. "You're not seriously buying—"

"Now." The steely cut of his words stopped me in my tracks. "You've done enough. We'll talk about this when I get home."

I stood there staring at the two of them as if I were seven years old and being scolded for breaking a window. My stomach flopped and my throat tightened. SHE attacked me first, yet he hadn't listened to a word I said. That's what hurt the most. He really didn't have any faith in me, and I was done trying to convince him otherwise.

"When will that be?" I managed to ask.

"I'm taking April to lunch, as planned. I want to make sure she's all right." He kept his arm around her shoulders, dipped his head closer to hers. "Do you think you need to go to the doctor?"

"I think I'm okay." April rubbed her neck. "Did she bruise me? I swear, I thought she was going to choke me to death."

"If I wanted to choke you, I would have." I planted a foot in their direction.

"Juli," Chase warned, but I didn't listen. All I saw was April's smirk against the dark blue cotton of his uniform.

"All I did was pin you to the floor after you attacked me first, and you know it. She's lying to you, Chase."

Chase left April's side and approached me with such intensity I backed away. Taking me by the elbow, he escorted me through the door and to the sidewalk. His voice was dead calm when he spoke.

"I'm not discussing this in front of her when she's visibly shaken. I don't know what you were trying to do but you are way out of line, Julianna. Whatever I ask you to do, you do the opposite. Nothing has changed. I've had it. I don't understand you."

"No, you don't. You never did." I thrust my chin up. It was either that or have him see it wobble.

He inhaled in a deep breath as if counting to ten, then added in a weary voice, "Go back to the house, please. We'll talk later." He left me and returned inside to be with April. I walked home with my head low, wondering if I'd turned into a complete nut-job over this case and lost my best friend in the process.

When had I become so desperate?

Fourteen

"Do you mind telling me what possessed you to go after April like that?" Chase asked me later that day as we sat on his patio enjoying a batch of cheesecake brownies from Mrs.Bailey. We'd both had time to cool off and could come at the conversation reasonably now.

"I don't expect you to understand or be impartial at this point." I pulled at the fringe of my cut offs and straightened the hem of my pink tank top.

"I'm the sheriff. It's my job to be impartial." Even Chase had changed out of his uniform and into a pair of black shorts and white athletic cut shirt. I'd thought he was muscular before, but the thin material made his biceps look huge.

I shook off the distraction and focused on the conversation at hand. "Not where she's concerned. I'd call this a conflict of interest."

"Explain."

"I want to tell you everything, I really do. But you and April have this 'thing' now and no matter what I say, you're going to take her side because of your relationship." I shoved a huge, moist bite into my mouth, comfort food endorphins kicking in.

"You think so, huh?" He masked his expression by taking a long drink of milk.

"Of course." I took another bite. "She's always liked you, Chase."

"I know," he admitted.

"She's had you to herself for the last ten years. God, she's practically naming your children."

"Come again?" His eyes bugged wide.

"Even you can't be that stupid."

"I know, I know." He held up his hands, splaying his fingers that held the milk glass. "There's only one thing."

"What's that?" I thought for a minute if I really wanted to know the answer to this question, then decided I'd better try to answer it myself. "You're actually going to believe me?"

"Remember when I said my relationship with April was complicated?" I nodded and he continued, "It still is. I know perfectly well she wants a future with me. I don't know when I'll be ready to give it to her."

"Chase." I eyed him curiously, wondering what was going on with him.

"I told you, it's complicated." He snatched another brownie off the plate.

"Does it have anything to do with me?"

"Maybe a little." He smiled. "You see, you always had a special place in my heart. You always will."

"She knows this, right?"

"Of course, we've talked in depth about it. I will always care about you."

"And me you." My chest felt tight, and my stomach quivered deep inside, like during a scary movie when something bad was about to happen.

"While April is great, I don't feel the way I think I should feel if I'm going to commit to someone. Do you understand what I'm saying?"

"Absolutely. And now you know how I felt." The words slipped out before I could take them back. You would have thought I'd physically slapped him before he covered up whatever emotion I'd unburied by the gruffness in his voice.

"We're not talking about us."

"You're right. I shouldn't have said that." The truth was, I wasn't ready to talk about us. So, I did what any good friend would do, which was more than anyone had done for me. Not that I would have ever let them, even back then. I took his hand and tried to help him make sense of things. "Then why do you continue to go out with her? Aren't you giving her false hope?"

"Eh, sometimes I think so. Then there are times where we really do get along so well and it's easy, and I think that maybe I'm not trying hard enough to move forward."

"Guess I didn't help matters by coming home." I laced my fingers in my lap.

"Not really, but I'm glad you're back." He nudged me until I looked up.

"Are you? Because I feel like I've made a complete mess of things."

"Trust me, you haven't." He entwined his fingers with mine, and I swear my heart skipped a beat. "I want you to understand that April is April and I'm only human. If something clicks with us down the road that's great, and if it doesn't, I'll deal with it. But I'm letting whatever this is play out on its own."

"Wow, no rule book?" I slipped my hands free, trying rapidly to process what he'd just said.

"Someone once advised me to put the rules away."

"Really...wise person," I coughed out, "whoever that was. But I believe the advice was to toss the book, period."

"Something like that." He flashed a toothy grin before switching gears. "Do you understand what I'm trying to say here?"

"I get it." At least I thought I did. He liked April, but not enough to marry her. Inside I felt content with that, and thrilled he still held what we had in such high regard.

"Are you ready to tell me why you would accuse April of breaking into your house and killing Pete?"

I explained my reasoning and to his credit he listened to every word, not interrupting once. For a split second I think he even believed I'd solved the case. When I was through, he sat back in the wicker chair and clapped his hands.

"Well done, well done. Too bad you're wrong. April isn't a suspect."

"Why? How can you say that? She makes those dolls."

"The dolls aren't voodoo dolls. I know for a fact she was at a Dark Room Conference in Morristown. Several of her students had work on display and up for awards. She sent me pictures and we were texting after I said goodnight to you."

"You, texting? Miracles never cease," I chided. "Was she really there? She could have been staking out my house and making it seem like she was in Morristown."

"I said goodbye to her that morning. She showed me her ticket and the program."

"Maybe that was part of her cover so you wouldn't suspect anything. Pretty smart to have the town sheriff as your alibi."

"Stop. If you think about it, deep down, you know April isn't capable of something like this."

"You didn't see the burning destruction in her eyes before she jumped me. She is capable of more than you think."

"I'm sure everyone is at one point or another."

"You're picking a heck of a time to be diplomatic." I placed my hands on my knees.

"It's my job, along with doing damage control once everyone hears about this."

"Oh, yeah, small town gossip, how quickly I forget." I raised both hands in the air.

"You're messing with New Hope's sweetheart." He winked, knowing full well it would set me off.

"Blah, blah, blah, and you're the most eligible bachelor. Oh, please." I distorted my face, making exaggerated goo-goo eyes at him. We both laughed even though we were aware of the seriousness of the problem. "I want them to accept me and like me like they did my mom."

"They will, Julianna, they will."

"Not if they think I go around killing people or beating them up. They'll think I'm crazy."

"Don't worry about this. Even though you are suspiciously implicated in the murder of Pete Seaver, I know you aren't capable of killing anyone."

Finally, he believed me. Maybe he always had. Leave it to Chase to mess with me for so long. "I thought you just said everyone is capable at some point," I asked to be sure my suspicions were right.

"Not you, and not murder." He paused and I sensed a serious question coming. "Unless there's something you want to tell me about Boston?"

"Nah...it's complicated."

———

THANKFULLY, I'D AVOIDED TALKING WITH CHASE ABOUT the most recent parts of my life.

There were many bad decisions he didn't need to know about, ending with my on-again-off- again-but definitely off-again-relationship with David von Hoffster. Returning to New Hope would be my clean slate. I would take Chase's advice and trust April had nothing to do with the break-in or the murder, but that raised my worry meter about who might be after me and why. I knew Chase believed in my innocence regarding the murder, but I also knew his job required proof, which meant I wasn't out of the woods as far as being a suspect.

There had to be something I missed along the way. There was so much stress and negative energy lately, I needed to recharge and relax. Rita's salon would be the perfect place to go. Being pampered with a mani-pedi always worked to clear my head.

So did a peaceful morning walk. Me, nature, and the awakenings of my sleepy little town. While I loved the excitement of Atlantic City, the hustle in New York City and the busy trendiness of my Boston life...today, unlike any other day, I felt in my heart that New Hope was home.

"Good morning, Juli," Simon Banks said from across the quiet street.

"Good morning, Mr. Banks." I waved back, surprised when he crossed to my side. "Call me Simon. I see we have the same idea for a morning stroll." He held up his camera as he came closer.

"I have an appointment at Rita's salon. Nothing relieves stress better than a little self-care. And I couldn't resist a walk on such a beautiful morning." I tilted my head at the large lens of the camera. "I thought you were a food blogger. Yet I always see you with your camera outdoors."

"Staging a photo shoot for a plate of spaghetti and a glass of Merlot can be fun, but what nature does on her own is simply striking. A far cry from Misty's pancake special I shot last week." Simon scuffed some loose stones with his sneaker. "What can I say, I have a love for art in all its forms. Being from Boston, I'm sure you hold some appreciation for fine art."

"I'm originally from New Hope. I only lived in Boston for a while." I felt the strangest need to correct him. Since we were on a first name basis, and in a small town where everyone knew everybody's business, I didn't have a problem asking, "How did you know about Boston?"

"Small town."

"Ah, right." The summer breeze and chirping of sparrows filled the quiet void, and I realized I'd never seen Simon without sunglasses, not even at the pancake breakfast. Just as my worry meter clicked on, Simon broke our awkward silence.

"I should be moving along. I've been enjoying the walking trails here. The dew in the meadow this morning will make for some spectacular shots."

"Of course." I glanced at my watch as my worry meter jumped. "Look at that time. I don't want to keep Rita waiting."

"Enjoy the salon time. My wife swears by it. I'm sure whatever it is you're holding on to will be released in no time. See you around town." He waved with his camera and walked away.

I continued toward Rita's, wondering if Chase had investigated Simon at all. I passed by Harry Henderson straightening his garden tool display. I swear he saw me coming but continued as if he didn't see me at all. Obviously, April had cried her story to her aunt and uncle. Today was a new day, and Mom would be proud of my positivity meter refusing to shut down this morning.

"Hi, Harry." I decided to speak first and be the bigger person, even though I was less than half his size. "Do you have any beige putty? I'd like to seal up some cracks along the molding I painted at the café."

"Just white." He kept straightening hand tools that didn't need to be straightened.

"Oh, I see." I stood quietly, wondering what to say, if anything at all. Maybe I should move on and let him get over this misunderstanding in his own time. "Well, enjoy your day." I started to walk away when the giant teddy bear spoke.

"Betty and I are very disappointed in you, Juli. How could you think our sweet April is such a monster?"

"It's hard to explain," I countered, needing that energizing manicure more by the minute.

"She's no murderer. You were all friends."

"I know. It's kind of complicated." I hated to keep using that phrase, but darned if it didn't seem to fit this whole sordid mess.

"Betty thinks if you'd never come back, none of this would have happened. Chase and April would be happy right now."

"Maybe they would be." I remembered Chase's words. "Then there's a chance they would be right where they are now. You can't rush love, Harry."

"You know, we always understood your reckless side, but what you did to April is taking it too far. What would your poor mother say?" Harry shook his head, still not meeting my eyes.

"She'd say she understood, then she'd tell me I acted impulsively." I breathed deep through my nose, knowing this was truthful and exactly what I would have to do next to make things right. "She'd tell me to apologize."

Harry raised his head. Pleased by the sincerity on my face, the corners of his mouth tipped up. Without saying a word, he snatched the broom with one hand, waving me off with the other and humming while he swept the sidewalk in front of his store.

And just like that, all was right in his small corner of New Hope.

I felt relieved his acceptance had been so easy. Betty might be a tougher nut to crack than Harry. Then again, all I had to do was be honest and let her know it was a huge mistake on my part. Of course, I'd have to save face and say the same things to April. With a little luck, she wouldn't hold it against me for too long.

"Hey, pretty lady, where are you headed?" Gary slowed his patrol car to a crawl and followed me as I walked. His smile was so genuine, and his dimples were to die for.

"Rita's, to have my nails done."

"You don't strike me as the type."

"Trust me, I enjoy being pampered once in a while."

"How about tomorrow? I'll make you dinner at my place." He stopped the car, waiting for me to answer. "I've got to work the late shift tonight and I'm meeting some buddies in the afternoon so how about eight o'clock?"

"How can I resist those puppy-dog eyes?" I smiled wide and laughed. "Dinner at eight, it is! I'll bring the wine."

"Make it red, I cook a mean filet mignon."

"No filet for me. I stay away from meat."

"No worries," he said without missing a beat. "I also have a veggie lasagna recipe that's out of this world."

"Sounds amazing, I'm hungry already."

Gary's next words were cut off by a ruckus in Miller Park.

"Is that Jimmy O'Toole with his niece? Who's the other guy?" I asked as Gary put his cruiser in park and sprung from the door.

"Perez...." Gary ground out and stalked across the grass, leaving dewy footprints in his wake. I recognized the name from when I was at the police station with Chase. Not about to miss any of the action, I hurried behind him, hating the feel of the wet grass on my sandal-clad feet. Gary reached the trio just as things heated up under the towering oak tree.

"Get your filthy hands off my niece, do you hear me!" Jimmy yelled and clenched his fists.

"You don't own her, old man." The younger man didn't back down.

"She came here to get away from the likes of you."

"She wasn't given a choice." The younger man took Andie's hand and pulled her against him. "Isn't that right?" The minute their bodies touched she nodded her agreement. I hoped Gary picked up on her body language, but he seemed hyper-focused on the man.

"Oh, she had a choice, but we all knew you'd come sniffing back around if she stayed. And here you are."

"I love him, Uncle Jimmy."

"Girl, your heart is too good for this lowlife." Jimmy's eyes softened when he spoke to Andie then switched to a deadly glare as they zeroed back on her boyfriend. "Take your hands off her or you'll lose them."

"Okay, folks, let's take a step back," Gary said diplomatically.

"Andie, are you all right?" When she nodded, he smiled and said, "Why don't you go stand over by Juli so us men can have a talk." The girl reluctantly came over, and I wiped her tears with the back of my hand.

"It's going to be okay," I assured her even though I had no idea what would happen next.

"Jimmy, what seems to be the problem?" Gary stepped closer to the men, and I could feel the tension bouncing off all of them.

"This delinquent has come to town to take Andie back to Chicago. He's dirty, I tell you. He's just going to involve her in his drugs and gambling schemes again and ruin her life."

"No, he's not!' Andie rushed forward and I caught her arm before she could get too close. "He's here for me!"

"Do you even know who this guy is? Andie, he's no good for you." Jimmy pleaded, and I could see the worry in his eyes.

"Max Perez." Gary turned toward the other man, keeping his voice deep and calm. "I wondered when you were going to show up."

"Just here to play some cards," he sent a seductive glance toward Andie, "and some other things."

"Why you son of a—" Jimmy lunged, Gary held him off, and Andie screamed.

"Jimmy, take Andie home," he ordered, "or we'll all have to finish this at the station."

"You've got no grounds to take me anywhere. Shall I call my lawyer?" Max sounded overly sure of himself, and my worry meter spiked so hard I shivered even though the morning temperature was seventy-two. Jimmy approached and reached for Andie's hand, but she held back.

"No, you can't arrest him. He didn't do anything. We were having coffee. Uncle Jimmy, don't let Max go to jail!"

"It's okay, babe, no worries." Max's voice still held a cool, cocky tone. "Keep doing what you're doing, okay? It's important and I'm proud of you. Remember what we talked about?"

"Yes." Andie sniffed. "I love you." This time she allowed Jimmy to put his arm around her and walk to where his silver pickup sat parked with the engine running. Relieved Andie was going to be okay, I returned my focus to Gary and Max.

"What's it going to be?" Max opened his arms wide.

"Whatever you're really doing here, keep the townspeople out of it."

"Andie's an old connection. Can I help it if she's easily impressionable?"

"I'm going to need you to un-connect."

"Sorry, no can do. I helped her get a job, and she's great at it. The company would hate to lose her. Besides, I happen to like all the benefits."

"I'm watching you, Perez."

"As I'm watching you, Detective Maxwell." Max picked up a paper coffee cup from the grass, opened the lid and poured it at Gary's feet. "Don't threaten me. My attorney is on speed dial." He then crushed the cup, tossed it into a nearby trash can and walked to his shiny black sports car.

"Sorry you had to witness all of that," Gary said as we walked toward his car.

Actually, I'm glad I was here for Andie." I meant it. Whatever was going on between her and this Max character was more than just a crush. Maybe she would see me as an ally and talk to me about it. Lord knows I'd had my own experiences with shady characters.

"She shouldn't have been here either. There's something more than cards that brought Perez to New Hope."

"Any idea what it could be?" I wondered if Max Perez was one of the loan sharks Chase talked about. Could there be a connection with Pete's death? I waited patiently for Gary's response, but he seemed too deep in his own thoughts when we reached his car.

"I'll see you tomorrow for dinner." Gary slapped the side of his door, gave me a salute, and drove off. I continued down the street with a million questions filtering through my overactive brain.

Did Max and Gary know each other? When did Gary become a detective? There was a story here and I wanted to find out more. Was Jimmy involved somehow and now poor Andie was too? I never did get a chance to check out the fish market. Oh, and how would Chase react when he found out I had an official date with Gary?

I stopped outside Nailed It! salon to contemplate the situation. Rather than have a huge discussion where Chase points out all of Gary's faults, I decided I'd tell him when I had one foot out the door. In this case, the less he knew the better. If he could have April, then Gary should be fair game for me.

I walked into the salon, to a cheery group of women apparently there for the same reason I was. Two were in massage chairs while three were having their nails painted. I couldn't wait.

"Come on over here, girl!" Rita called and flagged me to her tidy glass and chrome table lined with several bright bottles of polish. "I'm so glad you called me for an appointment."

"I'm glad you had one available. I've been so stressed out."

"Yeah, we heard about the incident with April Henderson."

"Please, I don't want to talk about it anymore. I made a huge mistake and I'm sure I'll be paying for it for months to come."

"April's not that vindictive. You might suffer for a while, but she'll get over it fast. She's too stuck on Chase Hargrave to let anything come between them, and she knows how close you two are."

"So I've heard." I sighed, trying to release some of the tension. I'd need more than a mani-pedi and massage before making the big apology to April. "I was thinking of a nice shade of pink. I have a date tomorrow, and I'm going to wear my fuchsia shorts and white sleeveless blouse."

"Ohhh, nice. With Chase?"

"No, um, with Gary."

She arched a brow in surprise. "Good for you! So, you thinking of hot pink or pale

pink?"

"Hot pink, why?"

"You see, I have a policy that I don't duplicate colors for my repeat customers." She rolled her chair over to a display stand and surveyed the bright colored bottles. "I know what you're thinking, it's crazy, but it works. People feel special and they continue to come back."

"Everyone has their own color? How can you not duplicate that?"

"I only do it for a month. That way the person can come in and get touch-ups without worrying someone else is wearing the same color. If they chose an entire polish change, then the color goes back in the lineup for someone else to use."

"Interesting."

"Oh, it's a big hit come prom and semi-formal time. No one wants the same dress or the same polish. Even the bridezillas love it."

"I can see why. It's a unique concept. So, you don't have any hot pink or neon pink available?"

"No, I'm sorry. I have four different shades of hot pink, and they are all out." Rita scanned a clipboard with her finger. "Betty, Sandy, Lily, and my niece Cheryl who was headed to an out-of-town wedding, so she took the entire bottle."

"Betty, Sandy, and Lily?" My curiosity peaked. Betty and Sandy I understood, but Lily handled animals all day and sometimes performed surgeries. She didn't strike me as the kind of woman who cared about her nails.

"Yes. Speaking of Sandy, did she hit you up for the fundraiser?" Rita pulled two pretty pink polishes for me to choose from.

"That one." I pointed to the rose-colored bottle in her left hand, still wondering what Lily seemed to be hiding and what she'd been talking about the night she jogged with Rita. "She did, and I'm excited to put together a gift basket and maybe even some antique items from the attic. I think this is going to pull in a lot of money for the high school."

"And give your business good exposure. When Sandy does something, she does it up big. You watch, she will advertise, and people will come from all over."

"Then I'd better start digging through my attic."

"Not until these nails dry."

Fifteen

The high school fundraiser gave me good reason to sort through Mom's attic. There were interesting pieces of costume jewelry, some vintage clothing in excellent condition, a variety of crystal vases and books galore. They would make some amazing gift baskets by the time I was done.

Every trip I made downstairs, I kept an eye on the oven and the clock. I wanted to get ahead with some of the baking for the café, since I'd be making a ton of food items for the fundraiser. Chase didn't like the idea of me being at the house alone, but I assured him I wouldn't take long, and he was right next door if I needed him. I baked and sorted, and promised I'd package everything at his house. I also had in mind to take a late-night run of my own before returning to his house, hoping to casually bump into Lily.

She seemed so nice, and I honestly wanted to know her better, thinking we could become good friends. My worry meter continued to plague me, and I knew enough when something was off. I couldn't put my finger on it, but I thought with a bit more conversation Lily would either give me something solid or put my worries to rest.

At nine-thirty, I made sure the oven was off and put on my

running clothes. This time, I wasn't wearing all black. I wore a hot pink camo print tank and matching capri leggings. I'd even slipped on a reflective safety vest. No way Sheriff Do-Good could give me a lecture this time if he were to ever find out.

One peek through the curtains told me Chase was dozing in his recliner in front of the television, Major sound asleep at his feet. Perfect. I'd be able to sneak out undetected and return before he even knew I was gone. Then, once I had some more answers, I could present them to Chase, and I'd let him know about the confrontation with Jimmy O'Toole and Max Perez. Oh, and the whole Gary thing, too.

I tip-toed off my porch and headed in the direction of the marina. Since that was the last time I'd seen her, it stood to reason this was her route. The night was clear, and the summer temperatures had cooled slightly once the sun had set. Now I understood why she exercised late at night. This was so peaceful.

Peepers chirped from the trees and the soft summer breeze tickled my skin while I ran. I felt totally one with nature and self. This was better than any yoga class I'd ever attended.

The full moon mirrored on the water at the marina and the waves lapped the shoreline. I could see lights from those who stayed on their boats or who used the marina as a stopping point during their travels. Faint laughter cut through the quiet of the night. It must be romantic to spend the night on the open water with nothing but the stars above.

That was one adventure I hadn't been on yet.

I kept one eye out for Lily as I jogged along. The farther I went, the more my troubles seemed to disappear. As I looked to the path ahead, I dreamt of my future. This could easily become a new habit for me, and a healthy habit at that. The next time I went to Rita's I would be sure to mention this to her. Maybe the three of us could all jog together sometime.

"Oof!"

Someone rammed me from behind and I face-planted on the

ground as we slid. I tried to turn over, but their body weight was full across my back. A vice-like grip on my head forced my face repeatedly against the ground.

I fought to stay conscious, not knowing what this person planned to do to me or if there were more waiting to take their turn. The salty-sweet taste of blood filled my mouth. I tried to turn my head to the side, but all I could see was a form dressed in black.

A siren blared and the figure jumped off me. I lay still, my body aching. With the pressure of them gone, I panted to try and catch my breath. Footsteps thudded across the ground, but I couldn't tell if they were leaving or coming closer.

"Juli? It is you!" Gary's voice held concern as he carefully checked me over first, then supported my head and neck as he rolled me over. "Are you hurt?"

My mouth moved to speak but no sound came out. My eyes fluttered, trying to focus and as I vied for consciousness. I felt so scared and vulnerable.

"Stay with me, okay? It's going to be all right. I called for an ambulance, and I called Chase."

Those were the last words I remembered hearing before I blacked out. When I awoke, I was in a crisp, clean hospital bed with Chase sitting by my side. His eyes were bloodshot from lack of sleep and his usually crisp attire was covered in wrinkles.

"You look like hell," I managed in a raspy voice and cringed because laughing hurt something fierce.

"I look better than you," he said and brushed the hair off my forehead. "You were supposed to be baking cookies. What were you doing jogging by the marina, and don't tell me it's because you couldn't sleep."

"This is a heck of a way to get out of a date," Gary said from the other side of the hospital bed, appearing just as tired and worried as Chase judging by his messy hair and cloudy amber eyes.

"Date?" Chase narrowed his gaze on Gary and then me.

"I was going to tell you," I blurted.

"When? On your way out the door?" Chase frowned.

"Wait, you didn't tell him?" Gary's eyebrows raised.

Ugh, what a mess, I thought, but said, "Something like that. Oww!" I groaned and held my head. "It hurts."

They both made a move toward me, then remained in their seats, the awkward tension filling the space around us.

"It should hurt," Chase finally reprimanded. "Do you realize you pulled this crazy stunt with no identification or cell phone on you?"

"I wasn't thinking."

"That much is evident." Gary ran a hand through his hair and massaged his neck.

"I'll tell you what I'm thinking." Chase stood and paced at the side of the bed. "I'm thinking these loan sharks are coming after you now because of that statue. We need to find it and until we do, you're not safe. They could have killed you."

"I'm not so sure it's the loan sharks." Although I hadn't had the chance to check the connection with Max Perez.

"What?" both Gary and Chase said in unison, their gazes meeting before settling back on me.

"I've been following some leads on my own. I'm almost positive Lily Johnson has something to do with this. She was involved with Pete and she's holding back information, I know it."

"Go on, I'm all ears," Chase said, giving me a stern look.

"I know she runs late at night, so I decided to try to catch up to her and maybe get her to, you know, talk to me. Honestly, I think she was on to me. I think she was the one who jumped me from behind because I'm getting close to proving she is Pete's killer."

"There's only one way to find out."

"You're not going there without me." I tried to sit up, but it hurt too much so I eased back against the pillows. "If she did this, she won't be able to hide it." I wanted to see her face when we showed up to interrogate her and I wanted to see Chase's face when he realized I'd figured this out and solved the murder on my own.

Then I would properly thank Gary for saving my life.

———

CHASE PICKED ME UP THE NEXT MORNING AFTER Doctor Porter cleared me with nothing more than bumps and bruises. My body still felt like I'd been hit by a bus, and I had a whopper of a headache, but nothing would keep me from this meeting with Lily Johnson. I think by now Chase even knew it, that's why he didn't put up an argument about me joining him.

He parked in the back lot of Lily's animal hospital, where we sat for a moment watching people come and go with their pets. He flipped through some pages in a notebook, jotted down things I couldn't read and kept glancing at his watch.

"Hot lunch date with April? It's only ten o'clock, you've got a long wait." I bounced my knees up and down trying to rid myself of the anxiety zipping through me. Why weren't we getting out already?

"No."

"Then what are we doing sitting here like a bunch of dolts. We should be in there grilling her about the night Pete died."

"Grilling her?" Chase lifted his head as a smirk spread across his face. "You watch too much television. Let me remind you that you are the silent partner here. I am the sheriff. I will do the questioning."

"Really? We're partners?" I reached across the seat and rested my hand on his forearm.

"No."

"C'mon." I threw myself against the back of the seat and winced as pain shot through my back. "We could play some good-cop-bad-cop with her. Give me a chance."

"Juli, I'm serious about this. I don't want you saying anything, got it?"

"Okay, okay, whatever you say. Can we go in already?"

"Not until ten-fifteen. I had one of the secretaries at the office call and make a fake appointment so I could be sure no one else would be there while we talk."

"Oooh, you are a sneaky one!" I punched his bicep. "Nice play."

"Behave yourself in here." Chase opened his door.

"I wish you'd stop telling me that. You know darn well it's not likely to happen," I said while climbing out and shrugging. I was who I was, whether he liked it or not. At least Gary accepted me for who I was.

"I can hope, can't I?"

"You can, but it probably still won't happen." At least I was honest.

Chase sighed as he guided me by the shoulder through the door of New Hope Animal Hospital. Lily seemed surprised to see us and motioned she would be just a minute as she finished a conversation with a client she was checking out. The little white Terrier led its owner out the door, and we were alone.

"Chase, Juli, what brings you by? Is everything all right with Major?" she asked before taking a closer look at my face. "Oh, my God, what happened to you?"

"As if you don't know," I grumbled under my breath to which Chase elbowed me in the ribs. "Ow!" I couldn't help myself. I was sick and tired of people I thought I could trust taking advantage of me. First my house, and now my person; enough was enough.

"I'm sorry, what? I didn't hear you."

"She said she doesn't know," Chase answered. "She was attacked while jogging by the marina last night."

"How awful." We watched for signs of guilt but didn't see any. "I jog there all the time, and I've never had a problem."

"Precisely why I wanted to go that route," I spoke up and stepped aside to avoid another jab but not the warning glare.

"I didn't know you were a runner," Lily continued, oblivious to why we were here. "You and Rita made it sound like so much fun I had to try it out."

"How do you know I jog with Rita?" Lily questioned and for the first time appeared nervous.

"She—" Chase started to speak, but I cut him off.

"I was out walking one night when I couldn't sleep and overheard you two as you were jogging by."

"What exactly did you hear?"

"Something that you didn't want getting out because there could be trouble," Chase jumped in before I could. "Lily, I need to ask you questions about Pete Seaver's death."

Lily turned as white as the terrier who'd walked out the door, only she didn't try to leave. She dropped into the nearest chair, holding her face in her hands. When she lifted her eyes, she seemed more emotionally upset than guilty. I frowned.

"I told you everything before, Sheriff."

"I understand, but in light of what Juli heard, I want to revisit some areas and make sure we didn't miss anything. Do you mind if we proceed?"

"I can't believe it's come to this. I kept hoping it would all go away like any other crime. I don't know what to do." Lily lowered her head and cried. I straightened my spine, nodding an affirmative in Chase's direction that we had caught ourselves a killer.

"Lily, are you saying you killed Pete Seaver?" Chase asked, taking the chair next to hers.

"What? No!" Her face registered pure shock. "Is that what you think? Are you here to arrest me?" She jumped to her feet.

"Yes, for Pete's murder and my assault last night," I chimed in angrily. "And just when I was really starting to like you."

"I didn't kill Pete, and I didn't assault you," she pleaded, sounding genuine and sincere.

"Can you tell us where you were then?" Chase stood between me and Lily.

"That's just it, I don't know if I can."

"What do you mean? Either you were there, or you weren't. You all but told me you wanted him dead." I leaned around Chase to stare her down.

"No, no, that's not what I said." Lily sat, rubbing her face as if suddenly exhausted. "Of course, I was furious with Pete. I gave him everything and I never questioned anything. I knew he had a gambling problem, but I thought the longer we were together, he would realize he didn't need that way of life anymore."

"He was so much older than you. Why weren't you with someone your own age?" I asked out of my own curiosity. Pete was no prize, and Lily was young and beautiful.

"Guys my own age don't understand me. Pete did and he had this sense of adventure that was contagious. We were together for a while, and I really thought it would be forever."

"Which was why you got the tattoo." I pointed to the infinity symbol on her wrist and noticed Chase watching me in surprise.

"Yeah, we got matching ones. His on the top and mine on the bottom so when we held hands we'd be as one...forever." She stopped to wipe a stray tear. "So much for that, huh?"

"What happened between you two anyway?" Chase interrupted.

"Pete started acting differently and I thought it was the gambling, but I couldn't be sure. He wouldn't let me come to his house anymore, saying he was having some plumbing problems, and the place was a mess. When he'd come to my house, I'd find blonde hairs on his clothes. One day he came smelling like perfume and I knew he'd been cheating on me."

"Do you know who it was?" I asked.

"No, and he wouldn't tell me. He made up some excuse how he needed someone more mature, and he was on the adventure of a lifetime with his beach girl."

"I'm sorry about that. When was the last time you saw him?" Chase whipped out his notebook.

Lily's forehead wrinkled. "Come to think of it, I guess it was the day he died. He approached me after work, saying how sorry he was for dumping me. He knew how badly he'd hurt me, but I was the only person he could turn to."

"For what?" Both Chase and I asked.

"Money. Pete came to me to borrow money." Lily straightened in the chair, glancing from me to Chase as she spoke. "I told him I wouldn't give him a dime. I didn't want anything to do with him anymore."

"That's when he made you angry, right?" I prodded, standing straighter myself.

"Angry yes, but not angry enough to kill him," she said, snapping her head in my direction. "It had taken me six months to get over him. I just wanted him gone. I didn't want any ties to him. I'd started a new chapter in my life."

"Which leads us to the night he was killed," Chase interjected. "Lily, you previously told me you were tending to an emergency at the Sharpton farm. Oliver Sharpton confirmed that with my deputy. Is there anything else you need to tell me?" Chase closed his notebook and the most serious expression I'd ever seen shadowed his face.

Lily wrung her hands in her lap, her bravado suddenly slipping. "This is where I don't know what to do."

"Tell the truth," I encouraged and sat down next to her.

"Can you promise me it won't get out? You have to promise me," she pleaded, searching our faces for affirmation.

"I will do everything I can under the law to protect you," Chase said.

"I was meeting my boyfriend. We have a secret place just outside of town where we can be together, and no one will see. I was with him when I received the call from Mr. Sharpton about his cow who'd gotten tangled in some barbed wire. She was cut up bad, and he didn't know what to do. We went together."

"You and this boyfriend?" Chase once more opened his note-book, pen at the ready.

"Yes."

"He can corroborate this?" Chase asked.

Lily shook her head. "I'd rather you didn't ask him. He's married."

Chase leaned in, his voice softer when he spoke, "You need to give me his name."

"Vinnie," she responded.

My mouth hung open "Vinnie Minetti?" I exclaimed, and they both stared at me. "You're the mystery woman I saw in the truck with Vinnie?" Whoops.

"You've been spying on me?" Lily asked, her mouth gaping like mine.

"No, I was following Vinnie," I quickly clarified.

"Why?" She tilted her head.

"Yes, tell us why." Chase folded his arms across his chest.

"Because I thought Vinnie had a motive too." I sighed. "Maybe not to kill Pete, but more so to set me up for murder, because he doesn't like the competition." I told them what Vinnie had said about my mother and her pies being competition for his and how he didn't want the same thing to happen with my organic treats. Hearing the theory out loud made me realize how silly it sounded. "Now I understand he was only being sneaky because he's involved withyou."

"This can't be made public. He's finalizing his divorce, and this would ruin everything he's worked to set up. We've done everything we can to keep us a secret and it must stay that way until he has the papers. Please."

"What about last night when I was assaulted?" I asked, wanting someone to be accountable for my bruises.

"Vin and I were at Pepper's Motel. That's our secret spot."

"Lily, thank you for being honest, I know how difficult this is for you." Chase stood and shook her hand. "We will keep this information private, you can count on that." He shot me a firm look, and I nodded.

"Thank you. I really appreciate it, and so will Vinnie."

Chase and I were silent when we returned to the car. This had been a complete dead end, and I had run out of leads. I glanced over at my friend who seemed deep in thought.

"What are you thinking?"

"There's got to be something we're missing." He gazed out the window as if searching for the answer. Then he turned his stormy eyes to mine. "Until I can figure it out, I don't want you going anywhere without me."

"What?" I twisted in the seat to face him. "You can't do that. I'm already living under your roof."

"We know how well that's been working out. You seem to have a problem with keeping your nose out of this case. I can't trust you not to investigate on your own, so from now on I'm like gum on your shoe."

"Oh, that's original." I returned to facing the dash.

"I mean it, Juli. Things have gotten worse for you, and I'm going to be hauling you in if I don't figure it out. I don't want to have to do that."

"Then I guess this makes us official partners," I stated with a sideward glance.

"We're not partners," he confirmed, gripping the wheel, and putting the car in gear.

"Speaking of partners, since when is Gary a detective?"

"He isn't."

"Why would Max Perez call him one?" I jerked forward when Chase hit the brakes, thankful for my seatbelt.

"How do you know Max Perez?"

"I don't know him. I was with Gary when he broke up an almost fight between Jimmy O'Toole and Max. It was over Andie.

I guess Max is her boyfriend." I shrugged. "Who knew, right? But between you and me, I think there's a lot more going on."

"Oh, you do, do you? I think you've given me even more reason to put you under house arrest."

"Do what you must, Sheriff." I held my wrists out to be cuffed.

"Don't tempt me." He took his foot off the brake and the car moved forward.

He could say what he wanted but I knew after all of this he would stand true to his word and keep me close. By doing so, I'd be able to convince him to fill me in on all the details of the case, and whatever else he knew about Max Perez. The more I thought about it, house arrest could be a win-win.

A win I desperately needed because right now, I felt like I was losing.

Sixteen

"Let's go, partner," I said while tying an apron around Chase's midsection, appreciating the woodsy smell of his aftershave.

"We're not partners," he repeated for the umpteenth time, and I grinned.

"If you think you're going to be my shadow and not help me bake for the fundraiser, you've got another thing coming."

I opened one of the antique wardrobes at the café, where I'd installed shelves, and pulled out my ceramic mixing bowls, measuring cups and wooden spoons. I had more than enough space to store my gazillion cooking gadgets now that I'd started my own business. I never had a chance to have my open house, so I was counting on this fundraiser to not only help the high school but raise awareness about my café in plenty of time for my grand opening.

"I don't bake." He stood there in his dark-wash jeans and grey dri-fit shirt, hands up, looking totally lost in the kitchen.

"Expand your horizons." I spread my arms wide. "You might surprise yourself."

"I've been told as much."

"I won't give you anything too taxing, I promise. With you here I can work on two different recipes at once, so I'm taking full advantage."

"You, taking advantage of me? My dreams are coming true." He raised his hands to the heavens, and I was pretty sure that beam of sunshine spilling through the window—as if on cue—was my mother.

"Trust me, you're still dreaming." I bumped him with my hip. "I'm going to make organic corn chips and fresh organic pineapple mango salsa."

"Eww, too fruity. Whatever happened to good old-fashioned hot and spicy salsa?" "This has zip to it, don't you worry." Chase watched over my shoulder as I laid out some paring knives and a couple cutting boards.

"Who's worried? I think it sounds too fruity."

"Again, give it a chance." I reached for a pineapple and pointed toward the two mangos on the counter.

He handed me the fruit. "I'll give it a chance if you stop telling me to give things a chance."

"Deal." We shook hands, and I was glad for the extra help and the company. Neither Chase nor I had any idea who might have jumped me. Chase seemed to think it wasn't a random act, which spiked my worry meter immensely. At least I would go from Chase's capable hands to Gary's on our date tonight. It was going to be like having my own personal bodyguards.

"What are you grinning about?" Chase asked, following me to the cutting board. "Or don't I want to know?"

"I feel like a celebrity with my own bodyguards. I have you all day and Gary—"

"All night?" Chase tilted his head as a brow arched high on his forehead.

"At night," I emphasized. "I really hadn't thought about all night," I teased, handing him a knife.

"Let's not." He watched me dice a mango and then imitated my moves.

"Gary seems like a nice guy, what's your problem? Is it because he's a detective and you're not?" I dumped our chunks into a large stainless-steel bowl.

"From what I know of him, he is a nice guy." Chase wiped his hands on the front of his apron. "He's never talked much about his family or having a serious girlfriend. And I think your new friend Max must have misspoken."

"Maybe...." I pursed my lips in thought. "If you could have heard them though, they had a definite connection. And as far as a girlfriend, maybe Gary hasn't found the right one yet." I cored the pineapple.

"And you think you're it?"

"No, are you jealous?" I peeked from under my lashes, forever enjoying our banter.

"No. I just don't want you to get hurt. Apparently, there's more to my new deputy than meets the eye." He stuck the tip of the knife repeatedly on the wooden cutting board, avoiding eye contact. "The county-wide Play Makers Game is tomorrow. After that, Perez should be gone along with any trouble Gary seems to think the man is stirring up."

"Do you think there's a connection between Max and Pete Seaver?" I had to ask.

"It would make sense. Max is a big league, big city card player. Not sure what lured him to New Hope, unless it was Pete or his loan sharks."

"Give it up on the loan sharks already. I think it's time you ask Deputy-Detective some questions."

"I would be more than happy to do that except I'm being held captive making organic treats." His tone still held the teasing quality I loved, and I was thankful he took my Detective jab in good jest.

"Now that we have that settled, let's resume our lesson in baking corn chips." I didn't want to think of what else the two of them would talk about. Plus, I still needed to check out the fish market after hours.

"Great." He sounded relieved. "What will you be doing?"

"I'm going to make more of the Kitty Krackers. I bought some catnip at the farmers market and fresh tuna at the fish market. I'm going to add a little powdered milk and they should be fantastic."

"I thought people could eat them, too? Who's going to eat catnip?"

"The cats, silly. This batch will be for animals only."

"Got it. What do I need to do now?"

"I've put everything you'll need on the counter except the corn meal, that's in the back. Take the big bowl with you and scoop three full scoops of meal into the bowl."

Chase left and I started thinking about how successful I could be in New Hope. Sure, there had been some misunderstandings with people, but there was also plenty of time to regroup and adjust. Lily was a start, and April would need more time which was fine with me. For as much as I knew I'd forever ruined things with Chase the day I left town, I wasn't ready to see him with anyone else either, especially April Henderson.

"Juli," Chase called from the back.

"It's the yellowish looking grain." I shook my head and laughed thinking he didn't know which barrel contained the cornmeal. "The barrels are labeled," I yelled back.

"That's not it. You need to come here."

"For crying out loud." I dropped what I was doing and headed to his rescue. "We will never get anything done if I have to keep doing every ...." My voice trailed off when I noticed his pale, bug-eyed expression. "What? What's wrong?"

Chase pointed with the wooden scoop, and my gaze lowered to the corn meal barrel. Sticking half out of the corn meal was Pete's statue. My stomach clenched and my throat tightened as I swallowed to force the rising bile back down.

"What is that doing there?" I voiced the question on both our minds.

"That's what I want to know." Those accusatory green eyes of his didn't blink.

"Do you think I'd be stupid enough to hide the murder weapon in the grain barrel?" I approached the barrel and gripped its metal rim. "It's contaminated everything. I won't be able to use any of this corn meal now."

"Who said this was the murder weapon?"

"Well, I assumed because the statue was missing, and the medical examiner said he was hit with a blunt object, that the object in question was the statue. Didn't you?"

"I'm asking you."

"It makes sense. I mean, look at that pale pink spot right there." I pointed as close to the object as I could without touching it. "That could be a stain from blood that someone wiped off."

"Or paint." He glanced around the room at the molding I had recently painted in a deep burgundy to match my logo and containers. "It almost comes close to the color of your nail polish."

"Sorry to burst that bubble, but this is a fresh manicure. I didn't have polish on my nails until now. Besides, anyone could have put the statue there. I've had problems with the locks since day one." I marched toward the back door and rattled the knob just to prove my point.

"Did you have them fixed?"

"No, not yet," I said, sounding more than irritated, "I've been kind of busy."

"Busy investigating a case you have no business working on, or busy trying to throw me off track?" He shoved the scoop back into the cornmeal, shaking his head in disappointment. "If you put half that energy into your business, you'd be all set for the fundraiser and grand opening."

"I'm the one who's been implicated from the start, and your office doesn't seem to care."

"I care. When are you going to get that through your head?" He rounded the barrel to stand beside me, resting his hand on my shoulder. "I know in my heart you didn't do it. I know you're not capable of something like this. But I also have a job to do. Even you have to admit this doesn't look good."

"W-What are you saying?" I didn't like the look in his eyes or the way his hand traveled like a breeze down my arm. "This is for your own good." He wrapped his hand around my wrist.

"What is?" I craned my neck to see his face as he maneuvered my hand behind my back. "Chase?"

"Julianna Butler, you have the right to remain silent. Anything you say can and will be used against you in a court of law." He secured the cuff with a click.

"Oh, my God, you're arresting me!" I tried to wriggle around, but he'd already taken my free hand and connected it to the open cuff.

"If you cannot afford an attorney—"

"Stop right there, I know what my Miranda Rights are. You can't do this."

"Let's go, Julianna," he said only after finishing reading me my rights. Sheriff Goody-Good always stuck to the book. "At least if you're in my jail cell I won't have to worry about you getting in more trouble, or killed," he added to soften the blow.

I didn't know what else I could do at this point but surrender.

———

THE ONE GOOD THING ABOUT SITTING ALONE IN THE jail cell was it gave me time to run through my list of suspects in peace. One of them must have thrown me off track somehow, but who? Someone who had access to my café? Since I didn't have the locks fixed, that technically could be anyone.

There was no telling how long it was going to take before they realized finding the statue at the café was completely circumstantial and they should let me go. I had a business to run, an important fundraising project to prepare for, not to mention a dinner date with a sexy deputy-slash-detective. Chase wasn't going to be happy with me, but I needed to find a way out of this cell.

"Juuuli."

I whirled around to see Scallywag perched on the desk. "How did you get in here?" I changed my tone when the fickle bird looked in the other direction. "Never mind, you crazy-er, loveable bird. I'm so glad you're here now. Come help Auntie Juli out of this jail cell."

Scallywag bobbed and danced across the edge of the metal desk, stopping occasionally to tap-tap-tap with his beak. Walking to the center of the desk he paused in front of a large, brass key ring. Tapping it with his beak, he tilted his head at the *'ching-chang'* sound it made.

"You're a genius!" I yelled. Startled, he flapped his massive wings, hovering for a brief second above the desk blotter. "No, wait! Stay there." I had to con that con artist into bringing me the key ring. Who knows how much time I had before Chase or Gary returned?

Scallywag stared me straight in the eye before pruning his wings as if I didn't exist. Was the rascally bird taunting me? He lowered his head and pulled at something stuck in his talons. It looked like a piece of paper as he plucked and tore tiny shreds onto the desktop.

"I'm a genius." He squawked and beat his wings in the air.

"Yes, yes you are," I agreed though it pained me to do so.

"Where's the money? Who are you? Gonna kill you."

"Oh, my gosh." Listening to his annoying chatter suddenly connected the mental dots in this case. "You're repeating the night of the murder, aren't you? You heard it all before you escaped out the window."

I tried not to make any sudden moves to scare him away, but I felt an instant sense of relief that my troubles might be over. I needed to keep Scallywag talking until Chase or Gary came in to corroborate the story. My gut told me this was an all too important break in the case, and I'd learned to listen to my gut.

"What else?" I inquired in a sugar-sweet tone and made kissy noises at him.

"Stupid Juli."

"Argh!" Nice hadn't worked, so I thought I'd try the bad cop angle and slammed my palms against the bars. "You crazy nasty bird! Tell me what happened that night, or I will pluck you like a chicken."

"What have I done? Pete's dead!"

"I know Pete's dead. Who did it, Scallywag? Tell Auntie Juli who killed Pete."

"Someone's coming. Stay away from my wife. What have I done?" The parrot flew toward me and clung to the steel bars of my cell. I slowly picked the piece of paper from his foot.

"Can't wait to get away with you. Love, your sandy beaches." I read the note, not quite understanding it at first.

"Don't do it. Oh, no, Pete's dead," the bird squawked.

"Away from my wife?" I echoed Scallywag's words. "Whose wife?" I thought of Vinnie and his affair with Lily. Had Pete been after Connie? Or was Pete going to tell Connie about the affair because Lily turned him down?

Scallywag shot from the cell back to the desk, obsessed with the key ring now that his foot was free. I stared at the note in my hand, trying to think of the other married men in town who could have tangled with Pete that night I never did make it to the fish market to investigate Jimmy O'Toole. This could be the first solid lead since finding the statue in my grain bin.

"Billy, no!" Scallywag screeched and beat his wings in the air.

"Billy?" I scowled at the bird. I didn't have a Billy on my suspect list. Had I missed someone? "Billy...Billy...Bill...Bill Perkins?" Then sandy beaches must be referring to Sandy Perkins. Had Sandy sent the note to Bill and then Pete interfered with their romantic rendezvous? Had they caught him red-handed stealing the statue from Mrs. Bailey? Maybe they threatened to call the police. What if there was a struggle?

Scallywag clucked and tapped his beak on the desk. A strange cooing noise resonated deep in his throat, and he moved his head round and round in the shape of a circle. He rocked from one foot to the next and then tried to latch on to the brass ring.

"What if that pink mark on the statue isn't blood or paint, but a scuff from Sandy's hot pink nail polish," I deduced aloud. Rita had listed Sandy as one of the women who wore pink this month. Or what if Vinnie had already killed Pete? That meant Bill and Sandy happened upon the body and hid the statue to protect someone. Who was it and why?

Now I really needed the bird's help. If I didn't get out of this cell, I'd never know the truth about Bill and Sandy. What if they were leaving town like her note said? They weren't on Chase's list of suspects, so he'd never think of detaining them.

"Give me the keys, Scallywag. Right there, on the desk, Big Fella," I coaxed by pointing and wagging my finger. The frustrating fowl didn't budge. "Scallywaaag," I warned.

"Juuuli."

"Yes, that's right. Auntie Juli needs the keys. Who's a pretty boy?"

"Juuuli. Pete's dead." Scallywag mimicked and I forced a swallow to keep my curses to myself. I fisted my hands and shoved them into the deep pocket of my apron.

"Sesame Peeps!" I exclaimed as I fingered the little gems. Holding one between the steel bars, I tilted it like a reflector to get his attention. "Look, come and get the treat."

The birds head stopped bobbing and his big eyes blinked several times. He'd seen the cracker. Would he bring me the keys for it? He was a rascal all right, but how much did my feathered friend really understand.

"Coooookie," he cooed, followed by clucking and more bobbing.

"That's right, a cookie for the pretty bird." Scallywag moved to the edge of the desk as if he were about to take flight. I had a moment of panic. "Not without those keys," I ordered then quickly softened my tone. "You pretty, pretty bird."

To my astonishment the parrot picked at the key ring with his foot. Could this be happening? The bird was going to break me out of my prison. This would be one for the record books.

"C'mon, Scally. Bring me the keys."

Scallywag used his beak to maneuver the large ring between his talons. He'd taken off from the desk when Major bounded through the door. The keys fell from the bird's grasp, and they slid across the linoleum.

"No!" I cried, sticking my arm as far as it would go through the bars in a failed attempt to catch them. I slid to the floor, feeling defeated. My freedom lay only inches from my reach. "This is all your fault," I ground out between my teeth as I smooshed my face against the bars. Major ignored my tone, trotted over, and licked at my face.

"Eww! Knock it off, fur ball. The bird and I had a good thing going until you showed up." Major whined and lay down. Big brown pools of love gazed at me from under shaggy brows. "Oh, for crying out loud," I huffed, extending my hand to pat his head. "Sorry."

Major sniffed my hand and whined again. When I didn't do anything, he nudged me with his moist nose. "Woof."

"What?" I asked when he nudged me again. "I suppose you want a treat too?" He sat up and cocked his head. Maybe all wasn't lost yet, I thought as an idea came to me. "You're going to have to work for it." I pulled the crackers from my apron and tossed it close to the key ring to get his attention. "Bring it." I pointed to the brass ring next to his fat fuzzy paw.

Major gobbled the cracker, sniffed the key ring then returned his gaze to mine. Unbelievable! Didn't Chase train his dog? If I got out of here, it would be a miracle.

"Get it, Major. Keys," I ordered, realizing he wasn't as sensitive as the finicky fowl. "You can do it," I encouraged, as he sniffed and licked the ring. When he clamped it between his teeth, my heart soared. "Yes! That's my boy!" Major dropped the keys in front of me and I held the rest of the crackers for him to eat.

Moments later I was free and heading out the door with my animal menagerie close behind. I snuck home unseen and returned Scallywag to his cage before Mrs. Bailey worried. Loading Major in my truck, I set out across town to the Perkins residence.

My freedom relied on either of them knowing what really happened the night Pete Seaver died.

$$Seventeen$$

"**I** could arrest you for speeding. Oh, wait, you're already supposed to be in jail," Chase said the minute I stepped out of my truck.

"Where did you come from?" I glanced up and down the street thinking Gary wouldn't be far behind. I didn't see either of their cars.

"I never really left. Something told me you'd find a way out. You haven't done a darn thing I've asked since you came home, why should I think a jail cell would hold you."

"Why didn't you say anything?" I ignored his jab.

"I wasn't sure what you were up to. At first, I thought you'd broken out of jail and were going to leave town, until you took Major with you." Chase reached up and ruffled the dog's head hanging over the tailgate. "What's really going on and why are you here at the Perkins' house?"

"Because of this note." I pulled the tattered paper from my apron pocket and handed it to Chase.

"And this relates to Bill and Sandy how?"

"When Scallywag kept repeating what he'd heard the night of Pete's murder, I thought he was talking about Vinnie. But we already knew about Vinnie and Lily. The same Lily who dated Pete and who wouldn't take him back, and wanted their relationship kept a secret because of Vinnie's upcoming divorce!" My eyes grew wide as I started putting the pieces together. "I think Vinnie might have killed Pete to keep him from telling Connie about the affair with Lily."

"Then why didn't you head straight to Vinnie's place?"

"Because Sandy is sandy beaches in the note, I'm sure of it. She wrote it for Bill. They were planning a romantic getaway only Pete ruined it."

"That's nice for them, I guess, but it still doesn't explain why you came here instead of leading me to Vinnie."

"Because I think they either happened upon Pete stealing the statue from Mrs. B's, or Pete was already dead."

"Then why haven't they come forward with any information?"

"I'm not sure. That's why I wanted to speak to them to find out what exactly happened and ask them who they are protecting."

"What makes you think they are protecting someone?"

"If they found Pete already dead, then they found the statue. That pink mark could be a scuff from Sandy's nail polish. Why hide it unless they knew the person who killed Pete."

"You're right about the nail polish."

"I am?" I didn't try to hide my shock.

"Lab results showed high amounts of nitrocellulose and acetate, components of nail polish."

"Yes!" I made a fist pump in the air in victory.

"Hold on. Do you know how many women could be wearing the same color nail polish? That mark could have been on there for a long time. While you have a good theory, this needs a little more investigation before we barge into their home with a million questions."

"But—" He wouldn't let me explain about Rita's Salon, so I gave up trying. He'd find out soon enough.

"Our first stop should be a talk with Vinnie and Lily. Maybe

I'll call them both to the station and question them together, see if they are on the up and up. In the meantime, I want you back in the cell for your own protection."

I couldn't let him take me back there. I had so much work to do, and for the first time I felt like we were about to close this case. He needed to let me spread my wings like he did ten years ago, only this time I wouldn't be going anywhere.

"Can I at least sit in when you question them? You got this lead because of me, remember?"

He stared at me for a long moment, and then finally sighed. "You can't say a word, not one peep."

I was ready to agree with him when I recapped the pieces of information from Scallywag. Once more the clues rearranged themselves in my head. There was something about the note Scally found that I couldn't let drop.

"Can I assume by your silence you're going to behave?" Chase dangled the handcuffs in front of my dazed face. I waved them off, trying to gather my thoughts.

"Wait. When Lily first told me about her and Pete, she said he dumped her for some beach girl. And then later, she mentioned he wanted someone more mature."

"So? Guys do that kind of stuff all the time." I gaped at his remark, and he clarified, "Some guys. I don't do that."

"Of course not," I uttered, then jumped back into my ah-ha moment. "Why didn't I think of this first!"

"Spill it, I'm not sure I like that gleam in your eye."

"Sandy is sandy beaches, right? She's the beach girl Lily was talking about, the more mature woman Pete dumped her for! Pete was having an affair with Sandy Perkins. That note was meant for Pete, and they were going to run away together!" I'd nailed it. Chase should ask me to be another deputy, or maybe the town lawyer.

"Do you know how outlandish that sounds? Bill and Sandy have been together for years, college sweethearts, as Bill will tell you. They are upstanding citizens in this town." Chase began to burst my bubble. "They adore each other. There is no way she was cheating on Bill with the likes of Pete Seaver. I'm not buying it."

"You'd better believe it, because Scallywag repeated the murder scene."

"He what?"

"Think about it. Pete broke into Mrs. Bailey's house to steal the statue and Scallywag escaped. He was up in my tree when Pete was murdered. He heard everything."

"That still doesn't prove Bill and Sandy are involved."

"Scallywag repeated the name Billy, who I wasn't sure of at first until I figured out Sandy had written the note, only I thought she'd meant it for her husband. Which is how I came to the conclusion they found the dead body."

"Where did you get this note anyway?"

"It was stuck to Scallywag's foot. I don't know where he picked it up, but I'm thankful he lived up to his name."

"You expect me to arrest Bill and Sandy on the basis of this note?"

"Now I do. Between this note and Lily's testimony, I think one of the Perkins' killed Pete."

"This isn't going to be easy, you know. It will be bad for all of us if you're wrong."

"Bill had access to my café and could have easily hidden the statue in my grain bin. You said the lab verified that reddish mark as nail polish. She wears a specific color every month, and this month it's pink, so I'm betting my first sale it's a match. Rita will be able to confirm if Sandy came in that day for a manicure."

"You think you have this all figured out, don't you?"

"It makes perfect sense."

"Actually, it does," he grudgingly admitted.

"You don't say...." I shot Chase a smug grin. "What's our next move, partner?"

"My next move is to call Gary here and then we, meaning Gary and me, will go in and question them."

"Not without me. I practically solved this case on my own. I was wrongfully accused, wrongfully put on house arrest, and now wrongfully jailed. It's only right that I'm there to see this all go down."

Chase knew I'd win so he didn't bother trying to argue with me.

———

We waited outside the Perkins' house until Gary arrived. Leaving Major in the back of the truck, the three of us proceeded to ring the doorbell.

"What brings you all around today?" Bill asked when he answered the door.

"Billy? Who's there?" Sandy called from somewhere in the house. I couldn't resist a poke at Chase's back.

"It's Sheriff Hargrave with his deputy and Juli Butler."

"For heaven's sake, invite them in." Sandy appeared, nudging Bill out of the way, and extending an arm to welcome us into their home. "Is everything all right? Juli, darling, I heard about your ordeal. I see you're out now, so they must have caught the nasty person."

"That's what we're here to talk about," Chase stated. Gary cleared his throat, and I noticed Bill glancing about the room as if looking for something. "Is there a place we can sit down?"

"Certainly, come in the library, it's more comfortable." Sandy ushered us into a gorgeous room with wall-to-wall books and thick leather furniture you could imagine sinking into while reading. "What is it you want to talk about?" Sandy asked once we were all seated.

"Where were you both the night of Pete Seaver's death?"

Chase's question brought immediate eye contact between Sandy and Bill, but I couldn't read the silent message they shared.

"I, I—" Sandy started, but Bill interrupted.

"She'd gone to visit her sister."

"Is that why you had your nails done?" I asked, and Chase scowled at me.

"What were you and your sister doing?" Chase questioned. "If I call her, will she verifythis?"

"We were going to go shopping," Sandy said nervously. "Yes, she will verify it. Sheriff, what exactly is going on here?"

"We have a note that implicates you in the murder of Pete Seaver," Gary added and produced the note for them to see.

"That's a bunch of bull." Bill grabbed the note then stared adoringly at his wife. His eyes seemed to glass over, and I swear I saw his lip quiver.

"Were you having an affair with Pete?" I asked.

"What Juli is asking," Chase shot me a warning glance, and I slouched slightly against the supple leather, "is if you and Pete Seaver were together the night he was murdered. Did you write him this note?"

"Of course, she didn't," Bill interjected, sounding agitated. "My Sandy wouldn't be caught dead with someone like him."

"Maybe she killed him to make sure of it." The words slipped out before I could catch them. Everyone, including Gary, stared at me with mouths open. "I'm sorry, but all signs point to Sandy."

"All right, all right." Sandy stepped forward, waving her hands in front of her face. "I was seeing Pete. While I love my husband, I longed for adventure. Call it a mid-life crisis. In hindsight, I don't know what I was thinking. Pete Seaver was my wild adventure. We were going to sail the Caribbean together. He told me he'd been longing for someone like me."

"What happened?" Gary asked in a soft voice which encouraged Sandy to continue.

"I don't really know. Pete started acting strange. One minute he couldn't wait to be with me, and the next he was pushing me away saying it wasn't going to work."

"Because I found out," Bill added, jumping to Sandy's side. "The night I was working on the security lights at Harry's, I-I saw you with him. You're always doing for others, so I thought you were helping him out. But then when he hugged you and kissed you, I knew there was something more." Bill took a moment to catch a breath and visibly calm the anger we all saw building. Sandy couldn't quite look at him, staring at the floor instead as he continued. "A man like Pete was out to take advantage of you and I wasn't about to let that happen. Not to my wife! I talked to the lowlife a couple of days later. I told him to leave my wife alone because she didn't need him."

"Oh, Billy, if I'd only known." Sandy latched onto his arm. "I'm so sorry for everything."

He patted her and in response, said, "It takes two, Sandy. I could have done more to make you happy."

"How did Pete respond? Did he threaten you?" Chase asked.

"No. He told me to mind my own business, and that he was through with her anyway. He said his sister was coming to town and he had to get the statue back. Made me mad how he could use my beautiful Sandy like that. I knew a loser like him would hurt her. I didn't want that to happen, but he did it."

"Then you hurt him back," I piped in under the watchful glare of Chase.

"I followed him, and sure enough I caught him breaking into Mrs. Bailey's house, but he didn't see me. I was about to call the sheriff when Sandy showed up."

"I was trying to stop him because I was angry with him. I'd seen him that afternoon falling all over Lily Johnson. She's too young for him, he'd told me as much before, and I didn't want him making the same mistake and ruining both of their lives."

"What exactly happened, Mrs. Perkins?" Again, Gary's soft tone spurred her forward. "We started to argue. He held the statue and claimed it was going to solve all his problems. He didn't want me or my money any longer and kept repeating the statue held the key." She paused, looking thoughtful and said, "He'd only been interested in my money, not my love. I grabbed the statue from his hand. I wanted to break it, to throw it away and show him he didn't need it. We could still be happy on our adventure together. While we were tugging, Bill tried to help. Pete's hand slipped. He teetered back and we both let go. The statue hit him on the head as he fell."

"You were the 'What have I done?'" I mimicked Scallywag.

"He wasn't dead then," Bill concluded. "Sandy was so distraught I couldn't let her take the fall for someone like him. He'd go to the police for sure and report us, ruin the love of my life. I needed to protect her. I figured he didn't have many friends in this town due to all his cheating and gambling, so he'd never be missed. When he started to move, I hit him hard enough to knock him out." Bill paused to put his arm around his crying wife. "We made a pact never to speak of this. We planned to call in an anonymous tip and let the police take care of him. If he did decide to get the sheriff involved, we were going to pretend it never happened. It would be his word against ours, and who would believe him?"

"You see, I've always loved my Billy. I just lost sight of that since we've been together for so long. I thought I needed adventure, but what I really needed was more time with him."

"Why did you trash my house? Were you trying to scare me with the voodoo doll? I mean, you planted the murder weapon in my grain bin. Why not just leave it for the police?"

"That's not true." Bill's eyes pleaded with me to believe him. "You are such a nice person. We just wanted to return the statue to Ida Bailey, but it was already so late. I decided I would return it in the morning, so I put it in my toolbox in the trunk."

"How did it end up in Juli's grain bin?" Chase asked, and by the slight squint of his eyes, I could tell he wasn't sure about the tale being spun in the library.

"As you know, you found Pete dead the next morning. You've got to believe me, he was still breathing when we left him. Sandy and I panicked because our fingerprints were all over the statue. We couldn't be associated with the thing now that it was thought to be the murder weapon. I was doing the work in your shop, and I'd taken it out of my toolbox, ready to throw it in one of the dumpsters when you came in. I tossed it into the grain bin without a second thought."

"What about the doll?" Gary asked.

"I never broke into Juli's house. I don't know anything about a voodoo doll."

"It's true," Sandy said, edging closer to Bill. "Ever since the incident with Pete, Bill has always been by my side. We like Juli. We'd never want to see her in trouble."

Wow, Sandy was a far cry from my mom's nemesis. She had a heart and despite her bad judgment call with Pete, she was a good person who loved her husband. But one of them was responsible for Pete's death.

"Bill, I'm going to have to bring you in," Chase said, shocking us all. I moved to comfort Sandy.

"Bring me in for what? I didn't kill him. Don't you believe me?"

"I'm sorry, Bill. I'm arresting you for the murder of Pete Seaver."

"I won't go!" Bill yelled. "I didn't do it!" He raced through the house and out the door. Chase and Gary were right behind him.

At the top of the porch Chase stopped. He put two fingers in his mouth and sent a shrill whistle through the air. Major's head popped up from the bed of my truck. The shaggy deputy took one look at the fleeing Bill Perkins and another at his master, who gave him the signal to pursue.

In one giant leap, Major landed on the ground only to pounce on Bill. With the hefty sheepdog on top of him, Bill wasn't going anywhere. Major kept him pinned to the grass until Chase arrived with handcuffs. Poor Bill. I'm sure this wasn't the kind of adventure either he or Sandy planned on.

"Do you really have to take him in?" I asked as Chase helped Bill into his squad car.

"It's my job and we have probable cause. You were right, it makes perfect sense."

"He said he didn't do it. I said the same thing, remember? You let me go." My heart was breaking as I watched Sandy and Bill stare at each other through the car window. "This is my fault."

"I have to take a formal statement. You don't have to be there."

"What about Sandy? We can't leave her alone."

"How about I drop her off with Mrs. Bailey. Will that make you feel better?" I nodded and turned toward my truck. I'd been confident in my analysis. Now, I wasn't so sure. "Hey." Chase reached down and took my hand. "Justice isn't always easy, especially when it involves people you know."

"This is one time I wish I wasn't right."

Eighteen

Chase did his best to assure Bill that Sandy was in good
hands with Ida Bailey. After taking his formal statement,
he settled Bill into a cell. The heaviness in my chest
weighed me down where I sat behind Chase's desk, stroking
Major's large head.

"Comfortable?" he asked when he walked into his office.

"No." I barely recognized my voice. My theories made sense,
even as I ran through them again for the umpteenth time since
leaving the Perkins house. "Something doesn't feel right."

"For once, Scarlett, I think we're on the same page."

I perked up in his chair, not caring he'd called me Scarlett.
Right now, Sheriff Goodie-Good not only validated my theory,
but was including me in his process. We had become a team.

"By same page...are you talking about—"

"The statue," we said in unison, and I rose to my feet.

"The evidence room," he said in answer to my unspoken question and dashed out the door. I swear I was on pins and needles
until he returned holding it high like an Olympic torch. "The
statue holds the key."

"Yes! That's what we've been missing. But how? I would have

noticed if there was a keyhole when I first examined it." I rushed to his side, reaching to inspect the statue with him. Only Major had other ideas. The giant dust bunny must have thought Chase had a fancy stick because he launched into the air and snatched it out of his master's hand. "No!" I yelled as he ran out the door with us in hot pursuit.

"Hey! What's going on?" Gary shouted, as he spun out of the way seconds before Major could take out his knee. "What's he got now?"

"The statue!" Chase and I yelled. "Stop him!"

Gary lunged at Major, causing him to divert his course. Chase and I split up, forming a triangle with Gary. There was no place for the shaggy demon to go as we slowly closed the gap.

"Major, sit," Chase commanded, then let loose a frustrated growl when the dog stood there with his head cocked and butt wiggling.

"Looks like somebody didn't get enough attention today," I scolded.

"We've been a little busy. Correct me if I'm wrong, but didn't he help you escape from jail?"

"Yes, he did," I said matter-of-factly, his use of the word we not going unnoticed.

"Wait, What?" Gary froze with his hands on his hips.

"He got to exercise his brain and take down Bill Perkins. I think that's a good mix of activity, don't you?" We closed in a little more and Major's giant paws danced on the floor, his jaw tightening with a distinct click against the statue. "Easy there, big fella," Chase crooned, and slowly crouched on the floor. "Major, come."

To our relief, Major hung his head and loped toward Chase. The moment he reached out to give the dog praise and take the statue, Major hopped back and without a running start leaped forward using Chase's shoulders to catapult him to the outside of our trap.

"That's it!" I bellowed and all movement ceased. Chase and

Gary watched me with slack jaws and bug-eyes as if I'd sprouted a second head. I turned my attention to the guilty pile of fluff having a hard time controlling his excitement. I had to admit, he'd been growing on me since spending so much time together. Right now was not the time to test my patience.

If the statue really did hold the key, then there could be proof that Bill Perkins did not kill Pete Seaver. We'd never know unless we had the statue.

"I've had it with your horrible behavior, mister. It is not playtime." I stomped my foot and pointed my finger at his adorable, twitching black nose, refusing to get sucked in by those mocha pools of love underneath his shaggy brows. I breathed deep, exhaled, and made eye contact with Major and then commanded, "Leave it."

I'm not sure what shocked us more, the fact he listened to me, or the pool of diamonds that poured from the statue once it hit the floor. I grabbed Major by the collar when he made a move toward the twinkling gemstones. Gary and Chase rushed over to take a closer look.

"Well, what do you know...." Gary said as he scooped some into his palm.

"Are those real diamonds?" I found myself asking.

"I'd say yes." Chase glanced up from the brilliant gems. "That would explain why Pete wanted the statue back after he sold it. Must be he found out a little too late what was inside."

"Or he was never supposed to know at all," Gary mused just as his cell phone rang. He poured the diamonds into Chase's hand and moved across the room to take the call. "This is Deputy Maxwell."

"Chase." I kept my voice low. "What would a man with a gambling problem be doing with a statue full of diamonds?"

"I don't know."

"I think I know who does." Before I could fill him in, Gary walked back over.

"There's a situation at the marina, boss. I'll take care of it."

"Nothing serious, I hope."

"I'll keep you posted."

I waited until the door closed behind Gary and chewed my bottom lip, trying to find the right way to tell Chase that his deputy wasn't the man he thought...or at least it seemed that way. I absently pet Major once more, running through all my clues and scenarios.

"What is it you think you know about the diamonds?"

"It's Gary. I think he's a dirty cop." I watched as Sheriff know-it-all arched a brow in disbelief. "How much do you really know about a guy in six months?"

"Juli—"

"No, listen. The day Gary was in the café helping me with Tess, he left his phone on a table. I went to grab it for him and saw a text message from someone named Mark. All it said was diamonds."

"And you think this implicates Gary in Pete's murder." He shifted his weight and crossed his arms in front of his chest.

"You don't? If he's not involved, he sure knows something about it." I stared wide eyed at the good sheriff. "He tried to tell me it was a bet with his brother-in-law about his sister's birthstone. I didn't think anything of it then, but now it seems suspicious."

"I know for a fact Gary is not a dirty cop."

"Is that in your rule book?" I couldn't help the sarcasm. We'd gone from teamwork to not believing me again, and I didn't like it one bit.

"As a matter of fact, I spoke with his commanding officer, who happens to be an old friend of mine, before Gary even came to town. He was calling in a favor."

"Oh, kind of like you owe me so take the dirty cop?"

"Again, you watch too much television." Chase shook his head and once more, I wanted to slug him. I shrugged my shoulders to ease the tension and let him continue. "Let's just say Gary had a problem with a stake out gone wrong. He was told to take time off, which he declined. Rather than have him stay in Chicago where he could get into trouble, they sent him here." He held up a hand to stop me from talking. "Before you jump to any more conclusions, he's been doing a fine job."

"I'm not buying it." I used his favorite phrase and saw the teasing glint flicker in his eyes right before his phone beeped three times. The flicker turned quickly to a dull burn as he read his text message.

"Gary needs me at the marina."

"Wait a minute, I think Chicago has something to do with all of this." Chase paused and I knew I didn't have long to finish. "Everything bad from Chicago has come to New Hope. Gary comes, then the O'Toole's niece because she got into trouble, then that Perez guy." In a flash I watched Chase put together the pieces he'd already known existed. A recognition I didn't understand lit in his eyes.

"Stay here with Major. I'll be back a soon as I can." He grabbed his keys, holstered his gun then turned to me when he reached the door. "I mean it, Juli. Stay put. He fixed his eyes on mine for a brief moment, and then he disappeared.

His voice had almost sounded laced with worry. I brushed it off as a scare-tactic, even though he knew better. I glanced from the door to the drowsy sheepdog. So far it had been an exciting day.

Far be it from me to stay away.

I knew I'd be in trouble once Chase reached the marina, but I couldn't help it. As I'd told him at the Perkins' house, I needed to see this case through. Chase should know by now that nothing was going to stop me. He'd been busy putting on what looked to me like tactical gear, so he didn't see me slip into the back seat of his cruiser. I'd wedged myself on the floor between the seats to make sure I stayed out of sight from his mirrors. After feeling every single bump during our ride across town, I'd wished I'd taken my lumps earlier so I could be riding comfortably in shotgun.

The car stopped and I felt an immediate jolt to my already tender ribcage. I bit my lip to prevent the whimper from escaping and giving me away. As if reading my mind, he exited the vehicle. I physically relaxed as I heard his boots against gravel and the 'pop' of the trunk release. I lay there for a brief moment of peace when suddenly the passenger door whipped open.

"Out."

I played opossum.

"Don't test me, Scarlett."

"All right," I moaned and slowly pushed myself up and out the door. "How did you know I was there?"

"I'm a trained professional, remember?"

"As a trained professional, you should have known better than to ask me to stay at the station."

"Forgive me for worrying about your safety." He cleared his throat, and I noticed his change of tone when he said, "You shouldn't be here."

"If I wasn't here then I'd be stuck back there alone with the dog worrying about you." I swallowed hard over that admission. His gaze met mine, and neither one of us said a word. We already knew this was a given, an unspoken promise that would never change. "So, what's going on?" I asked when I finally found my voice.

"I really don't have time to explain. Please. Stay here." He put both hands on my shoulders as if that action alone would cement me to the ground.

"That's not going to happen."

"Julianna, I swear, I will handcuff you to this car if I have to."

"You're wasting time, let's go." I started walking away reveling in my small victory when Mark Walker came running out of a small cluster of evergreens.

"Sheriff! I'm glad you're here. Gary's going to need your help for sure." Mark bent at the waist breathing hard and trying to catch his breath. "Jimmy's getting into it with Max Perez."

"Thanks, Mark. You stay here with Miss Butler and don't let her anywhere near the marina. Got it?"

"Yes, sir." Mark straightened up, still winded. "Hi, Juli."

"Hi." I smiled then cast my gaze toward Chase's retreating back. "I know what he just told you, but you have to understand that I can't do that."

"But the sheriff said—"

"The sheriff has been telling me those exact words for years, and it's never worked yet." I cocked my head, mentally sorting the years. "No, I was right, it's never worked."

"But he—"

"Mark, you can stay here like Sheriff Do-Good ordered you to do, or you can come with me." I marched off, following Chase's path. I hadn't gone ten steps before I heard Mark behind me.

"Then what are we going to do?"

"We're going to help."

———

I STOPPED FOR A MOMENT AND CAUGHT SIGHT OF GARY crouched below one of the windows of the fish market. He motioned for Chase to cut left toward the side of the fish market. Which meant Mark and I were headed toward the water.

"I still don't understand how we're supposed to help. Deputy Maxwell pulled me out because it was getting too dangerous."

"What?" I squinted in Mark's direction, not understanding what he was talking about. "Get down!" I whispered when Gary scanned in our direction. "We need to get to the front side of the market." I kept my eye on Gary, stopping every couple of yards when his 'trained senses' obviously picked up on something. If the men in my life would stop making me crazy and give me a chance, I'd march right in there..."That's it!"

"That's what?" Mark whispered back.

"I'm going in."

"Into the market? Why?"

"How did your wife not kill you?" I asked and patted him on the cheek.

"That's not very nice, Juli. I don't think your mother would appreciate—"

"Shush." I raised my index finger in front of his face. Now was not the time to think of Mom. I motioned him forward with me until we were underneath a set of double windows facing the water. "Listen."

"Let the girl go, Perez, she's nothing to you," Jimmy O'Toole all but growled.

"That's where you're wrong, Uncle Jimmy. Andie is everything to me, and I know you're something to her or you wouldn't be here right now. Isn't that right, sweetheart?"

"Uncle Jimmy, just let us go. Don't call the sheriff, and we'll be gone in the morning. Please. I don't want him to hurt you."

"This guy isn't going to hurt me. Don't you worry. Why don't you go home to Aunt Tammy and let Mr. Perez and I sort this out?"

"I can't go. I love him."

"Open your eyes, girl." There was a pause and I thought I heard a couple sniffles from Andie before Jimmy continued. "He's implicating this entire family and using you to smuggle these diamonds."

"Diamonds?" I whispered, keeping my head below the window.

"Yeah," Mark responded, "They are shipping them inside the frozen fish."

"Who's they, and how do you know this?"

"Whoever Max is working for. I happened to see something on one of the fish while I was waiting to pick up my order. I thought someone had lost a diamond from a ring, so I brought it to Jimmy. He went back to the display and noticed a small bag filled with diamonds inside the mouth of the tuna. About that time Max

Perez showed up. Jimmy gave me my order and told me to get out. That's when I called Gary."

"Listen, Jimbo," Max's voice boomed, and I realized he was right in front of the window we were under. "Andie wanted to help me in my new business venture, and I agreed. We're partners, aren't we, sweetheart? The fish come in already stuffed with the diamonds. My little beauty helps you out by putting them on ice while removing the bags of ice. Now, if it weren't for some young gun distracting her, she wouldn't have missed one and our job here would be almost over."

Scott Iverson. I swallowed the lump in my throat, praying this thug didn't do anything to Scott.

"Why aren't they moving in?" I whispered once I was sure Max had moved away from the window. The man had confessed to enough, what were they waiting for? Between the fish man, Sheriff Goodie and Deputy Hotstuff, they could take Max down with no problem. "I can't stand it. I have to do something." I pulled out my phone. "What's your number?"

"Why? I'm right here?"

"Who knew you were such a comedian. Have you stopped drinking?" This guy was not the Mark Walker I'd interacted with since moving back to New Hope. Something was fishy and it wasn't just the air at the market. "Call me right now. I have a plan." With a look of confusion, he hesitated. I snatched his phone and dialed myself before I lost what little patience I possessed. I placed one small wireless earbud into my ear then pulled some hair over to disguise it.

"What are you doing?"

"Creating a diversion. Keep the line open, you'll be able to hear me." I winked, shoved my phone into my back pocket and headed toward the door of the fish market. Taking a couple cleansing breaths, I made sure I walked hard against the deck planks as I approached. Oh, I wanted them to know someone was coming. No surprises. Apparently, local law enforcement needed a nudge.

"Mr. O'Toole! I'm so glad you're still open." I barged in with a pasted-on smile.

"J-Juli, what can I do for you?" I watched his blue eyes dart from side to side, and I gave a slight tilt to my head to let him know I understood.

"Poor Mrs. Bailey had a piece of whitefish she was going to serve at her knitting club meeting tonight, and Scallywag took it right off the counter." Hey, I needed a story so unbelievable it was believable, and that bird owed me. "I told her I would get her a replacement piece of fish, and she said you had amazing tuna filets. Is this a tuna here?" I moved closer to the smuggled diamonds. When Mr. O'Toole reached a hand to stop me, Max Perez hooked his muscular arm across my chest.

"Max, don't!" Andie yelled.

"So, Miss Butler, now I can ask you directly."

"Ask me what?" I said, squirming to keep his forearm from pressing too hard against my throat.

"Where is my statue?" He hissed against my ear. "The one my idiot cousin, Pete, sold to you."

"Julianna!" Chase's voice shouted in my ear, making me flinch in Max's arm. "You need to get out of there right now." It appeared my sidekick had panicked. Thanks Mark.

"Kind of hard to do, you know," I said mainly to Chase while trying to answer Max's question. "I sold it, and there's no going back."

"Pete said he'd get it back."

"You do know he's dead, right?"

"Oh, I know." He loosened his grip enough to spin me around and I found myself face to face with the barrel of a gun. "Why don't you tell me exactly where it is."

"Pete said he got it from his sister. I paid him far more than it was worth. Why don't you tell me why you want it so badly?"

"Juli, don't play games with this guy," Chase warned.

"That's where you're wrong." Max put the gun to my forehead and lightly trailed it down to the tip of my nose where he tapped it with the end of the barrel. "That statue is worth a half-mil."

"Absolutely not." I shook my head, hoping to create more space between my face and his weapon. "I have experience in fine quality pieces."

Max tsked, circling around me. I could feel my bravado slipping at his closeness. "You see, Pete wanted to help with my new business when he heard about my operation here in New Hope. I gave him the statue as a test to make sure I could trust him. I'm sure you're aware he had some gambling problems."

"I heard."

"The only problem was, Pete was so desperate to pay off the loan sharks he sold the statue hoping to keep them off his back until he could work for me." Max tapped the gun against my shoulder accenting each word, "He. Should. Have. Come. To. Me. First."

"Why? What happened?"

"The statue he sold to you had a half of a million dollars' worth of diamonds inside it, that's what happened!" Max growled and the gun resumed its position in front of my face. "My buyer's diamonds, to be exact. So, if you know where they are, now would be a good time to tell me."

"Juli...." Chase warned in my ear.

"I don't know." I shrugged.

"I think you're lying." He stepped closer and out of reflex, I stepped back.

"You'll never know for sure if you shoot me."

"Damn it. Let's go." I heard Chase say right before he and Gary breached the door. "Drop the gun, Perez," Chase ordered. He kept a steely gaze set on Max. Watching him in action I became increasingly aware of Chase, the sheriff. He knew exactly what he was doing, and I had never felt safer even though the increased tension of the situation deemed otherwise. "Let her go, or this isn't going to end well."

"Squad's three minutes out," Gary stated from where he stood slightly behind and to the left of Chase.

"Last I knew, your squad bailed on you, Detective Maxwell. How's it feel not to have friends?" Max taunted.

"Watch your mouth, Perez." Even Gary had taken on a new demeanor, shocking me with his almost predatory glare. I became more and more intrigued by the men in my life and their qualities I'd been blind to or had forgotten. "You'll be wishing you stuck to your card game instead of jumping in the sandbox with the big dogs."

"Ha! You have no idea, Detective, what I'm capable of. This is just the beginning."

Not if I have anything to say about it."

"Drop the gun, Perez. I'm not telling you a third time." Chase's voice was fierce and full of an edginess I'd never ever heard. Not even when he'd been so angry at me for...."

"Andie, Sweetheart," Max began, making me aware of the two silent people still in the room. "Remember when we talked about sacrifice and doing uncomfortable things in order to keep the business running?"

"Yes," Andie replied in a voice laced with fear.

"Shoot your uncle."

"Andie, don't listen to him. You love your uncle." Gary's voice sounded soft and in control, so different from the way he had spoken to Max only moments before.

"Do it for us," Max coaxed. "If you don't, I will." He paused waiting for her answer and directed his next words to the men in front of us. "I'm going to need you to lower your weapons, gentlemen. If not, I'll put a bullet in this pretty little head right now, and then I'll shoot poor Uncle Jimmy."

"Not before we fill you with lead." The deep reverberation in Chase's voice caused me to shiver.

"You want to be responsible for three deaths, Sheriff? Look what happened to your deputy? Your career will be over. My death will mean nothing."

"One less criminal off the street," Gary declared.

"And one beautiful little girl in prison. You see, Detective, Andie is in this as deep as I am. I have records and her name is all over them. My buyer has been instructed to go to her for anything if something happens to me. If you kill me, you indict her, or invite a slew of trouble you won't be able to protect her from. These people have more connections than you think. They will find her."

"You're bluffing."

"I'm a betting man, Detective. Do you want to find out?"

Listening to their sparring, knowing this was becoming more dire with every exchange, brought tears of genuine fear to my eyes. Max would kill me. There was no way his bullet would miss. Chase wouldn't be able to save me.

"Juli." His voice was sharp. I blinked to clear my vision and focus on his face. "It's going to be okay. I promise."

"For the love of God, Andie, shoot the gun!" Max shouted.

"Shoot the gun. Shoot the gun." Scallywag flew through the open door, a good-sized tuna hanging from his talons. "Juuuliiii...." The crazy bird swooped low, slapping the fat fish against Max's head, causing him to lose his grip on me. I scrambled out of the way as the gun fired into the air. The bird circled back and dropped his catch on Max's head. He hit the floor, and Chase and Gary rushed to cuff him. Seconds later four men dressed in black hauled a stunned Max Perez and a tuna full of diamonds out of the fish market.

"You okay?" Gary asked, his amber eyes full of concern. I nodded. With insides still quivering from my ordeal, I couldn't seem to find my voice. "I'm going to go check on Jimmy and Andie," he said, giving my back a rub as Chase approached.

"What am I going to do with you, Scarlett?" Chase pulled me

in his arms and hugged me. And just like that, the dam of tears broke free. He squeezed me tighter, and I hugged him back as every bit of tension left my body. "Promise me you won't do something like this again?" Through his sincerity, the statement peaked my funny bone, and I couldn't help myself.

I laughed.

He pulled back, not letting me go fully, a confused smile painted his face. "What's so funny?"

"You know I can't promise that, Sheriff."

"I know." He chuckled. Draping his arm across my shoulders, he said, "C'mon, let's go home."

And I couldn't think of a better place to be.

Epilogue

ONE MONTH LATER…

"Thank you all for coming to the grand opening of the Butler's Pantry and Petit Four Paws Café." I lifted my champagne glass, courtesy of Rita Davis, and gazed about the room full of people and their animals. Everyone raised their glasses in salute.

I'd hired the Iverson boys to be servers and carry trays around the Pantry, so full of herbal iced teas and organic treats. They were a huge hit, especially with the older women who loved the polite young men. In the café, customers allowed their animals to socialize while they enjoyed some organic espresso drinks and purchased healthy pet snacks. I'd also hired Andie as my barista. Every now and then I caught her and Scott trading smiles.

After being questioned by Gary's FBI 'friends,' Andie had admitted once she realized what Max's business entailed, she tried to break up with him, but he threatened the safety of her family if she left. She'd felt trapped and didn't think she had a way out. One of her good friends in Chicago verified the way Max pursued her from the beginning and acted possessively with her. The FBI considered her a victim in this case and no arrest was made. I was so happy for her. She had so much life yet to live.

Max had confessed to murdering Pete Seaver. He'd found Pete on the ground, and upon reviving him to demand the statue and his diamonds, began to beat him repeatedly to make him talk. Only Max beat him so hard he eventually killed him.

"You've done a great job, Juli." I turned around and was face-to-face with April. An honest smile formed on her lips, and she leaned in to give me a hug. "Congratulations."

"Thanks, April. I know we kind of got off on the wrong foot."

"I understand. If I were being accused of murder, I guess I would be paranoid too."

"I appreciate that more than you know." I hope she felt my sincerity when I smiled and hugged her back. I'd returned to New Hope feeling like a stranger. Now, everyone here supporting my business venture made me feel accepted and wanted. I only wish Mom could be here to see this.

"Are you okay, Dear?" Mrs. Bailey asked.

"I'm fine, just missing Mom."

"Look out the window at this glorious day. That's your mother. She made this day for her beautiful girl." Mrs. Bailey's words made me tear up. I took a minute before I could speak.

"Thank you."

"Juli, I can't thank you enough for everything you did for Billy and me." Sandy grabbed and squeezed both of my hands when she and Bill approached bearing smiles and a gorgeous bouquet of flowers. "These are for you."

"Sandy, Bill, you didn't have to do this."

"Oh, you bet we did!" Bill added and pulled his wife closer to kiss her flawless cheek. I took the colorful bouquet, breathing deep their floral perfume and felt extremely blessed.

"What a lovely gesture, Sandy," Mrs. Bailey added, and I wondered if she realized Sandy wasn't the dragon lady all the competitions with my mother made her out to be.

"Gesture nothing!" Sandy chimed. "I've been hearing all the chatter here today. Juli and I are going to make great partners for our town's events." My jaw unhinged and my eyes sprung wide. "Juli, you have worked so hard since the day you arrived. You never let anything stop you, so much like your mother. I would be proud to work with you if you'll have me."

"Sandy! Are you serious?" I couldn't contain my joy any longer. "Yes, and thank you. This means the world to me."

"Juli, girl, you sure have outdone yourself here." Betty hustled across the floor and wrapped me in her fleshy arms. "You will be the talk of the town after this."

"Betty, I'm so glad you and Harry could come. It wouldn't be the same if I didn't get to share this day with all of you."

"We wouldn't be anywhere else! We're practically family, darlin.'"

"That's right," Harry agreed and completed the bear hug.

All afternoon I mingled with the townspeople. We talked about animals and my thoughts on organic eating for everyone. I couldn't have asked for a better day.

"I'm ready for that date whenever you are." Gary placed his hand on the small of my back and I jumped. "Sorry, didn't mean to startle you."

"I guess I'm still a little jumpy."

We didn't know who broke into my house or left the threatening voodoo doll. I agreed with Chase to change the locks and fix all doors here at the Pantry as a precaution. My hope was, now that Pete's murder had been solved, whoever had been trying to cause trouble would fade away and things would revert to normal.

"Understandable. I hope you'll feel safe with me when we finally do have that date." Gary's dimples made my knees quiver.

"Aww, Gary, you're so sweet. How can I not feel safe? You're an officer of the law, a former Chicago detective, anything else you care to add?"

"That will be date number two." He winked and I laughed.

I still couldn't believe he'd secretly hired Mark Walker to be a mole in the card games in preparation for Max Perez to come to the Play Maker's Tournament. Boy did things change when they realized Max wasn't here for the cards, but his new diamond smuggling business. It made me wonder if there were other things Gary was keeping to himself. The good news was Mark and his family were reunited, the FBI had paid him graciously for his role. The town considered him a hero for helping law enforcement take down a criminal, and I was considering making him my store manager, that way I could focus on creating my organic treats.

"If you two are done gushing all over each other, I'd like a word with Juli." Chase stood like a rock-solid wall in front of us.

"Sure. Gary, will you excuse me?"

"No problem, I'll catch up with you later." His hand brushed my lower back and waist as he walked away, and I felt heat flood my face.

Chase hooked my arm in his, and we walked to the outdoor patio area where there were fewer people. Most others were inside enjoying the atmosphere. We found a quiet corner against the cobblestone wall.

"You seem so serious. What's up?" I asked, trying to disguise my attraction to Gary.

"How have things been at the house?"

"I'm not worried at all since we've changed all the locks. Do you think you know who broke in?"

"Still no leads on that. I'm holding firm it was Pete's loan sharks thinking you had the statue that they could pawn somewhere else for more money. Obviously when they didn't come up with anything, they left town."

"That's good."

"It is, if you're going to stick around."

"Why wouldn't I stick around? I've put in too much work here to up and leave."

"I'm glad to hear that." His face brightened and when he smiled, a very familiar ache stirred deep within me, pushing whatever I felt for Gary to the back burner. I had a lot to figure out, starting with my new business. As far as the men in my life, maybe I would take a page out of my favorite sheriff's rule book and let things play out on their own.

"I'm glad if you're glad." I knew that sounded lame, but the butterflies in my stomach were messing with my brain cells. "You know, I need to stay in the sheriff's good graces." I laughed, silently praying for my off switch to engage.

"I don't see a problem there." Chase moved closer. The tops of our champagne glasses clinked, and he set them on the edge of the stone wall without breaking eye contact. My pulse quickened as the scent of his woodsy cologne carried on the breeze. "You know, I can teach you a thing or two about good graces." His breath was warm against my skin, and I became thankful for his hands on my shoulders. Without them, I would have melted faster than gelato in July.

"I bet you could," I replied, not recognizing my breathless voice.

"What are we going to do about this, Julianna?" His voice was almost hypnotic, and all my body parts screamed for me to agree with anything he wanted.

"What do you want to do?" This had to be his call, not mine.

"It's been nice having you back, even though you cause more trouble than this town has seen in years." And there it was, the green-eyed twinkle full of love and respect that I'd missed dearly during my ten years of avoiding adulthood...and my heart. "Since it's been a while, why don't we start with a real date?"

My stomach flipped. Now, I had two dates with two great men to think about, and no clue what to do about any of it. If this was seriously my do-over, my chance to set things right and be happy for the rest of my life, there was no way I could say no to any of it.

"What can I say? I sure know how to make an entrance," I stalled, wanting the dramatic affect to give my nerves time to settle before confirming my response.

"You also know how to make quite the exit, darling," a deep

and familiar voice cooed from behind. I spun around, my heart in my throat, at the man standing between the open French doors, champagne held high.

"David!" I managed after forcing a swallow. "W-What are you doing here?" I left Chase staring in confusion as I walked toward my ex-boyfriend and gave him a hug, mostly to make sure he was actually here and not a figment of too much champagne. "You should be in Boston." I hoped he didn't pick up on the nervous pitch in my voice.

"I've been in Boston dealing with a very nasty mess. You just can't hire good help these days. Do you know what I mean?" David eyed me curiously through his black-framed Clark Kent-style glasses.

"Yes, I do." I nodded and stepped back toward Chase who stood patiently waiting for an explanation. "Sheriff," I emphasized the word, "Chase Hargrave, this is David von Hoffster, my prior employer."

"And boyfriend," David added while extending his hand.

"Ex-boyfriend," I clarified, putting my hands on both of theirs to separate them and stared at Chase. "Very much an ex."

"What brings you to New Hope, David?" Chase narrowed his eyes slightly and there was a bit of a strain to his voice. "Are you here for Juli's grand opening?"

"I was here calling on an old friend, when lo and behold I saw Julianna's picture plastered on the front page of the Chronicle. Something about murder charges being dropped, and a grand opening?" He drained his glass and handed it to me. "Be a love and get me another." Then he focused on Chase as if I'd vanished. "I'm surprised she settled here, it's so unlike her. Then I thought since she's started her own business and I'm close enough to town, it might be a good time for Juli and me to settle some unfinished business of our own."

I'd never mentioned my hometown to David at any point in our relationship, nor did he ever mention an old friend who lived in New Hope. I worked very hard at my independence, and I liked my privacy. David wasn't here for my grand opening.

"Business?" I piped up, not wanting David anywhere near Chase or Gary. "I'm pretty sure everything is finished between us, David." I handed him his empty glass and mouthed to Chase, "It's complicated."

"Not exactly." David tipped the glass upside down, showing his disappointment that I hadn't refilled it. "I believe you know the whereabouts of a certain piece of canvas that is no longer in my possession." I could tell by the increasing scowl on Chase's face, he deduced something was up.

He'd be correct.

"You know that thing we were talking about?" I said to Chase and chewed my lower lip while the wheels in his head assessed the current situation.

"Yeah?"

"I'm going to need a rain check." Trouble had a way of following me, and in this case, it came in the form of David von Hoffster, proof positive that skeletons didn't stay in closets.

But that's another story....

Also by Barbara Witek

A JULI BUTLER MYSTERY
Cracker Jacked

About the Author

I live in upstate New York with my very own alpha-male who puts up with my crazy author tendencies and my even crazier imagination!

I'm a firm believer in love at first sight, second chances and creating your own destiny. Isn't that what romance is all about? Being a hopeless romantic helps me write my touching, emotional and heartfelt romances. I also love a good mystery and trying to figure out whodunnit, along with the feeling of being swept into another time through historicals.

When I'm not writing, I'm in love with life on 2 wheels! I've recently gone from being a passenger to driving my own motorcycle. The thrill never gets old and I love the rush of starting that engine and taking off. Every ride is an adventure and I see the open road and world around me so differently. And of course when I'm not cruising, I enjoy a good glass of wine-or whiskey-and getting lost in a book. I also love cross-country skiing and ice-skating (although I admit to not having done either in years!) hiking, anything crafty, and competitive family game nights (scrabble of course)! And dogs. I love them and want to adopt them all!

I love to connect with my readers, fans, and other authors. Come find me and let's chat it up! Here's how: